Theater

of the

Crime

NEIL LOW

THE THEATER of the CRIME

A Tigress Publishing Book

ISBN: 978-1-59404-061-0
1-59404-061-3
Library of Congress Control Number: 2014
Printed in the United States of America

Book Design: Steve Montiglio
Editor: Peter Atkins

10 9 8 7 6 5 4 3 2 1

Requests for such permission should be submitted to:
Tigress Publishing
7095 Hollywood Blvd #369
Hollywood, CA 90028

*In loving memory of Bev Mallory,
whose advice and encouragement I
still treasure. Can you see me now?*

><><><><><><><><><><><><><><><><><><><><><><><><><><><><><><><><><><

Sitting in the front seats of the lower balcony of the
Paramount Theater on Vera Deward's birthday, Alan Stewart
grabbed his arm rests, leaned forward, and stood up at the
same moment the music in the orchestra pit stopped. He
scowled down at the stage and then glanced to Vera at his
side, shaking his head.

"Something's wrong there!" he said. "That can't be part
of the act!"

The applause in the theater stuttered to a stop, as if
taking its cue from the organ player, while the fire on
stage quickened and merged from the closed coffin to the
blazing curtains behind it, smoke billowing to the ceiling
and spreading out towards the audience like a colossal
tidal wave sweeping across a small Pacific island. The Fire
Chief, sitting in the front row, stood and turned toward the
audience and shouted what had already become obvious to
the unsettled crowd: "FIRE!"

Alan grabbed Vera's arm and tugged her toward him.
On the main floor below, others in the audience repeated
the alarm, telling those not sure of what they were seeing
that imminent danger quickly approached. From behind
the stage curtains, women's voices shrieked, and one called

out: "The door is locked!"

"Please exit the building," shouted the Fire Chief, while his deputy raced up toward the stage. "There's no need to panic, people! Please move smartly and take your belongings."

The smoke continued its push across the auditorium's ornate ceiling, obscuring the house lights, hovering over the audience, and gracefully descending onto the upper balcony. Alan passed Vera under his arm like a dance partner, and guided her toward the steps that led to the curtained doorway and ramp that would take them to the steps leading down to the front of the theater.

"If I lose you in the crowd, stay close to the walls and cover your mouth with this," he said, handing her his white kerchief.

As they hurried up the steps, the smoke lowered over them, and Alan glimpsed the stage, now fully engulfed in flames, with the fire climbing the velvet curtains in front above the apron, gobbling at it hungrily. The surrounding smoke tasted bitter, while its thickness blurred visibility like a dense harbor fog. A man in a military uniform of some sort, with a Van Dyke beard and fancy walking stick, seemingly appeared out of nowhere and rushed past them, bumping Vera into the wall as he bulldozed his way ahead of others to be first out the door.

"Hey, jerk!" Alan called after the man.

Vera clasped Alan's arm tightly and held it close to her as they started down the ramp, Alan ground his teeth while locking an image of the rude beast in his mind. Below them on the ramp, a fire alarm bell near the ceiling started ringing. Its incessant hammer repeatedly struck a red-colored bell, making a rapid clanging sound.

"Ignore him, and let's just get out of here!" Vera shouted through the kerchief. "My honor will survive."

2

They hurried down the crowded stairway, while more men ran past them. Inside the auditorium, the yelling grew louder, but did not completely obscure a shrill scream from the stage.

"That's not good," Alan grumbled as they drew closer to the main entrance, a clogged chokepoint where those escaping the first floor massed together into an unmoving clot of humanity. The man who had banged into Vera adjusted his hat while shoving past others, recklessly poking some with his walking stick, which had a shiny animal's head on top. He bulldozed into an older gentleman, who stooped forward, stumbled, and fell as his legs couldn't recover fast enough to catch his balance. A woman behind the fallen man stopped short of him but the surging crowd, fleeing the choking smoke, pressed up against her in terror and knocked her on top of the man, who cried out as someone else stepped on his hand. Others also fell inside the rolling stampede, which added to the panic, and that combined to increase the urgency of the people trying to escape the encroaching inferno.

"This isn't going to work!" shouted Vera over the fire alarm, with Alan's handkerchief over her mouth and nose. Her shoulders slumped as she leaned against the wall on the stairs. "We'll be trampled before we make it to the door..."

Alan leaned close to her protectively, as the stairs behind them filled with anxious theater goers, mouths agape and eyes wide and opaque—their brightness dimmed by the billowing smoke that hung near the ceiling. Its own momentum pressed the crowd into the tight knot of people clumped together, cursing and yelling orders to those in the front to move quickly.

Alan wrapped his arm around Vera's waist and steered her ahead a few feet, hugging the wall, to where a small alcove jutted out onto a small landing, deflecting patrons away from it like a boulder in a stream. Alan leaned into the small cavity for shelter and then his hip banged against a brass doorknob on an unmarked doorway.

"What's this?" he muttered.

"A metal door," said Vera. "So it probably leads to the machine room, furnace, and storage below."

Alan pressed his tie against his mouth and tried to breathe through it. "Heat and smoke rise," he said, leaning close and raising his voice over the alarm. "Fires create an air current that moves upward..."

"Something you've read?" asked Vera, gazing hopefully into his eyes.

"Of course—probably *The Boy Scout Handbook*—I'm not sure. Even if we have to go back underneath the theater we should have time before the fire starts settling down on us."

"I trust your instincts, Champ!" Vera shouted. "They've always worked for us before, my detective scholar."

The houselights flickered and shrieks filled the smoky air. Alan twisted the knob and opened the door a few inches. Lights reflected off glossy cream colored walls and a metal grated set of steps.

"You're right about the machine room," said Alan, "but it will take us right underneath the fire."

Vera pushed away from the wall, slid under his arms, and peeked down the stairway. "I'm not looking forward to running underneath a fire," she said, "but first we should find the machine room, and beyond that the prop room. At the far end, there should be a delivery door leading to the alley."

Vera pulled the door open further and slid through, with Alan following close behind. The door shut on its own, sealing off much of the noise of the crowd. Down two flights of stairs and forty feet ahead, midway up a wall, another

4

fire alarm clanged away, louder than the one on the ramp they had just left.

"What if we reach the stairs in back, which is below street level, and find the steps only take us back up to the fire on the stage?" Alan asked.

Vera took off her high heels, held them in her hand, and led the way down the steps, along a catwalk, past a large boiler and a mass of interconnecting steam pipes and valves.

"I don't see we have much of a choice," she said, over her shoulder. "There isn't much chance we'd make it out the front door through the stampede, and the fire escapes aren't easy to reach. We'd never make it through the smoke to get to them."

At the end of the boiler room they encountered a closed fire door with a Buffalo fire extinguisher mounted next to it. The large brass cylinder had a rubber hose attached near the top. The heavily embossed lettering said, *In case of fire—turn upside down.*

"I hope we won't need this," said Alan, as he took the extinguisher from its mounting.

"Me, too!" Vera said, placing the back of her hand against the door before cautiously pulling it open and stepping though to a large, dimly lit room. "I hope Chief Grayson's Department is on the way."

Alan and Vera serpentined their way through partitions and floor-to-ceiling wooden cages with what appeared to be chicken wire stapled to the frames, each filled with props. The one closest to them had large canvas screens with street scenes, portable signs, furniture, steamer trunks, a stuffed full size horse, a carriage, and a stage coach. The ceiling above sloped downward away from them to a height of about twelve feet, where it leveled off.

Ahead, footfalls raced erratically across a wooden floor,

supported by trusses. Loud shouts from men and women accompanied the running and banging, as if heavy items had been dropped carelessly in the orchestra pit, and then the shouting grew louder, as if a door had been opened, and then a gush of smoke entered their large chamber, suddenly making it feel smaller. The sound of running feet followed the bang, and the voice became clearer.

The lights flickered again, and Vera seized Alan's arm.

"I know you don't smoke, but did you bring a lighter?" she asked.

"I've got a book of matches in one of my pockets."

"Of course you do, you Boy Scout."

"They pass them out at The Five Point Café. They have their logo on them. I just picked up a pack to have on hand. Look, there's the organ on top of the scaffolding, so we've reached the orchestra pit. Behind it's the stage," Alan nodded his head toward an industrial elevator with steel screens that serviced the stage, situated below a large trap door with smoke seeping through it. To the right of the elevator stood a simple set of stairs without a railing, leading to a smaller trap door, which suddenly opened. Smoke began pouring through the hole, tumbling down the steps. Men's legs wearing a dark coat, like the dress tunic firemen wear, bounded downward through the smoke, before disappearing into the shadows in back, heading away from them.

Alan and Vera moved toward the stairs, past the elevator cage. Ahead, a pair of women's legs in Bedouin pants emerged through the hazy smoke, followed immediately by two more pair, belonging to young ladies. The threesome, dressed in bright silks, stopped at the foot of the steps, coughing, disoriented, glancing about quickly, finally settling on Vera and Alan.

Instinctively, Alan rushed toward them, offering his arm

to lead them away from the smoke. The one with red hair locked large fearful eyes on his.

"You have to help Tasha, please!" she bellowed in a thick accent, grabbing Alan by the shoulders with a grip that wouldn't let go. "We got separated up there and couldn't find her in the smoke. We had to leave her behind. She's going to die!"

Behind Alan the elevator cage door slid open and a menacing sword fell to the floor with a clang. A swarthy man dressed as a eunuch in an Arabian Night's fantasy slid from a pile of mattresses and raced past Alan and Vera, heading toward the back of the building.

"Like rats fleeing a sinking ship," snapped Vera.

A moment later, a gust of air swept across the basement ceiling, caught the fluffing smoke, and pushed it back up the stairs.

"We want that back draft," said Alan, inclining his head toward the rear of the building. "It will keep the smoke away. Take these three outside and prop that door open, would you, darling? I'm going up."

"No, you're not!" said Vera. "That's when people die in fires—saving their cats, their dogs, and their photo albums."

Alan shook his head. "You heard what they said. There's someone up there who needs our help."

Vera scowled at Alan. "You be quick and you be safe, Champ! If anything happens to you, I'll never forgive you. Or me—for letting you go."

"Trying to help people in need is in my gene pool," said Alan. "I'm a rescuer. It's what Mackie would've done."

Vera pinched her lips together and shook her head, as she took the young ladies by the arm and led them away. "And we saw how that turned out for him..." she grumbled to herself.

7

Alan hurried up the stairs with the soda water extinguisher in one hand. The smoke made a soft wall, brightly lit above the floor, keeping him from sticking his head through the opening. He inhaled deeply as much of the outside air as he could, preparing to stick his head through the hole and launch himself onto the stage. As soon as he took another step up, he felt the breeze gush by him, pushing the smoke up, clearing a way for him. *That's my girl, Vera!*

As Alan set foot on the stage, he caught a heavy wash of spray from a fire hose, the water coming from below the right wing of the stage. Either the fire chief or his deputy had stayed behind, while everyone else fled, giving the fire his best effort. Whoever had directed the hose now moved it to stage right and what little remained of the curtains. At the front apron, the klieg lights continued to shine brightly on Alan, as if he were a performer, while illuminating much of the backstage, now exposed with the curtains having burnt away. Immediately behind the magician's prop coffin, long strands of sopping black velvet dripped soot on a woman who lay twisted on her side next to a black box pushed against the back wall, as if she were a drunk sprawled in the gutter. She was no derelict though—instead, a dark-haired beauty with sinuous legs protruding through an exotic silk skirt, cut high in the front. Her barely-there kaftan top designed to allow a knife thrower freedom to cast her lethal spell.

From the Cancan routine during the set change, Alan recognized Natasha Zarenko. She had been the premier high kicker, and also the headliner for the main attraction that the fire had kept him from seeing. He saw plenty of her now, as he set down the fire extinguisher, bent low, and slid his arms underneath her, picking her off the floor as he stood and straightened his back, like Clark Gable carrying Vivien Leigh. But instead of Rhett Butler taking Scarlett O'Hara upstairs to the master bedroom, Alan stepped downward through the trap door and descended through the surprisingly strong breeze. Besides smoke and soot, Zarenko exuded the scent of an expensive perfume, something exotic from Paris or further east, such as a Crusader might have brought home from Arabia, a lot like what Vera would wear.

The lights flickered again as Alan hit the bottom step and spun toward the back of the building. Madam Zarenko's head flopped away from his arm, exposing redness near the base of her skull, where the neck hairs swirled back toward the hairline. Alan tossed her gently, catching her, and shifting her weight in his arms so that he could get his arms under her further, carrying her between the wired cages of props, letting her feet lead the way so he wouldn't bump her head into something. Twenty feet ahead of them city lights and night sky shone through an open door. Inside the basement, the lights flickered one last time before dying for good.

The high-pitched siren sang a welcome greeting to Alan as he carried Madam Zarenko through the Paramount's basement door. Walking under an alley light, he stole a glimpse of the beauty's face in repose. She had that Hedy Lamarr savage beauty that would make a tango partner go weak at the knees. Vera had wedged open the basement door with a large brick shard, before moving down the alley a few yards away from the building, closer to Pine Street.

No sooner had Alan cleared the door with Madam Zarenko than her three assistants deserted Vera and ran towards their leader. Red flashing lights from down the alley reflected off the oil coated mud puddles and shiny wet bricks, glaring brightly to where a few of the survivors now huddled around Zarenko.

"What's wrong with her?" the ginger asked, gazing up at Alan.

"I'd say she's been hit on the back of the head with something," said Alan. "Did you see or hear something fall?"

"No, we didn't," the ginger said, shaking her head while checking with the blonde and brunette. "Too much smoke and too many people running everywhere. She told us in the dressing room that there'd be a trapdoor and where to find it, and then we got there and turned around—no Tasha!"

"We need to get her out to the street and find an ambulance and a doctor," said Alan.

Vera took off her gloves, gently pulled Zarenko's hair aside and studied the bruise, probing it softly with her fingertips. She nodded and moved ahead of the group, leading the way. Alan followed with the two escorts hovering close to Zarenko.

"Maybe there'll be a doctor in the crowd," said Vera, "but he'll be dealing with the seriously injured."

Through the rear door two more stagehands stumbled out, coughing, and holding each other up with arms wrapped around each other's shoulders, while dirty hands held colored hankies to their faces. They crossed the alley and leaned their backs against a brick wall, catching their breath, as if they'd run a distance race in record time. A moment later, another figure fumbled at the door and stuck her head out. Yvette LaPierre, the disappearing princess, took a deep breath and then pushed her way through the door without shoes on, wild-eyed, clutching her tattered silk top at the middle. Her silk pants were torn and jagged above cuts to her legs that had drawn blood, as if cats had used them as scratching posts.

"Somebody shoved my box against the wall so I couldn't get out!" she cried while continuing to inhale deeply. "I could have died in there!"

Vera took off her coat and covered LaPierre, escorting the magician's assistant across the alley to where the other women gathered. Down the alley a second fire engine arrived, red lights flashing. It dowsed its siren when it reached the alley, where several of the musicians stood with their instruments, and cranked the large wheels in their direction. The stage hands stood up wearily, shoved away from the wall, and signaled for the truck to come their way.

"Did everyone inside get out?" Vera asked. "St. Laurent? All his assistants? The stage crew and performers?"

"I don't know!" LaPierre said, the tears now starting to flow. "So much smoke and fire...I couldn't tell—but no one came for me. So...you haven't seen Frederic? Did he make it out?"

"We're only sure of the eunuch we saw running ahead of us," said Vera, "but we have no idea who else might have gotten out before him. And we need to clear this area so that we're not in the way of the firemen."

They passed the stage hands and headed down the brick alley toward where they guessed the others might gather and moved to the side to allow the fire engine to pass, but then Alan stopped abruptly.

"You're right about the injured, Vera. The ambulances and emergency rooms will be flooded with crushed and burned bodies, probably the dead and dying, too. I say we load everyone into the Packard and find help on our own."

"Sure," said Vera, pausing for a moment to think. "The fire doors were locked on the inside. Someone expected Madam Zarenko to perish in the fire–possibly with LaPierre and several others."

Alan nodded, following Vera's thought.

"And in my humble, street surgeon opinion," Vera went on, "Madam Zarenko's breathing and color are fine—at least what I can see that's not masked by stage makeup. So maybe these ladies should hide out for a while with us. With Jenny at school, I've got room at my place."

"And just who are you?" asked the ginger in an Eastern European accent.

"We're private detectives," said Vera. "Alan Stewart and

Vera Deward at your service. You can trust us."

"You're a detective?" asked the ginger. "Like a Pinkerton?"

"Definitely not like a Pinkerton," said Vera. "Around here they're known as strike-breakers and thick-headed brutes—starting in Tacoma and going all the way back to Chicago. We work for George Brinkman, the president at the Washington Federated Union, doing fraud investigations, but he hires us out for special jobs—and on occasion we do pro bono work for the police department."

"You do what?"

"We assist the police with cases they can't work—for any number of reasons—without charging a fee for our services. We do it for the greater good—and reward money, when it's there..."

The ginger glanced at the blonde and brunette performers, who checked with each other. The blonde arched her brows, shrugged, and tossed her hair to the side.

"Okay," said the ginger, "but what about a doctor?"

"My place is minutes away, on Capitol Hill, and I've had lots of practice patching people up, usually from bullet holes, but I've dealt with concussions before. The Champ just might show you the stitches I've sewn into his noggin. But if you want a hospital to check out Madam Zarenko properly, we can stop by Columbus on Madison Street and probably beat the rush. The good sisters there will keep their mouths shut and keep any nosey reporters at bay."

"You've been shot?" asked the blonde, eyes wide, staring up at Alan.

He tried to suppress a grin, but it didn't work. "A time or two..."

The group continued up the alley, across the street, and stopped next to the Union's limo, a 1940 Packard Super

180, parked in a pay lot.

"The police and fire departments will need to do a head count when the smoke clears and the ashes settle," Alan said to Vera. "They'll want to know how many bodies are buried in the rubble."

"I suppose they will at that. I'll give Ben Kearney or Mike Ketchum a call. See who they recommend. I'm sure they'll know someone at SFD who'll play ball with us, if that becomes important."

Madam Zarenko stirred in Alan's arms as he laid her
down in the backseat of the Packard, her head resting on
the ginger's lap. Her eyes fluttered and then opened. She
stared unfocussed into the distance, and then she jerked
spasmodically, trying to sit up.

Joined by the blonde, the ginger gently held her back,
while stroking her forehead soothingly, cooing, "Golubushka,
golubushka. It's alright, golubushka, we made it outside.
We're all safe now."

Zarenko relaxed backward and sighed lazily, staring
at Alan as he relaxed his grip on her. "Spa-see-ba,
golubushka."

"Looks like we made it to heaven after all, girls," she
said, switching to English, in a voice not as accented as her
helpers. "Who's this dreamboat in the fedora? I know he's
not St. Peter."

"I'm Alan Stewart, private detective."

"Private detective you say? So there's no halo under
your bonnet? Where are we then, and how did I get here?"

"Detective Alan is the one who found you," said the
ginger. "Sophie, Star, and I told him where we last saw
you on the stage, and he waltzed right up the stairs and

17

into the fire—just as brave as you please—and carried you outside."

"Then you are a living, breathing angel!" said Zarenko.

"Just thought I could help out is all," said Alan, "We should get you up to the hospital and beat the rush."

"Why a hospital?" asked Zarenko, her brow drawn low.

Vera leaned over the front seat. "You've had a concussion," she said. "Someone or something hit you hard enough to knock you out. I didn't feel a fracture or find anything to think you might have one, but it would still be wise to check it out. Are you feeling nauseous?"

"My head has an ache for certain, like a Sloe Gin hangover gives you, but I'm not sick to my stomach, if that's what you're asking."

Vera nodded contemplatively. "You'll probably be fine, and we can take you to my place. I know a doctor friend who can make a house call, if necessary."

Zarenko reached back and touched the base of her skull lightly, patting it softly with her fingers and grimacing. "I don't remember how I got this. We'd changed out of our Cancan outfits and heard people screaming 'Fire' and hurried to the stage door, but it had a chain wrapped around it—with a padlock. So we ran back up to the stage. People were running about everywhere, slamming into us and not apologizing. Smoke everywhere. Somebody grabbed my arm like he knew me, I thought he'd be nice and show me the way out. He said something...and then BAM! Lights out, Tasha!"

Vera stared intently in Zarenko's dark eyes. "Do you remember what he said?"

Tasha shook her head slowly and touched her hair, pressing it into place. "Something familiar, like I should know him, but I don't remember exactly. Something close to: 'They're waiting for you...'"

"And who would that be?" asked Vera.

"I assumed he meant the girls, who had been right next to me mere seconds before that."

"So, you don't know who grabbed you then?" asked Vera.

"Too much smoke," said Zarenko. "I'm sure a man, because of the voice. His grip, too. My girls are strong , but I think the size of the hand would make it a man."

"What about you, Miss LaPierre?" asked Vera. "Are you alright going to my place for patching up, until we can straighten this mess out?"

"I have a room in the Paramount's apartments. Shouldn't I go there first? In case others show up there?"

"Would that be a room of your own or one you share?" asked Vera.

LaPierre thought for a moment. "Share..."

Vera nodded. "Since we don't know what happened inside the theater, it might be better for you to come with us for a little while at least."

LaPierre nodded. "Do you and I know each other?" she asked.

"Maybe a few years back," said Vera, "at The Palace Hippodrome on Second Avenue at Spring Street, if you did stage time there."

LaPierre eyebrows arched as she smiled. "Your place will be fine."

"Alan will drive us," Vera said, "unless any of you want to go to the hospital first."

"If you have plenty of aspirin and a bar that's well stocked," said Zarenko, "I say it's your place, lady."

While Alan climbed in the front seat and started up the car, Vera sat directly behind him on the jump seat. She reached across her seat and squeezed Zarenko's hands, resting on top of her abdomen. "I'm Vera Deward. You can call me Vera."

"I'm Tasha," said Zarenko, "and these lovely ladies are Rose Red, Sophie's our blonde, and Star's our brunette. A hair color for every taste." Tasha sighed wearily. "Since going to the hospital might require us to produce papers documenting who we are and where we're from, we would rather avoid that inconvenience. I hope you understand. It's not like we're hiding from the law or dodging bail bondsmen, we just don't want to draw close attention to us personally."

Alan eased out of the parking lot and headed east on Pine Street.

"Are you white émigrés from Russia?" asked Vera.

Rose, Sophie, and Star nodded, while Tasha inhaled deeply. "Mostly," she said. "As Soon as word of the Romanovs' demise reached my family, I fled from Gatchina, near St. Petersburg, to Turkey with many other monarchists. I lost track of the years in Ankara and then Istanbul, and then I eventually met up with these three. They're young and have no recollection of Russia, the Romanovs, or even their own families. They were destined to a life in the brothels when I met them."

"You rescued us!" said Sophie, patting Tasha's shoulder, "not found us!"

"Are you wanted by the police or J. Edgar Hoover?" asked Vera.

"Nyet," said Tasha. "But Immigration and Naturalization doesn't have any use for 'our kind.' They're worried we might be filthy communists trying to infiltrate your shipyards with lunch buckets full of propaganda to organize your labor force. We're better off pretending to be gypsies."

"Our boss wouldn't want the competition," said Alan.

"Why's that?" asked Tasha.

"Seattle's had a history of labor unrest," said Alan,

"particularly on the waterfront with the Wobblies and the Longshoremen. The Pinkertons hired unemployed thugs as deputies who squared off against the Wobblies, killing a few here and more up in Everett. We had much of the same with the dockworkers a few years back when they unionized. Mr. Brinkman didn't like the violence so, like the Teamsters, he'd rather bribe his way to labor dominance than break heads and knee caps."

"Is that how you got shot?" asked Rose.

Alan missed a gear while shifting, letting the clutch up too fast, the Packard cruising north on Broadway. "Not exactly," he said. "A damsel in distress needed our assistance."

"And did you rescue her?" asked Rose, leaning forward in her seat.

Alan nodded. "That we did," he said, glancing at Vera, "but in our business we respect the privacy of our clients, so I can't really talk about it."

"I thought about waiting until we got settled, but timing can be very important," said Vera. "I want to know what you know about the fire tonight, so we should probably start at the beginning."

"Where would that be?" asked Tasha. "When our train arrived in Seattle this morning, or when the show started?"

"Unless you can think of anything important before when the show started, let's start there."

Two Nights Before at the Orpheum Theater

A man stood center stage on a small Oriental rug, directly in front of the drawn curtain. His white shirt and tie were covered by a silk robe and he wore matching slippers and had a brightly colored silk pajh wrapped around his head, adorned with a large jeweled pin. To either side of him were large vases of cut flowers, in which lilies were prominent. The man held a white envelope to his head, closed his eyes, and waved at the organist to stop playing for a moment.

"I need complete silence," said Alexander Conlin, billed as a seer, as *The Man Who Knows All*. He lowered the envelope and smiled at the packed house. "These past few days in Seattle, I've noticed an increase in psychic energy. Yours is a raw city which blends cultures with those who were here before your arrival. The psychic disturbances all started on a walk through your Pioneer Square, where I discovered a new totem pole honoring Seattle's link to Northwest Indians and Alaska. I touched the carved cedar and instantly felt a disquieting sensation, as if the wood were talking to me. I learned that this new totem pole had been purchased to replace the original—which had been chopped down and stolen from a native tribe only to be destroyed by an arsonist two years ago. I don't think you are aware of the horrible karma such a theft brings, and then to destroy a sacred icon with fire is only asking for the wrath of the gods—but I digress.

"My point is that when there are disturbances in the psychic field, I am often flooded with multiple messages, much like a young boy who can't sit still in school. My job is to sort through the voices shouting for attention inside my head and find those here in my audience tonight, who crave an answer to a question that is dear to them."

"Nice intro!" whispered an unseen woman's voice through earphones hidden inside the swami's headgear. The speaker had a hint of an Irish accent. The electric wires to the headgear ran down the back of Alexander's neck into his silk slippers, which had copper plated soles. When the seer stood on his magic carpet, the soles made contact with slightly protruding electric contacts, connected by wires that ran across the stage, down through a trap door to the orchestra pit, where the speaker had a view of the audience, from behind the organist.

"If you're ready," the woman's voice continued, "a Mrs. Pierpont is in the audience. She lost her son Andrew two weeks ago. Drowning. Lake Washington."

Alexander spread his arms as if he were a conductor getting ready to lead an orchestra. He nodded, touched the envelope to his head again, and closed his eyes. He held the envelope between his fingers while he rubbed his temples with this thumbs. He drew in a large breath of air and exhaled.

He opened his mascara-traced eyes wide and stared across the audience, brooding and unfocused. "I'm afraid the author of this note has lost someone very dear to them recently," he said. "I'm feeling sadness and the suddenness of the event. The death came as a shock on an otherwise happy day for others."

Alexander rubbed his chest and rotated his head around his neck, as if he were having trouble breathing. "I'm hearing a name that starts with an A," he said. "A young man's name."

A woman's voice cried out in the audience.

"She's six rows up and on the left side," whispered the voice in Alexander's ear.

Alexander gazed to his right and up into the balconies, avoiding the row his assistant had pointed out. "Is there a mother here who lost her son, Andy?" As he finished asking the name, he turned to the seating area six rows up and to his left.

A woman in her forties, holding a hanky to her eyes stood up, gazed around her, and sat down on the edge of her seat.

"You are Andy—Andrew's mother?" asked Alexander.

The woman stood again and shouted loudly, "Yes, I am!"

"Please join me on the stage, if you will?"

The heavyset woman excused herself as she passed in front of others, working her way to the side aisle, and then she all but ran to the stairs leading up the right apron to the stage. Alexander stepped off his magic carpet and met the woman a few feet away. He held up his left hand as if cautioning her not to get too close while he channeled psychic energy.

"Have we ever met before?" he asked.

The woman shook her head vigorously. "No!"

"Does your last name start with P?"

The woman nodded assuredly.

"Pied—"

The woman shook her head. "NO!"

"Now don't help me," said Alexander. "It might take me a minute."

The woman nodded.

"Not Piedmont but Pierpont!" said Alexander.

"Yes!" said the woman eagerly.

"And you're worried about your Andy. Please tell the audience how old."

"Sixteen!"

Alexander shook his head. "So young. So tragic. A Lake Washington drowning?"

"Yes!"

"Picnic?"

"Yes."

The audience applauded along with the question and answers, and the organist started an accompaniment of background music, a clever interpretation of eastern music.

Alexander held up a finger signaling to the audience that he needed a moment, while the organist continued, adding to the mood. "Your son wants you to know that he is in a happy place," said Alexander, "surrounded by relatives who've gone before and were waiting for him."

The audience clapped enthusiastically as the woman wiped tears from her eyes with the already soaking handkerchief. Alexander bowed slightly at the waist and stepped back toward the carpet. Mrs. Pierpont lurched forward and grabbed Alexander with open arms, trying to wrap him in a hug, and catching him mid-stride while he was partially turned, knocking him against one of the cut flower vases. "Thank you!" she blurted out.

Alexander dropped the envelope in an effort to catch and steady the falling vase, which slopped water onto the stage floor and carpet. He righted the vase and back-pedaled away from Mrs. Pierpont, who came after him again, tears brimming from her eyes.

The audience gasped in unison.

"This means so much to me!" she blurted out.

Alexander stepped onto the carpet, which sparked sharply, sending a staggering jolt through him. He recoiled, fell away, dropped to one knee, his pajh tipping backward off his head, precariously hanging from his neck by the narrow wires that went up his collar.

A man sitting in the second row, near the aisle, sprang out of his seat, ran to the stage, and jumped up onto it, like an Indian climbing up on a pony. He slid several feet across the apron and stopped in front of Mrs. Pierpont, rising quickly to his feet and bracing himself between her and the fallen performer.

Mrs. Pierpont held her hands to her face in terror as she stared over the man's shoulder at the fallen Alexander, still down on one knee. "Are you alright?" she asked fearfully.

Alexander opened his eyes halfway and robotically rose to his feet. He raised his hands and rubbed his temples as if dialing in a radio only he could hear, while his eyes remained hooded, unfocused, as if heavily sedated.

"Beware of the fire and pretense of magic!" said Alexander in an accented voice, sounding like a Russian woman's. "It comes in two days, on opening night. You have a different name now, but your treachery will be punished. There will come a reckoning that will unmask your cold heart and shallow tricks. Вы ответственны за смертельные случаи в моей семье! May all of your deaths be long and painful!"

The audience gasped.

Alexander's female assistant climbed up through the trap door. She squatted low, reached through the curtain, grabbed the carpet by an edge and yanked it hard, tossing it safely into the middle of the stage behind the closed curtain. She stood up, slid through the curtain, and approached Alexander, who rolled his eyes and shook his head.

"Are you alright?" she asked him, while grabbing the pajh and holding it in place against his back.

"I'm fine, Sylvie. Just a little stunned is all. What the hell happened?"

She leaned in close. "We need to rewire the carpet and clean up the water spill. Probably take twenty minutes. Do you want to continue with the show?

"Certainly. The show must go on!"

"Announce an early intermission then, and I'll escort you back stage and fix you up."

"Of course. My foot feels like it's on fire."

"We'll check it out. You might have a burn. I didn't know you spoke Russian."

Alexander gazed into Sylvie's eyes, a puzzled look on his face. "I don't. Why would you say that?"

The chattering in the packed Paramount Theater quieted as soon as the houselights dimmed. Below the stage the orchestra played a lively introduction with reeds, horns, and strings, showing off their range, while the spotlight shining from high above broadcast a large beam onto the closed curtain, drawing the audience's attention to the front apron. The bright light panned across the draped burgundy fabric, narrowing and increasing its intense focus until it locked on the left side of the stage, where a tuxedo clad Master of Ceremonies brushed back the crushed velvet curtain and stepped into the light, marching energetically to the forefront of the apron. He nodded to the conductor and the music stopped.

In the front of the second balcony, Alan and Vera sat together, with Alan taking the seat closest to the side aisle. He shifted his weight subtly and laced his arms through Vera's arm, sliding underneath her wrap, clasping a gloved hand. She squeezed a response, acknowledging the gesture, tugging the hand into her lap without glancing his way.

"You be careful doing that," she whispered. "You're out in public, and someone might see you."

"Welcome, ladies and gentlemen, to tonight's double bill

presentation at the Paramount, Seattle's premier theater!" boomed the on stage voice, "I am Nikolai Ivanovich, and it's a true joy to have so many in our audience tonight. Although we love presenting the latest movies from Paramount, we're pleased to see that the persistent rumors of vaudeville's eminent demise have been grossly exaggerated. The world will always have an appetite for live entertainment, where there are no cinematic re-takes and camera fakery. In tonight's magical opening act, remember that anything is possible when a master magician takes the stage. It's up to you to determine what is real and what is illusion—not an easy task, I warn you. Please enjoy yourselves. You're in the presence now of the renowned Frederic St. Laurent."

The packed crowd applauded warmly, and the announcer waited patiently for the audience to settle down.

"Following his magical conjuring, in which Monsieur St. Laurent promises to entertain you with his act, the likes of which you've never seen before, we will present our feature performance: the amazing Madam Natasha Zarenko, who will display her deadly skills in the impalement arts with knives, bullwhips and of course her exquisite target girls..."

The audience erupted in cheers, whoops, and whistles. Alan gave Vera a sideways glance, his brow knitted.

"From what I hear," said Vera, "she's decent with the whip but not much of a knife thrower—but these guys don't care. They know that before it's over, her girls will be naked on stage—trust me."

Alan flicked his brow high. "Wow! This is going to be much better than I thought!"

"Sure! Like you didn't know..."

"I wanted something vaudevillian for you tonight."

"Looks like we're going to get a healthy dash of burlesque."

"You don't mind?"

"Of course not. Maybe I'll pick up some pointers—in case being a detective doesn't work out for me, I could always return to the stage."

The crowd laughed at something the announcer said, and he held up his hand, as if begging their indulgence a moment, before continuing. "The Paramount is very proud to present to you, all the way from Paris, France, the world's most famous prestidigitator, Frederic St. Laurent!"

The Paramount's celebrated organist led the musical accompaniment as the curtains drew to the side, seemingly chasing the master of ceremonies off the stage. The spotlight narrowed its focused beam on a dapper gentleman standing center stage, wearing a swallow-tailed tuxedo with a top hat. The audience applauded, but it somehow lacked the enthusiasm Alan had expected to hear, given the size of the standing room only crowd. *They must have come because of the newspaper stories—or maybe the strippers*, he figured. Like gawkers to a train wreck, many of them hoping the predictions of death on stage during tonight's opening would prove true.

Alan didn't buy into the prediction, but local and national news organizations had fun with Alexander's vision, laughing it off as old-fashioned theatrics, a modern day version of the Old West taunt: "This town ain't big enough for the both of us!" They dismissed it as trivial banter between performers with over-sized egos and enormous bank accounts—Alexander's in particular. Unverified rumors had him as one of the country's richest men, a con man with a scurrilous hunger for women, including multiple marriages and bigamy.

St. Laurent took a deep bow and nodded his appreciation to the audience, showing no traces of apprehension. Immediately behind him stood a beauty wearing a strapless bustier, high heels, and black stockings with a fancy bow at the top, halfway up her thighs. She stepped out of his shadow into the focused light, and stood at his side. She bent over stiff-legged and picked up an empty bird cage from a small table. The low, nearly flat cage appeared to be mounted on a tray with a small drapery edge, and while holding it underneath with one hand, she drew a felt strap over her head and across her shoulders. She stretched her free arm over the top of the cage and opened a light-weight door on the top. Her every move in the high heels required several steps, shifting her weight from one leg to the other leg, often locking her knees, which somehow required her to flex her muscles and accentuate her strong limbs, firm derriere, and small waist, strategic actions Alan knew were not lost on the predominantly male audience—or the man directing the spotlight's beam.

St. Laurent joined in conspicuously watching his assistant, and then he glanced back to the audience as if reading their minds. He smiled knowingly. "I see that some of you are quite taken with my new assistant, Miss Yvette LaPierre. But I don't want you to worry about her tonight, because Alexander's prediction of death is more likely a wish for my demise, not hers."

"That's not her name," said Vera. "I recognize her but can't think of her real name. By the end of the show I'll have it."

Because Vera had once been involved in burlesque and had been around a number of vaudeville acts, Alan thought taking her to a live show would be the perfect surprise for her birthday. His tastes ran more toward Gary Cooper Westerns than magic and knife-throwing, but this happened to be the closest thing in town to vaudeville. He had purchased the tickets days before Alexander made his prediction, when sales for the performance were anything but brisk. Alan wondered if the traveling magician had encouraged his arch rival to make the far-fetched prognostication to help drive business to both of their shows.

"Don't worry, ladies and gentlemen," boomed St. Laurent in a French accent, as his assistant fussed with the cage and a butterfly net. "The Paramount's management has taken necessary precautions and spared no expense for your safety this evening."

"The accent's not right," whispered Vera.

"In what way?"

"I'm not sure. Maybe it's too formal, but it's not like any I've heard before. So I suspect the name is fake, too."

"Where's he from?

"Overseas somewhere, but not France. I'm not as skilled with European accents as I am American. I'll have to hear more before I can say. Need to catch him off guard to be sure."

"You will note that the Paramount has engaged Fire Chief Bill Grayson and his second in command, Al Jeffries, to be on hand for our fire display later in the show," said St. Laurent. "They're seated in the front row and have come here tonight to reassure you of the many measures taken for your personal safety. They of course will not hesitate to stop tonight's performance—if they thought any of you were in peril."

The two oversized fire commanders stood for the polite applause, doffed their hats in salute to the crowd and waved awkwardly before sitting down.

Alan leaned close to Vera. "Everyone loves firemen," he said. "Wonder how much this is costing the Paramount?"

Vera nodded but kept her eyes straight ahead. "If they were here for our safety," she said, "they'd be stationed backstage with charged hoses—right next to the fire props. Problem is that magicians are notoriously paranoid. They don't want anyone seeing their secrets. So St. Laurent undoubtedly nixed that idea, and their seats in the front row are bought and paid for by the house. You can bet Chief Grayson has his chubby fingers crossed, while patting the fat wallet in his tunic. He brought a lackey with him to blame, in case anything goes wrong."

"You spent a lot of time in theaters," said Alan. "Did you learn magic tricks?"

"Actually, quite a few. After my start in the circus, I took a stab at dodging swords inside the closed coffins, but then I got too curvy and outgrew the props, so they found other outfits I could wear—and things I might do to sell tickets."

"How come I didn't know this?"

"Being a box jumper has never come up, and don't ask me to reveal magic secrets, because I've taken the oath."

"What oath is that?"

"The Magician's Oath..." Vera trailed off softly through pursed lips. "Now, shhh! I'll tell you later. Watch the show."

Yvette LaPierre handed St. Laurent the sturdy butterfly net, and then curtsied, while steadying the bird cage with her free hand.

"If your hearing is finely tuned," said St. Laurent, cupping his hand to his ear, "then you might also hear the fluttering of wings about the stage, where it seems doves are circling about us, invisible to the naked eye. I use my hearing, much like a bat does, to track the doves, but it's very unlikely that you'll be able to see them until they've been caught and caged. Here, let me demonstrate."

St. Laurent's brushy eyebrows knitted low as he stared off into the distance and raised his net slowly into the air. He took a half a step forward, and then retraced it, stepping backward, his eyes flitting around the stage as if his mind's eye were tracking a stinging insect. Standing nearby, LaPierre followed his every move, keeping herself close to the magician, shifting weight on her legs at every opportunity.

"The secret to catching these elusive creatures," said St. Laurent, "is to patiently wait for them to come to you. In that respect it's a lot like catching house flies, except you wouldn't want to pin these darling creatures to a window and squish them."

St. Laurent reached out with the net on the extended pole, like a cat pawing at a dangling strand of yarn, and then quickly he struck at something, wheeled sharply, and slammed the net down on the open cage while LaPierre bounced up on her toes to catch it. White wings spread quickly and fluttered around the cage to the oohs and awes of the audience. Inside the small cage, the dove sidestepped over to a corner, as if making room for company, and settled down to roost.

St. Laurent repeated the catch two more times, and as he slammed the invisible birds into the waiting cage, Miss LaPierre jumped up on her toes, lifting the cage up to the rapidly descending net, catching it with the open door as the two forces slammed together.

Vera tugged on Alan's arm and leaned toward him. "Have you got this one figured out yet, or are you busy staring at Yvette's heaving cleavage and shapely legs?"

"I'm happy just watching her," said Alan. "I didn't know I had to figure out the tricks."

Vera dropped Alan's hand on her leg and then brushed it away in faux rage. "Rascal!"

While the crowd applauded, Miss LaPierre took quick mincing steps across the stage and handed the props and doves to an attendant dressed as a eunuch in a harem, with a turban and silk slippers with curled toes. She returned carrying four silver rings, large enough to pass a grapefruit through and handed them to St. Laurent, who moved down stage, closer to the apron.

"Now, ladies and gentlemen, I would like you to observe these rings closely."

St. Laurent clanged the rings together, demonstrating they were solid, and then he tossed the first one to his opposite hand and smiled. He continued tossing the others while counting out loud, clinking the second, third, and fourth against those in his hands as he drew his palms closer together.

"Listen to them talk to each other," St. Laurent said with a smile. "I discovered these enchanted rings on my recent trip to Singapore. The story is that they had been smuggled out of China from up near the Great Wall, and reportedly cost all who touched them their lives. The person who gave them to me believed them to be cursed and spat on the ground as I took delivery of them."

St. Laurent held the rings up in front of him and splayed them out. "Now watch as I link them all together."

The magician did as promised, and then he passed one ring through another ring, even though they appeared to be identical in size.

"He's very smooth," said Alan.

Vera nodded. "Countless hours of practice go into every illusion before you show it to the public. You have to be able to make these moves in your sleep."

The crowd clapped enthusiastically and St. Laurent bowed graciously, before handing the rings to Miss LaPierre. She set them inside a box and covered them with a cloth, while he stepped forward, walking out onto the front apron.

"For our next trick," said St. Laurent, "I would like the Fire Chief and his deputy to join me on the stage. I need men with visual acuity and sharp acumen to bear witness to this next feat."

The spotlight lowered to the front of the audience. The

two firemen sat for a moment and then exchanged glances, the junior officer apparently waiting for a nod of approval. The chief finally gave it, shrugged his shoulders, and both men finally rose to their feet, accepting polite applause.

"Looks like he didn't see this coming," said Vera. "The best Grayson can do is be a good sport. Nobody likes to be made a fool of, but he can hardly say no to them with all their money in his pocket."

A spotlight followed Chief Grayson as he led the way up a set of stairs to the left of the apron. He ascended quickly, tipped his hat, and smiled to the crowd, as a few in the audience yelled out encouragement, calling him familiarly by his first name.

St. Laurent performed a version of the shell game, but instead of shells and a pea, he used a brightly colored ball and metal drinking glasses, visible to the upper reaches of the theater. His hands moved deftly and the fire chiefs picked the wrong glass on every occasion. Then one of them accused St. Laurent of palming the soft orange ball, only to find a white tennis ball inside the next overturned cup.

"This guy is very good," said Alan. "He could make a lot of money on the street corner with that."

"That's a good point, Champ. Don't ever play for money with guys on the street. They work in teams. Even if you somehow win, which you won't, they won't let you out of their sight before the friends take *their* money back."

"What about the police?"

"If there's a game running, the cop on the beat is getting a cut—and so is his sergeant. In a dispute, whose side do you think they'll come down on? The beat cop will tell you to move on and be thankful for the life lesson."

"Now if you will excuse us a moment," said St. Laurent, "the Paramount has a surprise number for you while we prepare the stage for our grand finale."

The curtain drew together slowly as Nicholas Ivanovich once again took the stage, standing in the spotlight to the right on the apron.

"By now I believe you have learned to expect the unexpected," said Ivanovich, "and we have a little treat for you that we hope is unexpectedly enjoyable, although a touch naughty."

Men in the audience whistled and hooted in anticipation.

"Ladies and gentlemen, the Paramount Theater proudly presents for your pleasure an exotic sampling of the *Moulin Rouge Follies*, featuring the fabulous Natasha Zarenko Performers and the Cancan!"

The crowd hungrily applauded its approval mixed with cat calls, while from the pit below, the orchestra launched into a zesty rendition of the *Infernal Galop*. Almost instantly, four dancing girls appeared in front of the curtain, entering in pairs from each side of the stage, tossing their skirts above their knees, back and forth, as they skipped lightly to the center of the stage where they locked arms with the other pair when they passed each other, spinning like blades on a windmill. The dancers moving forward raised their knees high and shook their ankles as they skipped and turned, while the dancers moving backward bent over at the waist and tugged their skirts over the top of their white pantaloons, exposing dark hosiery and bare thighs at the top of shapely legs.

Vera tilted her head close to Alan's. "And you had no idea about this either?"

Alan grinned and shook his head.

The dancers separated but rejoined quickly, all four now facing forward in a line. In a synchronized movement they each grabbed the hem of their skirts with both hands, pulling them up as high as their faces and began high kicking, first in one direction and then the other. They separated into pairs again and while one performer danced in place, kicking her knees high, her partner raised a leg and grabbed it near the ankle, bouncing on the ball of her foot as she spun around a number of times to the delight of the crowd.

Vera elbowed Alan teasingly, and he lowered his head in mock embarrassment.

The dancers separated again and backed up closer to the drawn curtain. They took turns, first one and then the others running to the middle, performing cartwheels, where dark silk covered legs spun in front of white petticoats and bloomers, resembling flowers opening and closing all too quickly.

A dancer with dark hair and striking features stepped forward, gracefully alternating high kicks that would knock a top hat off a presidential candidate. After more than a dozen kicks with each leg, she suddenly dropped to the floor doing the splits, with her dress descending gracefully over her legs, like dandelion fluff.

"Ow!" said Alan. "Doesn't that hurt?"

"Not so much," said Vera. "You get used to it."

Alan smiled wryly. "Not that I could do those, but I'd be afraid I'd land on something important to the family tree..."

Vera grinned.

Once the lead dancer returned to her feet, the dancers huddled into a circle, bent over at the waist, and spun counter-clockwise with their skirts pulled high over their bloomers, shaking their posteriors on every step to a loud ovation from the audience. When they came out of the huddle they formed a line and linked arms across their shoulders. They high-kicked as they stepped sideways, hopped, and reversed direction, before finishing with each of them in turn doing a jump-split, landing on the stage facing the audience with their arms held high in the air.

While the crowded theater clapped appreciatively the women got up and sashayed across the stage, exiting to the right.

"Wow!" said Alan. "Tough act for St. Laurent to follow."

Vera nodded. "Although a short number, that's a strong act. The kind a theater likes to finish with. Makes me wonder what else's in store."

It took a full minute for the crowd to catch its breath, and while Alan and Vera whispered between themselves, the stage lights dimmed and the curtain opened to a very dark set. A swarthy man in Arabian Nights silk, short vest, and turban entered the stage, approaching St. Laurent, who seemingly ignored his presence while he began taking in the radiant glow of a narrowly focused spotlight.

"For this little adventure, we are going to travel deep into heart of Ancient India where the presence of a white man is almost unknown. Where their ancient culture, customs, and religions have long held beliefs we might find barbaric. While studying their culture, I observed a practice which still remains a part of their mystique, which I found quite fascinating and I thought the western world might want to see. It is the Hindu tradition of suttee, where royal widows self-immolate themselves on funeral pyres at their husbands' funerals so they can be with their spouses in eternity. On a practical level it clears up the messy business of estate planning and the passing of titles and property to the heirs."

The audience laughed.

"It has been reported that on rare occurrences the wives have not been willing to fulfill their expected role and need to have some spiritual guidance from community members to join their husbands in the afterlife."

The lights continued to dim on stage as St. Laurent and

the eunuch lit four torches positioned in tall stands, two on each side of a dark shape on a platform at the rear of the stage. Together, the men pulled a velvet cover off a black lacquered and polished nickel coffin, located on a raised platform, and folded the material neatly, while St. Laurent continued his narrative.

As soon as the cover had been folded, a similarly attired eunuch entered the stage, pulling LaPierre along behind him. She now wore silky harem pants, a slinky top, and a light veil that covered only the lower portion of her face. The eunuch led her to St. Laurent, where she obediently stopped and lowered her head. The two eunuchs took positions as sentries on either side of St. Laurent, their strong arms folded formidably in front.

"Tonight is the official debut of an act never before seen in America," said St. Laurent, "I am going to present for your wonder, awe, and amazement the *Witch of the Flame!*"

With a wave of St. Laurent's hands, the turbaned assistants crossed the stage to the coffin, lifting it up, and carrying it out to mid-stage, where they turned it slowly in a tight circle, exposing the ornate prop for the audience's inspection, before carrying it back to the platform, carefully setting it down, and closing its lid.

"Instead of burning on a pile of brush and chopped firewood like France's Joan of Arc, our Hindu princess has chosen a casket as her means of passage to the other side to meet her husband, a notorious Indian tyrant and philanderer, hated by his people but loved by this woman. The problem for her is not knowing which direction her husband has taken in the afterlife. Will this transitional method transport her to a blissful life in heaven or condemn her to the burning fires of hell?"

Without saying a word, one of the eunuchs bowed to the magician and exited the stage, while the other stood imposingly next to Miss LaPierre, seemingly unimpressed with her beauty or helplessness. St. Laurent indicated something on the platform with a tilt of his head to the princess, and she obediently picked up a blue wizard's robe adorned with bright dragons in a repeating pattern, holding it open for the magician as he slid into the robe one arm at a time, transforming into a wizard. She handed him a white wig with long hair and a matching beard to complete his ensemble. He slid the wig and beard over his head and deftly pushed it into place, before pulling up the conical hood, which made him appear taller, more menacing.

The wizard tugged at his sleeves, rolled his shoulders, and picked up another torch, lighting it from one already ablaze. With it he approached the princess menacingly. She bowed obsequiously and stepped backward to stand beside the eunuch. Wordlessly the wizard spread his arms wide, drawing the audience's focus to him once again, while he elegantly passed in front of the eunuch and the princess, circling the coffin, directing his torch into the deep shadows under and around the casket to show there were no concealments, his dancing gown visible through the brass trellis as he glided behind the coffin.

Having completely circled the coffin, he stopped in front of the princess and gestured with the torch for her to climb inside. She shook her head in protest as the wizard pulled opened the coffin and indicated again with the torch for her to climb inside.

She lowered her head and refused to move from her spot, clutching her hands to her bosoms. The wizard balled a hand into a fist and planted it on his hip, glaring at the princess, but still she didn't move. He shook his head and held the torch near the princess's face. As he did, the eunuch swept an arm underneath her legs, lifting her off her feet, and deposited her on the edge of the platform next to the coffin. She raised her hands in front of her face, palms out, and shook her head wearily. The wizard pointed again towards the shiny box with the torch. Reluctantly, slowly, the princess stepped into the casket, while members of the audience raised their voices for her not to enter it.

"Let her go!" someone pleaded.

The wizard spun half way around and raised the torch defiantly, as if threatening anyone who dared to challenge him. Then he returned his attention to the princess and motioned with the torch again. The princess sat down, dropped her head, and then slid into a prone position. The wizard handed the torch to the eunuch, pulled the lid closed and latched it shut. A few seconds later, the wizard picked up a shiny sword that had been on the platform next to the coffin. He gracefully swung it in an arc and caught it high in the air, his hands stretched over this pointy hood. Then he stepped up to the coffin, found a slot on top and drove the sword into the casket, the plunge met by a blood curdling scream.

"You beast!" yelled someone in the audience.

The wizard rolled his head and picked up another sword. He similarly swung it high and caught it as with the other. Again he stepped forward, found another slot on the casket and plunged the sword inside.

"Agghhh!" a woman's voice moaned from the coffin.

The wizard rested his hands on his hips and cocked his head, as if something weren't right, and then he quickly pulled the swords out and threw them down on the stage in front of the coffin. He took the torch from the eunuch to illuminate the latch, which he quickly opened. As Soon as he tugged the lid open, flames shot several feet into the air, forcing the wizard back. He reached up quickly and slammed the lid shut.

Many in the audience had screamed at the sight of the

flames, and now with the coffin closed, they sat in total silence.

The wizard inched forward and opened the lid a second time, and as before the flames shot several feet into the air, forcing him to withdraw and hastily close the lid again.

The audience grew alarmed and began chattering among themselves.

"You did this to her!" yelled one patron. "You must save her!"

The wizard cautiously opened the lid again. This time flames shot upward, but not as high—and then they died slowly. The eunuch inched backward as the wizard stepped forward, holding the lit torch out in front of him as if he were burning away cobwebs from a haunted house. As he leaned cautiously over the casket, a red-faced demon with a cape and horns suddenly sat up erect and lunged for the wizard, grabbing him by the neck. The suddenness of the attack took the wizard by surprise, and knocked the lit torch out of his hand, to the floor, where it rolled out of view into the curtains behind the platform and stage.

The wizard fought back, grabbing the demon with both hands around his neck and shoved him back inside the coffin.

Several in the audience screamed.

With one hand holding the red demon down, the wizard groped frantically with the other hand and slammed the coffin lid.

The audience screamed encouragement for the wizard, and below his hand the lid jumped from kicks and pushes coming from beneath it, trying to force it open, but somehow the wizard found the latch and clasped the lock shut. After a moment he backed away from the seemingly possessed casket.

"Save the girl!" yelled a voice from the audience, soon

followed by others echoing the sentiment.

His back to the audience and staring at the coffin, the wizard nodded and took a torch from one of the stands. He marched with purpose up to the coffin, unlatched the clasp, and threw the lid open. He swept the torch over the open casket, inspecting its interior, and then he climbed onto the platform, stood over the coffin, and drew his robe around him, while holding the torch in front. The flames on both sides shot high in the air, accompanied by a large puff of smoke that enveloped him. When the special effects flames subsided, the smoke continued to linger over the empty stage and coffin that continued to glow in places, like hot embers that had escaped a bonfire.

Many in the audience began clapping at the dramatic climax.

Vera nudged Alan with her elbow. "Isn't this about the time we should be seeing the rescued princess?"

Alan grabbed his arm rests, leaned forward, and stood up at the same moment the music in the orchestra pit stopped. He scowled down at the stage and then glanced to Vera at his side, shaking his head.

"Something's wrong there!" he said. "That can't be part of the act!"

Inside of Vera's kitchen, she removed an ice tray from the small compartment inside her refrigerator, levered it open, and dumped the ice cubes into a glass bowl on her kitchen table.

"Fancy-shmancy," said Rose Red. "I didn't know those things could make their own ice."

"They've come a long way since the ice box," said Vera, as she slid a few cubes into the top of an ice pack and twisted the cap shut.

Vera wrapped the ice pack with a fresh kitchen towel and sat on the edge of the sofa next to the reclining Tasha, who tilted her head obediently to the side. Vera pressed the cooling pack against the bruised area, took Tasha's hand and showed her where to press on it, to keep the bag in place. Then she sat back and gazed into Tasha's eyes.

"Your pupil dilation looks normal, so I think you're going to be alright. Would you like a couple of aspirin to go with that?"

"If I may be so bold, I'd like a glass of vodka to wash them down," said Tasha. "If you don't have any on hand, one of the girls can run out and get us a bottle. I'm sure our handsome driver can find a place."

"This is Washington State," said Alan. "We've got state controlled liquor stores that closed at 6:00pm."

"How primitive!" said Tasha. "The country repealed Prohibition years ago, and I know you have cocktail lounges all over downtown..."

"Lounges don't sell liquor for take out," said Alan.

"Sure they do, handsome. You have to know how to ask and do it in the right way. You'd probably have to bribe them, but Star knows how to charm it out of them."

Star rolled her lips slowly and flashed Alan a knowing smile. She shrugged her shoulders and arched her plucked brows high, confirming her skills at persuasion.

"Is Star your real name?" asked Alan.

The brunette gazed into the distance and shook her head. "It once said Mikala on a lost birth certificate somewhere. Nobody calls me that unless they're pulling my hair and whispering in my ear."

Alan cleared his throat and smiled. "Got it."

"I've got vodka on hand," said Vera, watching Alan with an impish grin. "If we run short, we'll try it Star's way. I've found the Fireside Lounge on Second Avenue has been accommodating for special requests."

"That's the spirit," said Tasha. "I'm starting to feel better already."

Vera retrieved a clear bottle of liquid from a dry bar, brought it back and set it on the counter near Sophie. "If you would take care of the drinks, I'll see to our other needs."

While Sophie brought out drinking glasses, Vera pulled a chair close to Yvette, sitting on the edge of a large sofa, picking at shreds of silk sticking to fresh scabs on her scratched legs.

"We should clean those up," said Vera, "before they get infected, and just maybe we can prevent scarring."

"You can do that?" asked Yvette.

"I know if we don't treat them right away, you'll have scars—or a lot worse."

"I don't want that!"

Vera nodded.

"Why don't you slip out of what's left, and I'll get some warm water, soap, and a cloth to scrub you up."

As Vera went back into the kitchen, Yvette stood up and promptly slid out of her silk pants, letting them drop to the floor, revealing flesh-colored underwear, made of the lightest material—the tiniest pair Alan had seen in his life—hardly enough to cover the essentials. Then she leaned over, hooked her thumbs inside her black hose, and tugged what was left of them down over her knees, one leg at a time. Yvette winced after she rolled the nylons past mid-calf, where she encountered a deeper gash on her muscle, where more of the clinging silk snagged hungrily at her skin.

Yvette sat back down, and Rose Red came over and scooted in next to her on the sofa, offering assistance, while lifting Yvette's feet into her lap.

"Let me help you with these," she said. "I'm no stranger to bleeding."

When Vera came out of the kitchen she slowed to a stop as she passed Alan. She slid a hand across his shoulders, up his neck, and scratched the back of his head playfully. She leaned close to his ear, almost touching it with her lips.

"Welcome to the girl's dressing room, Champ."

Alan flicked his brow high, while trying to hide his smirk.

"If you don't mind cleaning Yvette's wounds," said Vera, "Alan and I can concentrate on the theater fire, ask a few questions. Maybe we can get an idea of what happened up on the stage. Are we looking at an accident or arson? Did someone have murder in mind?"

Rose Red smiled at Vera and then Yvette, who also seemed comfortable with the nursing arrangement.

"If any of those cuts are deep, we can talk about stitches then. I'm quite adept at sewing a fine line, but should you want a real surgeon, we can arrange that too."

"So let's start with general questions and work our way in," said Vera.

Heads nodded from among those present.

"Alan and I have worked a number of cases together, and we don't have a set order of doing business. Whichever one of us has a question is the one who asks it. Are you ladies okay with that?"

Nods from all around.

"So, who told you to stay in the dressing room during St. Laurent's performance?"

"The owner, Nikolai Ivanovich," said Tasha. "He stopped by before the show to reminisce about the old days, and he told us St. Laurent had a deal for us. Niki held out a crisp hundred-dollar bill and told us we could have it. A gift from St. Laurent, if we did our Cancan number during his intermission—and if we promised to stay in the dressing room through the rest of his act."

"'Old days?'" asked Vera.

"Niki's an old friend. He got bit by the theater bug in Paris, cashed out his holdings, and immigrated here. We lost track. I didn't recognize the name on the contract, and the same went for him with me and the girls. He changes his name as often as he does his underwear. I barely recognized him when he came through the door."

"What name did he go by before?" asked Alan.

"Soloviev, last I heard," said Tasha. "He's another white émigré, not a Bolshevik. Likes to think he's connected to Russian royalty, but he's very much the commoner."

Alan nodded, weighing the information.

"And if we get this right," said Vera, "nobody approached you up until show time with the cash offer?"

Tasha shook her head slightly and closed her eyes a moment. "I grabbed the cash, shoved Niki out the door, and we dove through our steamer trunks to see if we had fresh panties. If we had to go bare bottom, we'd have charged Niki double."

Alan covered a broad grin, hoping his smile would escape notice.

"Oh, lookie," said Tasha, "I've embarrassed Detective Alan."

Across the room, Vera smirked and shook her head teasingly.

"Did Nikolai say why he wanted you to stay off the stage?" asked Vera.

"He said Frederic wanted to protect the secrets to his show, which is really not that big of a surprise. But we could really care less what his tricks are. He demanded that only people who worked for him be allowed backstage and in the wings during his act, especially for the finale. If we wanted to watch the show, we could buy tickets and sit out front with the others—which is ridiculous because there were no seats available, and he knew it."

"Did that pose a problem for you?"

Tasha closed her eyes and shook her head slightly. "We've seen a lot of magic shows, so we didn't need to see anymore tricks."

"Did they post anyone to watch you so that you stayed in your room?" asked Vera.

"We always have guys trying to watch us dress," said Tasha, "so I usually keep the door shut and don't pay much attention to it, unless they're going to pay for it. I'm thinking there might've been a Hungarian or Slav or two, dressed as eunuchs. Seems I heard them talking in their dialect."

51

"Do you speak that too?" asked Vera.

"I speak French, English, and housekeeper's Russian," said Tasha, "but I know a smattering of several others; enough to ask directions to the toilet and other necessities."

"You're a survivor," said Vera.

"All women are," said Tasha.

"I'm thinking one-hundred dollars is a lot of money for a three-minute Cancan," said Vera. "Makes me wonder about St. Laurent's motivation."

"I've never met him, so I can't say," said Tasha, "but I thought it presumptuous that he would be the one calling the shots with Niki, especially since we're the ones who put butts in the seats. Paying customers expect more for their dollar than watching some guy pull a rabbit out of a hat. If they want to see rabbits, they can visit farmer Bob in the country, but your average working stiff doesn't get to see girls strutting hot stuff, in the buff, nearly enough."

Yvette squeaked out an "Ouch," as Rose Red dabbed at one of her scratches.

"Not you, honey," said Tasha. "You've got stage presence. I can tell the men liked you. It's your boss who I think has a magic wand stuck up his ass."

"Probably where he pulls the rabbit out of," said Rose Red.

Vera rolled her eyes playfully at Alan.

"We don't have a rabbit," said LaPierre.

"I'm teasing, honey," said Tasha.

"I want to know more about you and St. Laurent," Vera said to LaPierre, "but first we need to do a head count of who we saw—and didn't see—get out of the building."

"Good idea," said Tasha.

"I'm guessing the orchestra got out all right, but we don't know that for sure," said Vera. "And then we saw a man run out while we were under the stage. I thought he might have been wearing a frock like the fire chief's, but we're not sure of that. One of the eunuchs ran past us, and then the five of you."

"There were the two grips who came out after Yvette," said Alan.

"The four of us are the only ones in our troupe," said Tasha. "We don't have grips or stage hands, so that leaves Nicholas, St. Laurent, and maybe some of his grips or cast, but I don't know how many that would be."

"Last we saw of St. Laurent," said Alan, "he had just made Miss LaPierre climb inside the coffin and went in after her..."

"Is there anybody else in your act?" Vera asked, addressing Yvette. "Do you have more stage hands or extras in your entourage?"

Yvette raised her brow and her eyes flared wide, innocently, as she shrugged her shoulders. "I'm brand new to the show," she said. "I've only practiced with Frederic the past couple of weeks, and mostly it has been just the two of us rehearsing in an empty theater in Los Angeles. I think the guys you call eunuchs and the other crew members were on a holiday break during that time, in-between tours."

"We're still trying to figure out how many that might have been," said Vera. "Did you get a chance to meet them on the train coming up to Seattle...or during the set up?"

"Frederic and I rode up in a Pullman sleeper. The others were in coach, and they speak different languages but seem to get along. I thought Latvian, but I wouldn't know... something Slavic for sure. I thought there might have been six or seven, but Frederic kept us apart, didn't want us mingling."

Vera wrote a tally down on a notepad she kept by her telephone, tore off a sheet, folded it in half the long way, and handed it to Alan.

"I'll stay here and entertain our guests while you go back down to the fire," Vera said. "Sorry to send you off, but this is my place and I need to stay. Column A is a list of who's here and those we're sure made it out. Column B is for the unknowns. See who's there from the police department that we trust. If you don't recognize any of our contacts, give this to whoever's in charge of the scene. I'll call Mike Ketchum at home and see if it will be his detectives or the fire department who investigate this. My hunch is that if there's a death, it becomes a murder, and the police department handles it."

"And when I'm done, then what?

"Drive by here and see if the lights are still on. I doubt we'll be going to bed early."

Alan parked in front of the Butterworth Mortuary on Pine Street, three blocks up the hill and east of the Paramount Theater. Gawkers, fire buffs, and back-up engine companies had taken all other available parking. Charged hoses snaked like giant Anacondas mating, crisscrossing as they passed through the front entrance of the Paramount. Firemen moved at a measured pace as they entered the theater with extra gear, giving the impression they were in mop-up mode. Onlookers filled the sidewalk across the street and continued to stare at the lineup of ambulances coming and going, like runners in a relay race.

Alan spotted Ben Kearney, an imposing detective in a coat, tie, and Homburg, standing close to the Fire Department's red command car, where the soaking wet deputy chief gave directions to firemen. Alan caught Ben's eye and his all-knowing nod, the ubiquitous non-verbal that suggested a less direct approach would be best for the moment.

Alan worked through the crowd and stopped next to Big Ben, who glanced sideways, nodded a greeting, while keeping his voice low.

"I got the feeling you're not easily entertained by watching fires, Champ."

"Saw enough of this one from the inside," said Alan.

"What? You were watching the show?"

"Vera's birthday today. She wanted a quiet celebration, nothing fancy."

"But she got a three-alarm fire instead."

Alan closed his eyes and shook his head slowly.

"Where is she now?" asked Ben. "You got her out alright?"

"You can rest assured of that. She's up at her apartment now, entertaining a handful of stage beauties who survived."

Ben creased a smile and shook his head. "Of course. You've got to love that woman, but then you don't need me to tell you that."

Alan grinned sheepishly and dug into his inside coat pocket, pulling out the list Vera had compiled. He handed it to Ben. "There's something not right about this fire. Madam Zarenko and her girls were supposed to be the closing act, following the magician, but he didn't want them to leave their dressing room during his performance, and either he or somebody working for him chained the fire doors shut."

"No kidding!"

"Although that's got to be against every fire code ever written, Vera and Zarenko said it's not uncommon for magicians to put restrictions on those who see how their tricks are done, the secrets behind the magic."

"I get that," said Ben, "but that's no excuse for locking fire doors. That's outrageous! Everyone knows about the 1911 Triangle Shirtwaist Fire in New York. Because so many young women were trapped inside and killed, fire codes were put in place across the entire country to prevent this exact kind of thing."

"We caught up with three girls from Madam Zarenko's act underneath the stage—"

56

"What were you doing down there?"

"We couldn't get through the crush of the crowd stampeding the front door, so we circled back underneath the theater. We met Zarenko's girls down there looking for a way out of the building, like us, but they couldn't find Tasha, so they had to leave without her. I went up through the trap door and found her flat out near the back of the stage, behind the props, knocked out by a judo chop, or so I'm guessing. She told us that right before that a man had hold of her arm, and that's the last she remembers. Now she's got a bruise on her neck."

"She's lucky to be alive," said Ben. "Did she thank you for saving her life?"

"She'd barely regained consciousness before I came down here. I don't need any thanks."

"Don't be surprised if it comes later when she's feeling better," said Ben. "My experience with theater is that the women working here have their own set of values and moral code. They're strong on watching out for each other and don't let society tell them how things ought to be done. They're never in town long enough to worry about the Legion of Decency coming after them with lit torches, tar, and feathers."

"A little thankful exuberance is not a bad thing," said Alan. "But right now, they're in protective surroundings, like our friends from Goon Dip Wong's Pleasure Emporium..."

"Exactly," said Ben, "they've got a lot in common, and far be it from me to tell you to avoid all the temptations in life."

Alan smiled dreamily and then shook his head. "We came up short on our head count," he said. "Have you seen the magician or the owner? Besides those two there could be a couple of Russians dressed as eunuchs and a grip or two who didn't make it out."

Big Ben indicated to the left of the doors with a tilt of his head. "There's four dead under the blankets, all trampled near the front door. This looks like a buffalo jump where Indians herded bison off a cliff for a large hunting kill. And the odd thing is that people from the upper levels who went out the fire escapes all seem to have made it down safely. Says something about human nature, but I'm not sure what."

"Vera and I were just a little ways back from the door when a man with a cane went down," said Alan. "Had it knocked out from under him by a thick-headed brute. It'd be a shame if the old guy is one of the victims."

"Fire or not, there's such a thing as grace and dignity," said Ben. "A lout that knocks down a guy with a cane needs a talking to in the alley with a leather sap and a firm fist."

"No argument from me on that," said Alan, "and I'll keep my eye out for him if you'll make sure he and I can have some privacy, so he can bone up on his manners."

"I'll run interference for you."

"So...who handles the investigation here," asked Alan, "you or the fire department?"

"From what I've heard the fire boys saying, it sounds like an accident, not an arson, which means they'll get stuck writing it up. This will be their baby. Police would only get involved if the fire had been deliberately set, like an arson fire meant to cover up murder—and even then, fire investigations aren't our specialty. We'd need to partner up with a fire supervisor for his expertise."

"What about Madam Zarenko getting knocked out from behind?"

"That sounds like motive for a crime, but does she know that's what happened for certain—or could it have been a prop that fell against her?"

"I didn't see anything lying on the stage near her."

"As soon as it's safe I'm going to join up with the Fire chiefs for a walk through. You can join us and show where you found Madam Zarenko, but even if there's nothing on the stage that might have hit her accidentally, that still doesn't mean your theory is wrong. Anything lying about could have been picked up and moved during the fire—just something to keep in mind."

"Did both chiefs make it out?

"Bill Grayson's at Harborview being treated for smoke inhalation, and you can see Jeffries right behind us."

"I'm not positive, but Vera and I thought we saw a man in a tunic like theirs running out the back door ahead of us."

"Wouldn't have been either one of these two, because they were inside fighting the fire, both of them working a hose, with Grayson on point, sucking in too much smoke and burns to his hands."

"We only saw the shape," said Alan. "Must have been wrong."

Ben's brow creased thoughtfully. "We can ask the crew if that sounds like someone from their act. No harm in that, but Grayson and Jeffries did a damn fine job keeping the fire from spreading to the rest of the building and apartments out front. We could have lost a lot more people if they hadn't been here."

*   *   *

Deputy Chief Al Jeffries stepped over large trunk hoses and led three of his commanders, accompanied by Ben and Alan, down the aisle of the theater to the stage, where two other firemen continued to hose down smoldering curtains and other draped fabric. The group climbed the steps to the side of the stage. Jeffries approached the fireman on the right apron and patted him reassuringly on the shoulder.

"Would you guys stand down a moment, please? We

want to take a look at the stage before everything gets shoved around and tells us a different story."

The fireman with the nozzle nodded and shut off the spray.

Jeffries gave Alan a friendly smile. "So you're the one who came up through the trap door and carried the woman off."

"That's right."

Jeffries shook his head. "I thought you were part of the act. People kept coming and going long after everyone should have cleared out."

"The doors in back were chained shut," said Alan.

"So I heard," said Jeffries, "but we saw a policeman up here getting people off the stage. Don't know where he came from."

"In a tunic?" asked Alan.

"Tunic, hat, nightstick, and handlebar mustache."

Alan canted his head towards Ben. "Must have been who Vera and I saw, but who is he?"

"He went through the trapdoor right before you came up, then after you carried the woman out, we lost track—no wait—the magician's assistant came staggering out on the stage on her own, right after you, and she ran down the steps. But there could've been a few more after that..."

"She followed us out, and then a couple of grips staggered out."

"I think everyone from up here must have made it out then," said Jeffries.

"While we're here, can we peek inside the coffin?" asked Alan, glancing back and forth between Jeffries and Ben. "His assistant said she got out of there and hid in another box, but then she got trapped against the wall or something. She's not sure how she got out of that mess."

"I'm fine with that," said Jeffries.

"I think it's a good idea," said Ben.

"Be careful with the metal handles," said Jeffries. "The coffin had been all ablaze and those are what Chief Grayson burned his fingers on."

Alan slowed in front of the coffin, and Jeffries picked up a long scrap of curtain fabric and doubled it over a couple of times like a kitchen towel. "Use this," he said, handing the drapery to Alan.

Alan shook his head and grinned more confidently than he felt. "St. Laurent might have ducked through here, but the last thing I know I saw had horns and looked like it wanted to get out."

The two fire commanders with Jeffries chuckled nervously. Alan wrapped the fabric around the still warm handle and lifted the top slowly, allowing trapped smoke to escape the coffin. But this smoke had a particularly foul smell to it, different from charred wood, melted fabric, charred paint, or lamp oil. It had the unmistakable smell of burnt flesh.

Alan pushed the lid all the way up, as far as it would go, and stepped away from the smoke and fumes. He waved the handful of fabric he still held, fanning it back and forth over the open casket, chasing away the foul vapors. Slowly the shape of a humanoid-like figure emerged through the foul haze, charred black, eyes bulging wide, and mouth open in terror—with horns on its head.

"Mother of Christ!" said one of the firemen standing near Jeffries. He followed the outburst by quickly making the sign of the cross.

Ben stepped forward, stopped next to Alan, and glanced toward the firemen. "I think his goose is cooked, but do any of you want to check his vital signs before we go any further?"

Jeffries exhaled and shook his head slowly. "I've got

this one detective, but promise me one thing. If this thing, whatever it is, suddenly grabs me around the neck and tries to drag me in the coffin with him, you'll shoot him in the fucking head!"

"I'll empty my gun," said Ben.

"And if that doesn't work, I'll empty mine, too," said Alan.

Jeffries stutter stepped, weighing what he'd just heard, and then he lifted one of the devil's legs and slid off the remnants of a red slipper.

"We've got a foot here, not a hoof."

"So we're dealing with what's left of a human, not the devil," said Ben.

"It would appear so," said Jeffries.

The deputy chief gently took hold of a deeply charred wrist, only to have the blackened flesh peel away as the hand dropped back into the coffin.

Jeffries shook his head again. "Alright, I'm going to check his jugular for a pulse, and this is where I want you on your toes."

"You've got it," said Ben.

Jeffries leaned in and reached his hand up to the right side of the devil's neck, finding a spot where the red hood had melted away.

"The skin here is as crispy as a Christmas Goose's, but I'm feeling nothing going on underneath. You guys want me to drive a stake through his heart while we're here?"

Nervous chuckles from the firemen.

"That won't be necessary, Chief," said Ben.

"I smell an accelerant," said Jeffries, "like he'd been drenched in kerosene or white gas. With the lid closed on the coffin, it doesn't seem there would have been enough oxygen to keep the fire going for long—like when you shut the lid on a cigarette lighter. So I'm surprised there's been this much burning."

"How about if the escape hatch had been left open?" asked Alan.

Jeffries nodded quietly as he thought a moment. "That would work and would also explain why all the fuel hadn't been consumed either, but where's this hatch you're talking about?"

Alan checked with Ben, "May I?"

"Certainly, Champ. I don't know the first thing about magic."

"I don't know much either," said Alan, "but I figure for Miss LaPierre to get out quickly and this guy to replace her so fast, the secret door has to be quite large. It also has to be on the side facing away from the audience."

Alan circled behind the prop and stared at the backside of the platform and the casket. He leaned over and closely examined a brass curtain rod with the remnants of a drawstring and curtain hooks. Then he knelt down and glanced underneath the platform. He stood up and nodded.

"When St. Laurent circled the casket, we could see his feet as he passed behind here. You can see mine now if you look underneath, because the blackout curtains have burned away. He'd set it up so either he or his assistant could pull the curtains closed during the act so we couldn't see what happened back here on the platform and the floor. So...somehow Miss LaPierre opened the side of the coffin, rolled out, and climbed into another box behind the back curtain...or house curtains that were right behind their set up, until the fire destroyed them."

Alan turned toward the back of the stage and gazed at the floor.

"There's the torch," Alan said, pointing to the smoldering prop on the floor. "It flew out of St. Laurent's hands when he fought with the devil—and that's what caught the drapes on fire. And there's the second coffin, back against the wall, like Miss LaPierre described. About half way in-between here and there is where I found Madam Zarenko on the floor."

Ben leaned into the coffin and canted his head in the direction of the devils feet. "I think I got something here. Much of the lining is gone and I see a treadle of some kind."

Ben reached past the devil and pushed firmly on what he'd been staring at. Following a soft metal click, the side of the coffin sprang open slightly at the top. Ben reached across the devil's body and shoved the door down, creating an opening big enough for the devil to easily enter.

"Very nice work," said Ben. "Quality craftsmanship. This must have cost your magician plenty."

Alan nodded, while studying the features of the devil. "So who is this guy?"

"It's not your magician?" asked Ben.

"I don't know," said Alan. "How about you, Chief? You saw him from much closer up than anyone else."

Jeffries arched his brow high and shook his head. "He's the right size and all, but with his eyelids burned off, I can't be sure. Is that a real mustache below what's left of his nose, or one of those show biz kits?"

Ben pinched a few of the whiskers to the side of the devil's mouth and tugged gently, as he leaned over close and stared.

"I'll go with 'real' on these," he said, "but then there's the problem of identification. This mug's fingers are so charred we'll never get fingerprints."

"So how can we tell who this is?" asked Alan. "Dental records?"

"Records from where?" asked Ben gently. "If this is your

magician, he's a world traveler. We would need to know who his dentist might have been and where he had his practice, if he had one. Performers are usually cash and carry sorts, the kind of people who don't leave a paper trail."

Ben leaned in close to the devil's face once again and sniffed the air. Then he picked up the charred hand and sniffed at the fabric. "I'll bet this is lighter fluid."

The large detective reached under the devil's shoulder and pulled the body upward, rolling the torso slightly, while feeling underneath it. Then he repeated the process, reaching across the devil, grabbing his other shoulder and tugging it toward him. Alan caught a glimpse of something yellow, red, and metallic. He slid his hand underneath the dead man's shoulders and pulled out a 19 cent can of *Red Devil Lighter Fluid.*

"That's rather apropos," said Ben. "It could be that someone wanted to destroy the face and fingers of this guy for sure, so there could never be a comparison made. This isn't what we'd call dispositive proof of a homicide, but this is beginning to look more and more like a crime—with an unknown victim. So to be on the safe side, don't handle that lighter fluid can anymore than needs be, Champ. We might try for fingerprints."

Alan sucked in his cheeks and his mouth made a small O.

Ben shook his head and gave Alan an easy grin. "Don't worry about it. Given all the fire props in this act, it could have a number of donor prints on it, and they'll all have a legitimate excuse why they'd be there..."

Ben raised an eyebrow and faced Jeffries. "What do you think, Chief? Do you see anything that positively cannot be explained away as accidental?"

"The lighter fluid can bothers me," Jeffries said, "but given all the fire in this act, there are a lot of plausible excuses why spilled fuel would be on Satan's hands. And then we had the two actors fighting with the torch in front of a packed house, whether real or pretend. If this guy had lighter fluid already saturating his clothing, the clumsiness with the torch could have easily set him on fire without it being deliberate. I'd like to hear from the other combatant to be sure, see what he's got to say."

Alan set the empty lighter fluid can on the platform next to the casket. "I'd like to take a look inside that other box on the floor, if you don't mind?"

Ben came around the side of the coffin and joined Alan. "How does this match up with the prediction the newspaper had about there being a tragedy here tonight?"

"It's right on the mark," said Alan. "St. Laurent even teased about it early on during his show. He suggested that Alexander, the seer who claims he knows all, might have hoped to eliminate him for some reason."

"Really? Jealousy's always a motive. We'll have to keep Alexander in mind if this turns out to be a murder."

Alan sat on his haunches next to the unadorned casket on the floor, wider at one end and tapered at the other. He grabbed the lid and tugged upward, but instead of opening, it slid across the floor closer to him, causing its sprung side to chatter on the stage decking as it moved.

"I can see how this could get pushed against the wall during a fight," said Alan.

"Or it could easily be shoved deliberately," added Ben.

Alan tugged on the lip of the casket and rolled the black painted box on its side, allowing the hinged side to flop wider open, exposing the purple crushed velvet lining, expertly upholstered with tuck and roll padding.

"I'm surprised the top doesn't slide off," said Alan.

Ben knelt next to Alan and ran his fingers along the edge, stopped suddenly and examined something black and

66

sticky on his thumb. He rubbed his thumb and forefinger together. He reached inside his pants pocket, took out a small folding knife and dug at a couple of spots on the lid.

"Shoe polish," he said. "Somebody screwed the lid down and covered the brass with polish. That implies a rush job, where a craftsman would've used putty and paint. Again, this isn't proof positive, but it's certainly curious."

"What do you make of this?" asked Alan, swinging the escape door up and checking its spring clamps, the kind common to kitchen cabinets. "Vampire fetish?"

"Too early for me to say," said Ben, shaking his large head. "I don't see any dirt in it, so maybe it's a leftover prop from another trick."

"I can ask Miss LaPierre what she knows about it," said Alan.

"Great a place to start as any," said Ben as he stood up. "I want to go along with you for that, but let's check the magician's dressing room first."

Being closer to the back of the stage, Alan led the way down the steps and stopped at the dressing room closest to the stage. The door stood partially open.

Alan shook his head. "Given what I'd heard about his need for secrecy, I thought we'd find a padlock bolted to a closed door."

"I'm sure the firemen probably opened it," said Ben. "They would've had to use an axe and break it open if it were locked. They'd have to make sure no one had gotten trapped inside suffering from smoke inhalation."

Alan flicked the light switch, but nothing happened.

"This circuit must still be out," said Ben, while pulling out a flashlight from his coat pocket.

"And Vera calls me the Boy Scout," said Alan.

"You were out on the town with Vera, while I'm on the job," said Ben. "In the police business you've got to carry one of these all the time, even when working the dayshift. You never know when you're going to have to go in a building without lights."

Ben stepped past Alan, shining his *EverReady* into the dark, like a miniature spotlight sweeping over the small enclosure, before settling down to illuminate one area at a time. Two steamer trunks sat on the floor with their lids pulled open, while a metal bar with a permanent sag held changes of costumes and after show clothes, seemingly broken into sections for men and women, with the men's side taking up the most room. Tubes of makeup, brushes, and eyebrow pencils took up the area in front of one mirror, while an assortment of theater make-up and spirit gum crowded the vanity's counter top.

"What's on that mannequin?" Alan asked.

Ben moved in closer and directed the flashlight beam at a bright blue robe with gold and red dragons, the hood pulled up over a white wig and beard on a dummy with carefully painted features.

"Yeah, the robe!" said Alan. "It's what the magician had on when fighting the devil."

Ben pulled the hood of the robe back to examine the mannequin more closely. "This is very well done," he said. "I'm thinking it has more uses than serving only as a coat rack."

"That's what St. Laurent had on when we last saw him," said Alan.

Ben nodded. "I'll get my camera, and we'll get some pictures of this and the coffin, but...could this be a spare or back up set?"

"If so, why would it be out?" asked Alan. "Why wouldn't they leave it in the trunk? That would be close enough for a quick change if they needed it. The mannequin takes up a lot of room."

Ben closed his eyes a moment and then handed Alan the flashlight. "Point well taken, Champ. Keep an eye on it, and I'll be back in two shakes..."

Alan's thoughtful smile turned into a scowl and he pointed behind Ben to a pile on the floor. Ben stepped to the side and Alan directed the light closely at another bright blue robe with the same dragon pattern. Ben squatted down and picked up the robe delicately, and charred pieces of the lower sleeve flaked away. Ben shook his head slowly.

"I think this one would be your magician's robe, and the burn marks would suggest the coffin fight had been for real."

Ben's gaze followed the robe to the floor and another wig and beard, this one pushed up against the wall like a forgotten dust mop. "I'll bring some paper bags for the evidence. These things will be going with us."

"Why two identical robes?" asked Alan.

"I'm going to have to give this some thought, Champ. Normally when on a case, we work with the premise that everything can be explained by the laws of physics, such as inertia and cause and effect, but with magicians the opposite is often where the truth is. Their whole livelihood is based on misdirection, sleight of hand, and smoke and mirrors. It's going to be very difficult to determine what's real versus what's a deliberate deception, designed to deceive."

"Things aren't always what they appear."

"Especially in magic, Champ. I'll get the gear and be right back."

While Alan turned off the engine on the Packard in front
of Vera's apartment building on Tenth Avenue East and set
the handbrake, Ben climbed out the passenger side, strode
up to the first step, and then spun around to wait for Alan.

"Bit of a hurry, aren't you Ben?" Alan teased.

"After what you told me about the girls and their Cancan
routine, yeah, I'm interested in meeting them. They sound
like a lot of fun."

Ben led the way, climbing the stairs to the top floor. Vera
greeted Ben warmly, welcoming him inside her apartment.
Alan made the introductions for Ben to everyone else. Ben
nodded politely, but then stepped forward when Madam
Zarenko offered her hand, clicking his heels together in a
courtly manner, bending forward at the waist, and kissing
her hand. Alan could have sworn she blushed.

"Call me 'Tasha,' my dashing giant of a man, and what
shall I call you?"

"You can call me 'your humble servant,' madam—but
'Ben' will do nicely. We're not sticklers on formality here."

"'Ben' it is then, and will you join us for a drink?"

Ben shook his head and smiled. "Afraid not. I'm on duty
at the moment."

"Such a pity," said Tasha. "How long does duty last?"

"Until I'm comfortable enough to call Chief Ketchum and advise him on whether we have a homicide or not."

"Someone died?" several of the women asked in unison.

Ben nodded, while making eye contact with each of them. "Four were crushed in the crowd at the front door, and then we found a burnt body inside the casket."

Everyone sat silently a moment, lost in their own thoughts, and then Miss LaPierre spoke first. "Frederic?"

"We're not sure, ma'am," said Ben. "Burnt beyond recognition, at least in my humble opinion, but we'd like you to take a look when the body's been transferred to the coroner's office, see if you can identify it."

LaPierre lowered her eyes and nodded her assent.

"Now, can any of you tell me about seeing a policeman on the stage?" asked Ben. "Is that part of anyone's act?"

Zarenko and her assistants all shrugged their shoulders in unison, while checking with each other to make sure they were in agreement.

"Nyet," said Tasha, "but I did see one outside our dressing room before the fire. Almost everywhere we perform we have that happen. In some countries they check our papers, other countries the police discourage us from meeting privately with patrons after the show, and sometimes the police wait to watch us dress and undress. No matter where we go, men are men, and they like being around pretty girls, particularly when the girls are not wearing clothes. I figured him to be one of those."

"Can you describe him?" asked Ben.

Tasha shrugged and shook her head. "He looked like every beat cop or Bobby I've ever seen. Helmet, mustache, and frock."

Ben thought a moment. "You sure about the helmet?"

Tasha nodded slowly. "I certainly think so, but now I'm not so sure."

"I saw him too—but only for a moment," said Sophie. "He had a helmet."

"Very curious," said Ben. "We haven't worn those in years."

Ben exchanged puzzled glances with Alan.

"How about you, Yvette," asked Alan, "Did you see him—or might a policeman be a part of your act?"

"If you ask me general questions, I can answer them," said LaPierre, "but if you ask me specific questions about how the act is done, I can't help you. I've taken the magician's oath and can't divulge secrets."

Vera hitched her leg up and scooted across the padded arm of Alan's chair. "I've taken the magician's oath, too," she said, "but that rule only applies to the key elements of the illusions that might spoil the surprise for future shows. What outfits you wear during your act are hardly proprietary information."

"Actually they might be," said Tasha, adding her two cents worth, "if the magician has doubles or stand-ins as part of the illusion. Knowing that information could tip the secret to others how the act is performed—

"I'm not trying to be a know-it-all," Tasha continued, "but years ago in Europe I took the oath too. I jumped boxes before I learned knife throwing."

"Not just body doubles," said Alan to Ben, "but that also could apply to dummies wearing the magician's clothes..."

"I see," said Ben. "How about I put the question another way, Miss LaPierre. Can you tell me, then, if there ever has been a police uniform with helmet inside your dressing room wardrobe?"

All eyes focused on LaPierre as she thought. Finally she sighed. "I saw something like that, but honestly I have no idea which one of the men wears it or when. I only know my parts. That's all I've rehearsed. I've never seen the end of the act, so I don't know who would be wearing it.

"We all share the same tight quarters," LaPierre went on, "taking turns dressing, and all of us have multiple roles and play many different parts."

"All right," said Ben. "That's helpful. Now we know the policeman could be one of the performers, but not exactly which one. So can you tell me if you saw anyone in a police uniform on stage when you were trying to get out of the building?"

LaPierre shook her head. "I only saw the top part of a figure going through the hole in the floor. I assumed it to be a man and decided to follow him out."

"We're going to need to talk to the other people in your act," said Ben. "Are they all staying in the Paramount Apartments?"

"Frederic told me the others had rooms on a lower floor," said LaPierre. "Room 410, but I'm not positive."

"How about your room?" asked Ben.

"Ninth floor, 907."

"Do you have the key?" asked Ben.

LaPierre shook her head. "I got out of there with what I'm wearing, and I'm lucky to have that. Maybe it's in the dressing room, or Frederic has it."

<<<<<<<<<<<<<<<<<<<<<<<<<<<<<<<<<<<<<<<<<<<<<<<<<<<<<<<<<<<<

Ben and Alan found the apartment manager outside the
Paramount Theater and Apartments watching the fire
crews clean up and stow their gear. With the elevator out
of service, Dimitri Chernikov rolled his eyes when asked to
haul his sixty-four year-old frame up the stairs to the ninth
floor.

"Don't you guys need a warrant?" Chernikov asked.

"He might," said Alan with a tilt of his head towards Ben,
"but I don't. I'm a private investigator working for a client.
Search and seizure laws don't apply to me."

"I don't know what that means," said Chernikov.

"It means we want to see inside Miss LaPierre and
Monsieur St. Laurent's quarters. We're not here to search
the apartment, we're only here to do a head count so we
can confirm who's missing from the fire, and right now St.
Laurent's still a no-show."

"What's that got to do with you needing a search
warrant?" asked Chernikov.

"Let's call it 'exigent circumstances' then," said Ben, "and
leave it at that. Otherwise I'll be forced to kick down the
door and put the Habeas Grabbus on your ass for hindering
our investigation."

"No need for the rough stuff," said Chernikov. "I just have to look out for our residents is all."

"That's what overpaid attorneys are for: looking out for the interests of people with money."

Chernikov stopped at the top of the ninth flight of stairs to catch his breath and held out the key ring to Ben. "I'm a life-long smoker and need a break. If you're going to go inside anyway, you might as well use the key. The master key is the light-colored brass with the large base. It's room 907, I'll catch up."

Alan glanced back, checking on Chernikov, while Ben knocked on the door. After a slow ten count, Ben inserted the key and turned the lock, pushing the door open slowly.

"Seattle Police," he said in a loud, firm voice.

After a five second pause, Ben leaned into the door with his shoulder and pushed it open. Alan followed Ben inside and found the unit to be bigger than he'd figured, with expert craftsmanship and extra trim details, such as built-in cabinets and arched doorways between the rooms, which included a kitchenette, bedroom, bath, and closet. Ben went to his left and Alan the right.

"Nobody here," said Alan from the kitchen.

"Not here, either," said Ben from the bedroom.

They regrouped in the living room near a steamer trunk and a set of suitcases. Alan glanced at the luggage tag on the steamer. "Frederic St. Laurent," he read out loud, then picked up and turned over the tags on the suitcases. "Wanda Collingsworth! That's interesting. Vera recognized her but didn't remember her real name."

"No guarantee that's her real name, either," said Ben. "It's not uncommon for girls in this industry to use stage names."

"This coming from the Teutonic Thunder," Alan said with a wicked grin.

"Exactly my point," said Ben. "I didn't want my wrestling past to follow me around, and Yvette—or Wanda—likely feels the same way. Nothing wrong with that."

Ben opened the closet, and Alan glanced over his shoulder. "I'm not seeing anything that indicates anyone raced through here after the fire."

"How about the water on the floor?" Alan said, pointing to a partial wet footprint near the front door. I'm all but dried off, so I didn't make that."

Ben knelt low and touched the moisture on the polished oak floor. Then he pressed his palm on the entryway carpet. "Good eye, Champ!"

"I got sprayed with a fire hose when I went up on the stage looking for Madam Zarenko, and the same could have happened to St. Laurent on his way out of the theater..."

"Or to someone else who'd also been on stage and ran up here right away..."

Alan nodded. "We should probably keep that possibility open."

"Let me see the bottom of your shoes," said Ben.

Alan placed a hand against the arched doorway for support and drew a foot up and caught it. Ben touched the pant cuffs and leather sole of Alan's shoes, and then repeated the process with the other foot.

Ben let go of Alan's foot and shook his large head. "The water's not from you."

"Didn't think so."

"And I didn't see an old beat coat or helmet, lying about up here, did you?"

Alan shook his head and pushed his cheek out with his tongue as he thought.

"We might want to check the building and nearby garbage cans," said Ben. "You never know what you'll find."

"What time do the garbage trucks come?" asked Alan.

"About 4:00 AM," said Ben. "I know because people complain to the department all the time about the garbage men banging the cans around, as if we would help them get their beauty sleep."

Alan stepped out into the hallway, ahead of Ben, who closed and locked the door behind them. At the end of the hallway, a dapper gentleman wearing a long cloak over uniform pants and boots, with a beard and full mustache, stood next to an overnight bag as he spoke with the apartment manager, handing him something.

Alan tapped Ben's beefy arm and inclined his head toward him, keeping his voice low. "There's the pushy guy from the theater. I'm going to have a talk with him."

Alan took brisk steps towards Chernikov and the gentleman, with Ben following close behind.

"I'll have a word," said Alan, staring at the man as he closed the distance between them.

The man gazed quizzically at Alan and grasped the barrel of his walking stick with one hand, while sliding one wrapped in gauze over the top of a polished lioness head. Ben caught Alan by the arm and slowed him down.

"Steady as you go, Champ," Ben whispered through a forced smile. "Don't lead with your temper."

Alan sensed that Ben had seen or knew something he didn't, he slowed to a stop, keeping his distance from the gentleman, and his eyes caught a glimpse of shiny steel blade extending from the man's walking stick.

"I saw you in the theater," said Alan, softening his approach.

The man sized up Alan and Ben, and then glanced back to Chernikov. "These are the detectives you let into my building?"

"Yes, sir, Mr. Ivanovich. They were going to break down the doors if I didn't give them the master key, so I saved you

$24.00 in repair costs."

"You're Nikolai Ivanovich?" asked Alan.

"You're in my building," said the man, tucking his bandaged hand into his overcoat. "Let's start with who you are first, and we'll go from there."

Alan detected a trace of a foreign accent that sounded more authentically French than St. Laurent's, but he didn't have Vera's practiced ear and skills at telling where he might be from. "I'm Alan Stewart, private detective."

"And I'm Benjamin Edward Kearney, Seattle Police Detective."

"And you are here why?" asked Ivanovich. "Why a private detective with the police?"

"I have been retained by a survivor of the fire," said Alan, "and at the moment we're trying to determine who else survived and who's unaccounted for. You were the master of ceremonies tonight, weren't you?"

Ivanovich gave an exaggerated nod. "Indeed."

"But now you have a beard and a uniform..."

Ivanovich touched his face with the hand holding the walking stick and nodded again. "I forgot I had it on," he said. "In the theater we all play many roles. I am of course the master of ceremonies, but tonight I had a part to play—actually a prank of sorts. Frederic offered me a crisp $100 bill to dress up as Nicholas the II, the late Russian tsar, and while in character introduce Madam Zarenko's act."

"But I saw you leaving through the front of the theater, where you shoved past people. How did you get from the stage up to the balcony?"

"There's a ladder connecting to a catwalk that crosses over the top of the theater, and it comes down at the projection booth on the top tier. It's a shortcut of sorts. Frederic wanted me to put on an officer's tunic, and then I remembered I have pieces that would make this even more authentic—an entire outfit. In a trunk in my room I have gold epaulets, braiding, and a sash. When everything is worn together, the outfit looks impressively regal. Would you care to see it?"

Alan made eye contact with Ben, who shook his head. "Not this time, but we are curious where you're going with the luggage?"

"I have a place at the Moore Hotel. I often stay there when I have a late night."

"You own both theaters?" asked Alan.

"Actually, I own the Paramount, the Moore, the Egyptian, the Coliseum, and the Palomar. So I thought I'd spend a few nights at the Moore, until things calm down here. With that nonsense about the crystal seer having predicted the catastrophe tonight, you can imagine I'll have reporters hounding me for a salacious quote because of the body count. People just don't seem to know what to do when there is a fire or a ship's sinking, like the Titanic. Instead of clearing the doorways so others can escape to safety, they have to stop and put on their coats, pick up their grips, and visit their neighbors. Seattle's the worst place for this, with everyone being so polite here. They stand like huge boulders in a stream and blather nonsense at complete strangers: 'After you.' 'No, after you!' 'No, I insist, after we've had crumpets and tea!' and in the meantime, while they're being so excruciatingly polite, good people get burnt to death or die from smoke inhalation. Or in the case of the Titanic, refuse to get in perfectly good lifeboats that sank along with the ship. It's illogical and insane and so terribly American and British. I sometimes wonder why you Americans fought for your independence when you're absolutely so much like your cousins."

"The Fire Department tells us four of those American 'good people' got trampled near the front door," said Alan, "and it looks like another twenty-nine were taken to the hospitals. The body count could rise."

Ivanovich closed his eyes and nodded, as if shutting it out. "What about those on stage?"

"We found a body there," said Ben. "Burnt to a crisp."

Ivanovich's eyes flared wide as he stared at Ben. "Man or woman? Can you tell me?"

"A man, inside the coffin," said Ben.

"Coffin? Sadly appropriate, but Madam Zarenko is all right then?"

"Detective Stewart found her knocked unconscious and carried her out," said Ben with a tilt of his head toward Alan.

"Thank you for that," said Ivanovich. "I'm glad the girls are okay."

"But not St. Laurent?" asked Alan.

Ivanovich rocked his head back and forth and nodded. "Of course Frederic and his crew, but which one died? I don't know that, do you?"

"We don't know whose body we found," said Ben. "We might need you to take a look later, see if you recognize him."

Ivanovich scrunched his brow into a painful frown. "Tonight?"

"I think the coroner will want to clean him up a bit first and figure out how he died, before a showing for identification. Fire is often used to cover up other crimes, destroy evidence. The Coroner will check for the consistency of the wounds and cause of death. And cleaning the body up might give us more to work with for identification, but the dead man had been wearing a devil's suit. A red one."

"Wouldn't that be Frederic?" asked Ivanovich. "After all, he's the star performer."

"He's still missing, so there's that possibility."

"How would St. Laurent have had time to change from his wizard outfit into the red devil's suit?" asked Alan.

"That's part of the magic," said Ivanovich, "but if I really knew that, I couldn't tell you. I'm still a card carrying actor who's taken the magician's oath."

"You, too?" said Alan, shaking his head.

"I'm actually not much of a magician. I didn't have the discipline to put in the necessary hours of practice to be proficient. I prefer mysticism and conduct private séances for discerning clients. What I do is more like what Alexander does over at the Orpheum, except I'm not that lucky, and that's what happened tonight—he got lucky with that prediction. I'm sure of that. Pure coincidence is all it is—but that aside, all serious practitioners insist that their assistants take the secrecy oath. They've put a lot of money into their illusions, and if everyone knows how they work, the magic is gone."

"And then so is the audience..." added Ben.

"So who else might be missing?" asked Ivanovich. "Is that what you're checking? Sort of a process of elimination?"

"We're not exactly sure how many helpers St. Laurent had, but everyone in Madam Zarenko's act has been accounted for."

Ivanovich moved his lips in and out as he thought, causing his mustache to roll about his lip like an overly large caterpillar. "I thought three, at least two from the Ukraine area. They had accents and were darker, like those from around the Black Sea, not like Muscovites or northern Russians."

"You speak Russian?" asked Alan.

"Very little anymore. Mostly French while growing up. English now."

"We're running into a lot of white émigrés lately," said Alan.

Ivanovich shrugged his shoulders. "Shouldn't be that surprising since Seattle is the main seaport to Alaska—which used to be Russian soil, you remember, and not that many years ago."

"Is that where you're from?" asked Alan.

Ivanovich shook his head. "Alexander Pantages and Alexander Conlin, the wizard who claims to know all. They both got their starts in Alaska near the gold fields, but I came here by way of France. Before that I traveled extensively through eastern and western Europe."

"I see," said Ben. "The stage hands and extras are down on the fourth floor?"

Ivanovich nodded. "You'll most likely find them curled up around a bottle of vodka. Now if you'll excuse me, you've taken enough of my time, I need to be going."

"One last question," said Alan. "How'd you burn your hand?"

Ivanovich's brow lowered into a scowl, he withdrew his bandaged hand from his pocket and flashed a smile devoid of sincerity. "My shirt needed a touch up, so I attempted to iron it myself with a fancy plug-in job that makes its own steam. I learned the hard way that it only takes a moment for them to heat up and scald."

"Try a healthy dab of *Vaseline* on it," said Alan. "It's what the oil riggers in Texas use for burns and cuts."

Ivanovich smiled indulgently, nodded, and resumed his conversation with the apartment manager.

* * *

Ben and Alan took the stairs down to the fourth floor but stopped at the landing on five. "So what are you thinking?" asked Alan. "Murder, arson, or accidental fire?"

"I'm still reserving judgment on this. There are some strange coincidences here, and you already know I don't believe in that sort of thing. So we're forced to treat it as an accident until we find clear, convincing evidence to the contrary. The guy's got a ton of money in real estate, but I can't see him starting a fire here, unless finances have been bad and he's looking to take the easy way out and cash in on insurance or fake a bankruptcy. If anything, though, trapping a man in a box and burning him alive would require a lot of rage. So if this turns out to be murder, I'm thinking the motives here are extremely personal and passionate."

"I'm with you on that."

"But as I told you earlier, these magicians are a clever group. We'll be hard pressed to show what really happened, unless we come up with a motive for murder or arson. Finding that would point us in the right direction."

"You knew all along that he had a sword hidden inside that walking stick?" asked Alan.

Ben nodded. "I did, but I'm not sure how. Might've been the way he held it, like he'd been a cavalry officer making ready to draw across his body, charging into cannon fire. I saw a few hidden swords while on the circuit in Europe, mostly in France and Spain. I think the burnished lion head gave it away. Seemed too fancy for someone to want to put weight on."

"Thanks for slowing me down. I might've walked right into a thrust. He seems to be the type who'd stick people first and apologize later—and then only if they were still able to stand and someone forced him."

"Guys like Ivanovich take care of themselves first. It wouldn't surprise me to learn he's made his dough clawing and climbing over a pile of bodies."

"Pantages might have been one of them," said Alan. "He got his bones picked clean by his attorneys while trying to clear his name. He won a reversal of his conviction on appeal, but it cost him everything he had."

"Fire sale prices," said Ben. "And speaking of fires, good

eye on the bandaged hand. How'd you know he'd burned it?"

"I didn't know, I played a hunch."

Ben nodded and creased a smile. "Hanging around Vera's been good for you."

"That it has," said Alan. "That is has..."

Alan and Ben took the steps and worked their way down the floors, checking the large collection of cans in the garbage rooms for the police tunic and helmet. While on the fourth floor, they decided to talk with the magician's assistants in room 410.

"If we had a crime and we thought they were our suspects, we'd interview them individually," said Ben. "But we're not sure of any of that yet. So I say we go easy and see if they give up something useful."

"Got it," said Alan. He stood to the side of the door and knocked, as Ben had taught him on another occasion, another hotel. Standing away from the door had paid off for them in Chinatown when a shooter fired through the door after they'd knocked and announced who they were.

"Who's it?" barked a male voice from inside the room.

"Police!" said Ben. "We need to speak with you."

Inside the room, voices spoke in low tones in a dialect unfamiliar to Alan. He guessed Russian, and glanced at Ben. He nodded back, apparently in sync with Alan's thought.

"Policia?"

"Da!" said Ben.

The door opened a few inches, and a dark haired man

with bushy brows stuck his nose into the large crack. Ben held up his police shield and Alan did as well with his P.I. badge. "Police," Ben repeated.

The man opened the door all the way. Another man of similar age and stature was seated, hunched over a small kitchen table with an overfull ashtray, an open bottle of vodka, and drinking classes with clear liquid. Both men gazed suspiciously at their new guests through the smoky haze.

"Were both of you in the theater tonight?" asked Ben.

The men glanced at each other, only their eyes moving. Finally, their heads nodded.

"We're glad you made it out safely, but we're wondering if you know if anyone is missing."

More shifting of eyes. "Pavel's not come back yet," said the one who'd answered the door.

"What about the magician, Frederic St. Laurent?" asked Ben.

The man's brow furrowed. "He stays on the ninth floor."

Ben smiled evenly. "We know that, but have you seen him since the fire?"

The man interpreted for the other, who nodded his understanding and then shook his head. "We haven't seen Frederic since the fire."

"I see," said Ben. "And what is Pavel's last name?

"Medved."

"How old is he?"

The man said something in Russian to the other man, and they quickly agreed on a number. "Forty-five."

"Are you the two who dress as the eunuchs?" asked Alan.

The man stared at Alan's eyes and mouth, puzzled.

"Eunuchs," said Alan. "The men on stage with turbans

and your arms crossed." Alan crossed his arms in front of his chest dramatically, as an example.

Both men nodded. "Da."

"What about Pavel?" asked Ben. "What does he do?"

The man lowered his head and rolled it back and forth. "We're not supposed to tell the secrets," he said.

"Does he dress as the devil?" asked Ben gently.

The two men exchanged glances and nodded sheepishly, like mischievous boys caught by a priest.

"How about dressing as the policeman?" asked Ben. "Does he wear the tunic and helmet?"

The spokesman shook his head. "He not wear that."

"Does Frederic wear that?" asked Ben.

The man lowered his head and gazed at the other at the table. "We get in trouble if we say too much, please. You understand?"

"I think we have enough to go on," said Ben. "Are you two close friends with Pavel?"

The talker rolled his head as he thought, while the other man looked away, glancing out the window. "He's quiet all the time. Keeps to himself. Wakes up screaming some nights, then he goes out and walks around. He's a lonely man."

"He tell you what the dreams are about?" asked Alan.

The man translated to the one at the table, who seemed irritated at the intrusion. After a short exchange he nodded knowingly. "I hear him sometimes say, 'Not the babushka! Not the babushka!' That's as close to English as I can make it for you."

"Does he have family?" asked Ben.

"Is something the matter with Pavel?" asked the talker. "Have you found him?"

"We're not sure," said Ben. "There's a body in the casket on stage. We might need you to identify it later."

The talker spoke excitedly to the other man, whose eyes flashed wide before his shoulders slumped. "So the seer's prediction has come true then? What about Frederic? Where's he?"

"We don't know yet," said Ben. "Does he sometimes wear the devil's outfit and one of you the magician's robes?"

The men looked at each other and shook their heads. "We play many parts, but you ask too much from us."

* * *

Ben and Alan continued checking the garbage rooms on each floor, working their way down the stairs to the back door and alley. Behind the theater were several 55 gallon drums for the building's garbage collection. They lifted the lids and checked each to no avail. Ben gazed down the alley towards Pine Street to the north and then up the alley to Pike Street.

"He wouldn't have gone out front," said Ben.

"I agree," said Alan.

"Let's check the cans on the way up to Pike and call it good," said Ben.

As they checked the next building's cans a figure stepped out of the doorway near the end of the alley, staggered and pushed his hand against a brick building, catching his balance. As the man tilted his head forward to unzip his fly, the oversized helmet on his head slid down the front of his face, and he had to catch it and push it back. Hands shoved out through over-sized sleeves of a police tunic.

Without saying a word to each other, Ben and Alan double-timed it up the alley and slowly surrounded the skinny dark man muttering to himself.

"Lorenzo Rice!" said Ben, startling the man.

Rice stopped urinating a moment, but then promptly continued. "Sorry, officers, but it hurts too much to stop once I start. You going to arrest me?"

"Not tonight, Lorenzo," said Ben. "But you can't be wearing that coat around, making people think you're the police."

"You like my coat?" asked Lorenzo. "You want to buy it?"

"If you throw in the helmet and tell me where you found it, I might be interested," said Ben.

"You got twenty dollars, and it's all yours."

"That's too rich for my blood, Lorenzo. I'm thinking for $2.00 you can buy yourself a bottle of Jack and disappear for two days."

"Two dollars ain't squat, Officer...I forget your name."

"Kearney. Ben Kearney."

"That's right, Big Ben Kearney, and who's your partner? I never remember you having no partner before."

"This is my partner, Detective Alan Stewart," said Ben. "We work together on special projects, and you look like you're wearing one of our special projects. I could arrest you for public intoxication and confiscate the get up, but I think giving you a few bucks for protecting this special project for us is only fair."

"Fair is right," said Rice. "Don't you forget that. I think ten dollars would be more fair."

"Oh, I see where this is headed," said Ben. "You drive a hard bargain, Lorenzo. I've got an Abe Lincoln in my wallet, and I bet you want every penny of that."

"That's right, I do," said Rice. "How many pennies is that?"

"I'm thinking 500 all together. What about you, partner?" Ben said to Alan.

"That's what I come up with," said Alan. "You take Abe Lincoln and you can trade it at any bank for 500 pennies."

"That's what I want then," said Rice, as he slid out of the coat. "I want that Abe Lincoln of yours and you can have this old coat."

"All right," said Ben, "but promise me you won't spend all those pennies on food or a warm place to stay tonight."

Lorenzo thought for a moment and then grinned widely. Chuckles followed. "You don't have to worry about that, Officer Kearney. I ain't gonna waste 500 pennies like that. No, sir!"

* * *

Ben took the helmet and tunic and stood underneath a streetlight. "Metropolitan Police," Ben read from the ornate cluster on the front of the cork and felt helmet. "British Bobby's custodian helmet, not one of ours, so most probably one that St. Laurent's company brought with them."

Ben handed the helmet to Alan for his inspection and held up the navy blue tunic. "Seven button front," he said, "which is pretty standard from a few years back, but we're going with five now—and this has a sewn on belt, which would never do for us. You'd never be able to unfasten all this and draw your weapon from under your coat when you needed it."

"That's always bothered me," said Alan. "How come you don't wear your revolvers on the outside of your uniform where you can get to them?"

Ben shook his head. "Image and tradition is all. Seattle's leaders wanted that friendly English bobby look with no weapon visible. They didn't want a Wild West sheriff with a low slung holster roaming the streets, scaring people away, making them think we're uncivilized. A lot of good policemen died during the early years, especially during Prohibition, because they couldn't draw their guns when they needed them. More often than not they died with guns still in their holsters."

"That's a shame."

Ben held up the embossed buttons to the light. "They've

also got M.P. initials," he said, "which fits with the London Constable theory. If this uniform doesn't turn out to be evidence in a crime, it looks like I bought myself the beginnings of a police memorabilia collection."

Ben methodically searched each pocket, dipping his fingers in and carefully exploring. Reaching into the inner breast pocket, he pulled out a folded piece of paper and opened it. He read out loud: "'Filipp. We are in grave danger. Remember all in your prayers to the Holy Father. Anna.' Dated June 21, 1918."

"Any significance?" asked Alan.

"I don't know. We've got an old coat here, so there's no telling how long the letter's been inside of it, let alone who wrote it and why. Nice feel to the paper," he said, rubbing the stationery between his fingers, "and you know my rules for collecting evidence: keep it until you know you don't need it. If you toss it, that's when you'll wish you'd kept it."

Ben refolded the letter and put it back in the coat pocket.

Ben and Alan sat across from each other in a booth at the
Five Point Café, studying the newspaper account of
last night's fire at the Paramount. At deadline the Post
Intelligencer placed the body count at six fatalities with
another twenty-nine injured treated at local hospitals.
The newspaper expected the numbers to rise after fire
investigators had time to sift through the ashes.

"Doesn't say if that includes the man in the coffin," said
Alan.

"They missed that detail," said Ben, "but they remembered
Alexander's prediction. They're making hay with that."

"What do you make of it?"

"By all accounts, I'm a college educated man," said Ben,
leaning over the newspaper and keeping his voice low, "so
I don't believe in hocus pocus and mentalists one damn
bit. I'll also tell you I'm not superstitious, but if I spill salt I
throw it over my shoulder, and I also knock on wood when
saying something I hope won't come back to bite me. I tell
myself that's not superstition, I just don't want to tempt
fate, take any chances. But this makes me wonder. I'd like
to say he got lucky with a wild guess, but this is spot on
specific. Either he's got a gift of some kind or he knows

more about this."

"Like who did it?"

"Exactly."

Alan closed his eyes a moment and nodded. "Vera and I are with you on the superstition."

Ben sat back and glanced up.

"We're with Ben on what?" asked Vera as she stopped behind Alan and rested a hand on his shoulder.

Alan scooted across his seat toward the window, making room on the end. Vera slid in next to him, her legs rubbing up against his as she got comfortable. He liked it that way, her being comfortable with physical closeness and touching. He hadn't been around that kind of closeness before. That wasn't how his family behaved. He liked this friendship and savored her company, which made him feel alive, always energized with her around.

"We were talking superstition and Alexander's prediction," said Alan.

Vera shrugged and nodded. "What's with that anyway? I try to be open to things I don't understand or can't explain, but all this sleight of hand is just that—it's manipulation. Once you know how the tricks are done, the principals behind them that is, you can figure out the new ones, but an out of the blue prediction like this doesn't have thin wires attached, or smoke and mirrors for that matter."

"You think there's a criminal plot and he knows who did it?" asked Ben.

"He calls himself 'Alexander—*who knows all*'," said Vera.

"I'm thinking we need to ask him what he really knows," said Alan.

"Me, too," said Ben. "As a showman, I imagine he keeps Vera's hours," he said, glancing at his watch.

Vera flashed her confident, make-men-weak-at-the-knees smile. "Had to get my company tucked in bed last night, but they were excited and we stayed up till the wee hours, a good old fashioned girls' sleepover. It's probably just as well that Jenny's in school. I'd say we had a pajama party, but none of the other girls had any to wear, so we went with panties and bras, with boobs everywhere."

Ben rolled his eyes toward the ceiling and sucked in his cheeks.

Alan closed his eyes dreamily. "Wish I could've been the fly on the wall."

"If the girls saw a fly on the wall with a boner, they'd squish it and pull its wings off."

"Ouch!" said Alan.

"And you trust these homeless waifs in your apartment without you or Jenny home?" asked Ben.

"Those girls have other skills for making money," said Vera. "They don't need to steal from me. Besides, there is a sisterhood for girls who work the stage. We look out for each other."

"What kind of skills?" asked Alan.

"I'm not saying who does what, but girls who work the circuit have been known to date for profit after hours."

"Seriously?" asked Alan.

Vera nodded. "Highest bidder wins their affection for the evening. That's true in my former business, too, but not always, not for everyone. The world would like to think we we're all whores, but that's not true. I just happened to be comfortable with my nudity back then, but my days of taking clothes off for money are over, if that's going to be your next question."

Vera nudged Alan's leg under the table.

"No, not a question from me." Alan said. "We've discussed that before."

Ben flicked his eyebrows and smiled. "I'm staying out of

this fight if you two go at it again."

Judy, the waitress, delivered a cup of coffee and a maple bar, setting them down in front of Vera, before topping off Ben and Alan's coffees. Vera slid her hand under the table and squeezed Alan's leg, as a peace gesture. She left her hand there a long moment, a comfortable one.

"Back to Alexander," said Ben.

"He's staying at the Camlin Apartment Hotel," said Vera. "The Orpheum has rooms there for their feature performers."

"Do you think he's up yet?" asked Alan.

"He's probably busy doing a Walter Winchell interview by telephone," said Ben. "He's going to get all the mileage out of this he can."

"The Camlin is only one block north of the Paramount," said Alan.

Ben nodded. "It is, but Alexander's got an alibi and 3,000 witnesses who'll put him on stage at the Orpheum at the exact moment the fire started at the Paramount."

"I remember the Camlin during Prohibition," said Vera. "They had a speakeasy in the basement and hidden rooms full of Roy Olmstead liquor, the real stuff from Canada. They used a dumbwaiter to send booze up to the rooms of discerning residents."

"I think just about every 'respectable' hotel had something like that going," said Ben. "That's the only way they could stay in business and be competitive. The Department's Dry Squad only went after those who didn't play ball with them."

* * *

Vera stood a short distance away and dabbed a hanky to her eyes as Ben and Alan approached the Camlin's concierge. Ben flashed his badge discreetly, and Alan did the same.

"We're investigating a complaint," said Ben, "about an underage runaway spending the night in your hotel last night. Her friends told her mother—" Ben nodded towards Vera "—that the young lady ran off with a noted stage celebrity and may still be in his company."

The concierge's face flushed as bright as his burgundy vest and matching bow tie. His eyes flared and he blew out air as if whistling, but no sound came out.

"The Alexander Conlin party in room 1007? I'm not surprised. Oh, dear, we've had complaints about him and his unregistered guests every time he stays here."

"We would like to pay Alexander a visit, recover Mrs. Hawthorn's daughter without making a scene. We would prefer you didn't alert him that we're on our way up."

"That won't be a problem," said the concierge, shaking his head and frowning dramatically, as if he needed sympathy.

"If he's the psychic he claims," said Ben, patting the polished desk top as if gentling a horse, "he should be expecting us about now. Don't you think?"

The concierge's brow knitted low, and then he smiled. "Right you are."

Alan took Vera's arm in his, assuming escort mode, and the trio entered a waiting elevator. "Tenth floor," said Ben to the tiny, elderly man, who cast his eyes low, "if you please." The man pulled the doors shut and shoved down on a handle, as if he were controlling a ride at an amusement park.

On the tenth floor, Ben stepped out first and led the way to 1007. While Vera and Alan hung back a few paces, Ben knocked on the door, stepped to the side, and listened where the door met the jamb. They all heard voices inside the room, and the patter of feet drew closer to the door. Ben stepped back and held his badge at the ready.

"Who ordered breakfast in?" said a female voice on the other side of the door, apparently to someone else in the room. "I thought we were going out."

The door opened, and a young woman in a silk robe frowned through mussed hair, hanging over her face. "Who are you?"

"We're detectives. I'm Police Detective Ben Kearney, and these are my associates, Vera Deward and Alan Stewart."

Alan held his badge at the ready, but the young woman didn't appear interested.

"Is Alex expecting you?" the woman asked, suppressing a yawn.

Ben shook his head. "Not at all. We were in the area and thought we'd talk to him about the fire."

"We haven't had a fire," said the woman, with a hint of an Irish accent, similar to Alan's mother's.

"Who you talking to, Sylvie?" asked a male voice from an interior room.

"It's the police," said Sylvie, holding the door ajar with one hand while clinching her robe over a sheer nightie at the middle with the other hand. The robe only reached mid-thigh and didn't cover her shapely legs and bare feet. She appeared to be in her early twenties, close to Alan's age.

"Put some clothes on," the male said to someone other than Sylvie.

"It's about a fire, they say," said Sylvie, raising her voice but still watching the detectives, glancing from one to the other, appraisingly.

"Of course it is, and it's about time. Show them into the front room. I'll join you in a moment."

Sylvie opened the door, stepped backward, and with a nod of her head indicated for the detectives to enter.

The well-appointed apartment reminded Alan of the ones he'd been inside at the Sorrento Hotel on Madison

Street, except for the women's clothing and liquor bottles strewn about the room.

Sylvie tugged a blanket off the sofa, picked up a pillow, and set them on a chair in the dinette. "Have a seat," she said, and then after a moment added, "Would you like a cup of tea while you wait?"

"That would be nice," said Ben, giving Alan and Vera a discreet nod, indicating for them to join him in the tea service.

"If you please," said Vera.

"Me, too, please," said Alan as he took off his hat and sat in the chair opposite the sofa Vera and Ben had taken, facing towards the kitchenette.

Sylvie quickly glanced at Alan as he casually draped one foot over a knee and slowly shook it, like a cat wagging its tail. Sylvie licked her lips self-consciously, canted her head slightly, trod quietly into the kitchenette, and began filling a kettle with water. As it filled she tugged at the forgotten belt to her bathrobe and cinched it shut around her narrow waist, before primping her hair, using the glass cupboard's reflection to spruce up.

Alan rested his chin on a bridge he made with one hand resting on the armrest, stroking the side of his nose with his index finger. He glanced over at Vera, who shot him her all-knowing grin. He knew she'd tease him later about flirting with Sylvie, while reassuring him it didn't bother her—as long as he didn't make an ass of either her or himself in the process.

After a moment the bedroom door opened and a dapper man stopped in the middle of its doorframe, wearing a silk robe, ascot, and exotic slippers, as if waiting for the spotlight to signal his entry, and then he approached Vera, offering an extended hand, palm upward.

"I'm Alexander Conlin, and I'm pleased to meet you," he

said, bowing at the waist, taking Vera's hand and kissing it between the knuckles.

Ben and Alan stood, introduced themselves and shook hands. As they re-took their seats, Alan snuck another peek towards Sylvie and caught her doing the same with him, checking him out. She quickly glanced away, and then looked back awkwardly, catching his smile. She's still a child, Alan thought. *All grown up physically and living the hard life on the road, but otherwise young.*

"This is about the fire at the Paramount?" asked Alexander.

"You are indeed psychic," said Ben, flashing a wry smile.

Alexander closed his eyes and grinned indulgently. "Touché, detective."

"I'm sorry," said Ben. "I'm not mocking you. That one screamed to be told."

"I don't mind," said Alexander. "I get teased a lot, but I'm the one who laughs in the end—all the way to the bank."

"So we've heard," said Vera.

"This is the worst fire in Seattle history that I can remember, casualty wise," said Ben. "The Great Fire in '89 burnt down the city—without taking a life. The losses were all property and a couple of cats and a lot of rats. Today, though, we have a city in grieving and people wanting answers to how you could have known in advance about this."

"Am I a suspect?"

Ben shook his head slowly. "Not at this time, but your knowing this in advance, when no-one else did, is suspicious. It could be coincidence, it could be you know something about Nikolai Ivanovich's financial situation we don't, it could be you inspired a latent fire bug who capitalized on the suggestion you gave him, or maybe you know something we don't."

"I understand," said Alexander, "but I'm not sure if I can tell you anything that will help you."

"I'm hoping you can tell us what you were seeing in the moment you made the prediction," said Ben. "Did you have a vision where you actually saw the fire? Or did your inner voice dictate to you what to say?"

Alexander sat forward on a companion chair and rubbed his temples. "The truth is I don't remember what I said."

"The papers said that you had some kind of awkward spasm during your act and started speaking in Russian," said Alan.

"I read the papers," said Alexander, "but I don't speak Russian. In fact, I don't know that I've ever heard more than a few words of it—and those back in my younger days in Alaska—but certainly nothing over the past several years."

"We're not planning on revealing secrets to your act," said Ben. "We have a need to know what the hell happened with the fire so we can get to the bottom of it. If you have—"

"I've got nothing," said Alexander, shaking his head. "We were in the very beginning of my act, when I felt a powerful jolt—I remember that much—and then I awoke later, still on my feet, like I'd been sleep walking when I woke up, now finding myself on stage in front of a packed theater. Rather disconcerting, I'll tell you. It took a moment to get my bearings."

"Have you ever experienced anything like that before?" asked Alan, before stealing another glance at Sylvie, who quietly followed the conversation, pretending to stare at the kettle.

"Nothing as dramatic as that," said Alexander. "I would just as soon not have this conversation repeated outside this room."

"Understood," said Ben.

"More than anything else, my act's foundation is based on skill, my showmanship ability, which I occasionally supplement with hypnosis—both individually and in group. I do a reasonable job of carrying this off. Consequently, I have signature methods I need to protect. That aside, and for purposes of your investigation, I neither saw anything consciously, nor planned to add this sort of prediction to my act, and as I've already said, I don't remember delivering it."

Ben nodded. "No grudges against St. Laurent?"

Alexander shook his head. "None. In fact I'd sent him a note suggesting we get together this week, but I never heard back."

"Does the name Medved mean anything to you?" asked Alan.

Alexander thought for a moment and shook his head. "Can't say that it does. Why?"

"We found a body inside one of the stage props," said Ben, "and please don't repeat that to Walter Winchell when he calls."

"Walter Winchell is going to call?" asked Sylvie.

Ben shook his head. "That's just me being psychic, but I expect you'll be dealing with reporters soon enough. My point is we've got a body and we don't know whose. Could be it's this Medved fellow or it might be Frederic, we haven't found him either. The burns were too bad to identify who it might be until the coroner's had a chance to clean him up."

Alexander lowered his eyes and frowned. "I won't deny there's a certain touch of pride in predicting the fire, I'm a showman after all. I feel like Babe Ruth calling home run shots, taunting the pitchers, but I have no memory of it to enjoy—and of course I take no joy in another man's death, whether Alexander's or the Medved fellow's."

"You were there, weren't you?" Alan said to Sylvie. "What do you remember about it?"

Sylvie smiled at Alan and then glanced at Alexander as if seeking permission, but he didn't acknowledge her. "Just as Alexander said, not something that's part of the act, and I've never heard him speak in falsetto."

"Did the voice name anyone specifically as the target?" asked Vera.

"I remember the non-Russian parts pretty well. She said, 'Beware of the fire and a pretense of magic!' and then warned 'It comes on opening night.' She said something more about having a different name, and the treachery would be punished.' I think that covers it."

"Pretense of magic," Vera repeated, "but no specific names given?"

"That's correct, but then there's one more piece..."

"Go on," Vera encouraged.

"She used the plural voice for the final part of the prophecy. She said, 'May all your *deaths* be long and painful!'"

"Very interesting," said Ben, "given we only die once, that is unless you believe in reincarnation."

"If this prophecy is real, there could be more deaths," said Alan, "but whose?"

Sylvie quietly nodded.

"What say you?" Ben asked Alexander. "Are we going to have more predictions?"

Alexander shook his head. "There aren't any in my plans, but I don't know what Anna has in mind."

"The voice who speaks has a name?" asked Vera.

Alexander shook his head again. "Not that I'm aware. Anna's the first name that popped into my head. It's Russian, isn't it?"

"Or Swedish, Finnish, Slovakian, or maybe even German,"

said Vera, "and all of those can be found in America."

"Have you been contacted by the news services and local reporters?" asked Ben.

"We haven't checked with the front desk yet," said Sylvie.

"I can't advise you on what to say or not say," said Ben, "but we'd appreciate if you keep these cards close to your chest for a few days, until we can sort this out. We have what we officially call a suspicious death, and at this point we're not sure if it's a murder or simply a tragic accident. We don't want you to fan the flames of rumor with speculation, which will only make our job more difficult."

"Understood," said Alexander, "but I can only promise that I'll try, because you never know what direction interviews on stories like these will take."

"We appreciate whatever you can do," said Ben.

"And if you would like tickets to tonight's performance," said Alexander, "I will have tickets left for you at the box office, front row or loge."

"Any chance if we came early we could get a backstage tour?" asked Alan, his attention focused on Sylvie.

She glanced again at Alexander, who nodded indulgently. "We would have to limit what you see," said Sylvie. "We protect the proprietary information on how our act works, which cannot be shared, you understand?"

"Of course," said Vera. "I understand how that works."

Ben smiled wryly, scratched the side of his face, and pointed at his eye so that just Alan could see it.

Ben stepped out of the glass and oak phone booth inside the Orpheum Theater lobby, rejoining Vera and Alan.

"There won't be any facial recognition of the victim," he said. "Too much tissue has been burnt away for that to happen. I told the coroner about the can of lighter fluid in the coffin, and he suggests it had likely been used to squirt combustibles inside the victim's mouth and sinuses, not just the fingertips."

Vera shook her head, and Alan rolled his eyes and let of a gush of air.

"Looking more like a murder to you now?" asked Alan.

"Grisly as that news is," said Ben, "the burns are post mortem. Cause of death, single stab wound to the heart from under the sternum."

"From one of the swords?" asked Alan.

"Not likely," said Ben. "Stage props don't have the *Wilkinson* edge to them. Doc is thinking a long, thin blade, like a stiletto. So it's probably a switch-blade, but that's my guess"

"So the murder happened on stage, right in front of us," said Vera.

"Does someone with that kind of wound die right away?"

asked Alan.

"Not necessarily," said Ben. "We had one in Chinatown a few years back, happened right in front of me. I came around the corner and didn't see the first part, but I watched the victim charge after the assailant, still carrying the knife he used to poke him, only to see the victim slump in the middle of the street, rolling over, and dying flat on his back. He didn't know he'd been stabbed until his pumper quit working. And he didn't leave a blood trail following him."

"That would explain the thrashing we saw on stage, among a couple of lid slamming shuts," said Alan. "I think we witnessed the murder."

"I agree," said Vera, "and to be sure, I can't figure out how stage assistants could stuff a body, post mortem, inside a coffin, anyways, especially right after Yvette had just gone through it. There wouldn't have been enough time. Even two burly grips would have their hands full with two-hundred pounds of dead weight that can't help the moving process—unless they had a levitation lift."

Alan and Ben exchanged glances, shook their heads. "We don't know what that is," said Alan.

"It's made by the Otis Elevator people for lifting lovely 'volunteers' from the audience," said Vera. "You notice they're always lithe young ladies wearing evening gowns. First they're hypnotized on stage, then slowly reclined backwards until they appear to be lying on the floor, and from there levitated four feet into the air—and most times made to disappear, leaving nothing but the silk that covered them."

"But St. Laurent didn't perform that trick," said Alan.

"He could still have the equipment available," said Vera, "stored backstage and shoved to the side."

Ben nodded slowly, closing his eyes a moment. "I can't say we were looking for that last night when we did the quick walk through. We'll have to pay the Paramount another visit. This time take you along with us."

"I'd be glad to go," said Vera.

"Stabbing is what's known classically as an intimate crime," said Ben, "in that you necessarily have to get close to the person you're killing, instead of shooting them from twenty paces across a courtyard or a stage with a pistol, rifle, or bow and arrow. You add into this the defiling of the body with the lighter fluid, burning the face away, and we're talking about serious rage here, like you'd find with romantic betrayal or deep seated hatred."

"Do you think there might have been forbidden love here?" asked Vera.

"Between the victim and his killer? That's always a possibility," said Ben, "but we haven't seen evidence to support or even suggest that yet. I'm inclined to think of revenge as a motive, where the killer wanted as large an audience as possible—so the whole world could see what he'd done..."

"Alexander certainly helped pack the house with his gruesome prediction," said Alan, "but I can't figure, if it were him, how'd he get from one theater to the other."

"Stunt doubles?" asked Ben rhetorically. "That works better for an act like St. Laurent's, but I can't see a mentalist utilizing a stand-in."

"Me neither," said Vera. "So...we watch his show tonight, time his intermission break, and see if it matches up with the start of the fire."

"And then he'd have to get back to the Orpheum and on stage," added Alan.

"Even if this part of the city had underground catacombs, like in Japan Town," said Vera, "I'm thinking it'd take at least thirty minutes to make the round trip—and everything would have to work perfectly. There'd be no room for error."

"We can ask Sylvie about last night's intermission," said Alan.

"We might have better luck asking someone who attended the show and not with close ties to it," said Ben, "don't you think?"

"I got a feeling about her," said Alan. "I think she's a lot more involved than just another pretty face."

"What makes you think that?" asked Vera, her tongue moistening her lips.

"I'm not sure," said Alan. "She had a keen interest in everything we discussed—like it meant more to her business wise. I think she's got a monetary stake in the show. I wouldn't be surprised if she does a lot of the management and personal assistant chores for Alexander."

"As opposed to his being her sugar daddy?" asked Ben.

"They might have that going on too," said Alan, "that is when he's not busy tapping the local talent pool, forcing her to sleep on the couch, but I got the feeling she has more of a business sense about her and a sense of her own independence. The looks are a bonus."

"I think we have a volunteer," said Vera, "but if she's the business brains, she might cover for him, because she counts on getting her paycheck at the end of the night."

Ben chuckled. "Is this going to cause a row between you two?"

Vera backhanded Ben's arm playfully. "Nothing I can't handle."

Alan shook his head sheepishly.

"You two can take the tour," said Vera. "I've seen plenty of theaters from every angle. I'll treat myself to a bag of popcorn and a soda. I'll wait in my seat like a proper school girl."

"Me, too," said Ben, "except for the proper girl part.

There's no sense in me tagging along on Alan's tour. Sylvie might feel more comfortable talking if she doesn't feel that she's being interrogated."

*   *   *

Alan knocked on the open door to dressing room B, where Sylvie leaned against a make-up station with her legs crossed in front, while visiting a man and a woman, seated across from her. Her pleated skirt stopped just below her knee, a far sight longer than the robe she'd worn earlier in the day. Sylvie glanced at Alan and smiled, nodding with her head for him to join her as she finished the conversation. The couple got up and left without making introductions, their business completed.

"Where are your friends?" Sylvie asked.

"Stage fright," said Alan.

"Seriously?"

Alan grinned, hoping to make the joke work and make her feel more at ease. "No, not really. Vera once worked the stage, and Ben sort of did too. He wrestled professionally for years on a circuit. They didn't figure things had changed all that much that they needed to tag along on a tour. When I left them they were talking about the history of the statue out front and not concerned about trap doors, secret passageways, organs, and klieg lights."

Alan extended his hand, and Sylvie slid her slender fingers into place making eye contact as they shook. She squeezed his hand politely before relaxing her grip. "I'm Alan Stewart, and I don't believe I've heard yours, other than Sylvie."

"Sylvie Jourdan."

"My pleasure, Miss Jourdan."

"You said something about a statue?"

"Yes, John Harte McGraw, once a King County Sheriff during the tough times and later the governor of the state,

111

second one in fact. His statue's planted on the plug of dirt out front of the theater. He's best remembered as the man responsible for Seattle's ship canal and major land work projects around the area, but most people here are new to town and never heard of him."

"Fame is so fleeting."

"That's my point," said Alan. "You have to capitalize on it while you can."

Sylvie nodded with a smile, her arms folded loosely across her chest. "So tell me, detective, did you really come early for a tour, or did you just want to talk to me alone?"

"You've caught me red faced and ashamed of myself," said Alan. "But while I'm here, can we do both?"

Sylvie stared at Alan a moment, smiled, lowered her eyes, then her arms, and pushed away from the counter. "Sure. Why not? And by the way, I can tell you're not ashamed of yourself."

"Really? Looks can be deceiving."

She took his hand and led him out the door and down a hallway. "The Orpheum has original paintings in the lobby that cost a bundle, I'm sure you've noticed, and for a while it had the largest seating capacity in the city, with 2,700 seats. The only theater with more seating is the—"

"Paramount," said Alan, "with 4,000."

"Correct," said Sylvie, "but we sell out every night here at the Orpheum, "which I seriously doubt St. Laurent can say about the Paramount."

"Really?"

"Really," said Sylvie, now letting go of Alan's hand as they walked. "What the Paramount has in size in seating, they lack in backstage facilities. We have fourteen dressing rooms, most with their own baths, and the women's lounges are magnificent. They're huge."

"Why is that?" asked Alan.

112

"Because the building designers are from the last century and were concerned about our delicate dispositions as the fair sex. They feared some of us might be taken with 'the vapors,' whatever the hell they are."

Alan stopped a moment to laugh, and Sylvie smiled appreciatively. "They're actually glorified smoking rooms for women who are worried about the disapproving looks their husbands or dates might give them if they smoked in public."

"I get it," said Alan. "Old school. Do you smoke?"

Sylvie shook her head. "No, but if I did, I wouldn't worry about where I lit up. But I saw what it did to my mother and father, who always rolled their own and died young. I never found it attractive or sophisticated for that matter."

Before long, their meandering course took them underneath the stage, behind the orchestra pit, which had a peek-a-boo view of the audience. The organist walked past them, greeted Sylvie familiarly, and climbed onto the elevated platform with the large organ console.

"Are there trap doors under this stage?" asked Alan.

"Naturally, but here we call them 'service doors.' I suppose 'trap' implies we were in the business of shanghaiing drunken sailors, shipping them overseas on Yankee Clippers or Chinese junks."

Sylvie pointed out a set of bare wooden stairs in the shadows, which reminded Alan of the ones he used at the Paramount Theater. A few strands of jacketed electrical wire draped through the stage floor and were fastened to the stairs, running down the steps and below their feet to the orchestra pit.

"Shanghaiing's not something you do?" he asked, smiling wryly.

Sylvie shook her head. "We don't do much white slavery either, if that's your next question. People get this idea that mentalists like Claude—Claude Alexander that is—can take over a person's mind, particularly virgins and young women, seduce them into performing lewd and lascivious acts that they would never do otherwise, encouraging them to run away from their husbands or families and never to return. That's old wives' tales rooted in superstition and jealousy."

"You call him Claude?"

Sylvie nodded. "He prefers Alexander on stage, as in Alexander the Great, the Greek conqueror of the world, but to family and close friends he's Claude, and sometimes Alex.

"I am curious about his reputation with women," said Alan. "I've heard he's been married several times, sometimes to more than one woman at the same time."

"Claude does like to be married, but you have to understand him. He grew up traveling on the road, raised by carnies and con artists. To him commitment is a vague concept. He actually has no idea what it means. Besides being married, he's like a sailor with a girl in every port— actually that would be several girls in every port. His penis doesn't have a conscience."

Alan caught himself starting to roll his eyes but stopped. He found Sylvie to be a younger version of Vera and didn't want to discourage her from speaking her mind.

"How long have you been with him?"

"You mean: how old am I?"

"That, too."

"I'm twenty-three, but in dog years I'm a lot older. My last four or five human years have been pretty intense."

"You like what you do?"

They had reached a cozy pit under the stage with a comfortable swivel chair, table, hooded desk lamp, and a lined wicker basket, like those used for taking collections in churches. On top of the desk sat an old microphone, the sort radio stations used for broadcasting their shows, with a set of earphones pushed to the side.

"This is where I hang out during the show," she said. "It makes me feel close to the action, like I'm a major part of it, without actually being a performer myself. I have the advantage of watching the audience without their noticing, and I see what parts of the act work and what doesn't."

"You run the business end of things, don't you?" asked Alan

"That's right."

"Including the bookings?"

Sylvie nodded.

"So how come if you can fill the theater every night, why didn't you get the Paramount, which has more seating?"

"I tried to, but their manager told me they'd already had a booking for these dates."

"Is that Nikolai Ivanovich?"

"Yeah, that's right."

Alan waited patiently, sensing more to come.

"I didn't want to appear arrogant," said Sylvie, "but I asked who they'd booked that could match our box office draw. Nick said Frederic St. Laurent, and I told him I didn't think vaudeville magic acts could fill the theater and he should consider us for these nights instead, because they fit our tour dates better. He agreed but said St. Laurent had guaranteed him a sellout performance, even promising a co-billing with Madam Zarenko's act."

"Let me get this straight," said Alan. "St. Laurent arranged the booking and promised to bring Zarenko's act with him?"

"That's right."

Alan shook his head as he thought. "I could swear that Tasha told us the contract offer came from Nick

Ivanovich."

"I don't know about that," said Sylvie. "Claude blew a fuse when I told him we could only get the Orpheum and would have to play more dates. When he heard what Nick said, he told me that had to be a lie, because Zarenko and Ivanovich were once married, and he couldn't imagine Nick signing any contract with her—even if it made both of them money."

Alan's mouth sagged opened as he stared at Sylvie. "Are you serious about this? They were married?"

"Years ago in Europe, according to Claude, and from what he said, there were parting shots—quite literally— but I don't know who shot at whom. So, detective, this fire you're investigating could very well have been deliberately set, with Zarenko trying to kill her ex-husband or get back at him by destroying his holdings."

"How does Alexander know this?" asked Alan, "and don't tell me 'because he's psychic'!"

"He's really close to Alexander Pantages," said Sylvie.

"Another 'Alexander'. How does that come into play?"

"This one's Greek. Between the Greeks and the Russians, there are a lot of them running around town, especially in the entertainment and restaurant business. That's why I call mine 'Claude,' which is his real first name. At any rate, Claude and Pantages got their starts in Alaska, back during the Gold Rush when they were kids. Rumor has it that Claude shot and killed a man named Soapy Smith, a notorious cheat who extorted Pantages, taking everything he had. Running a dodge on Pantages would have been one thing, but using muscle and threats another. Claude offered to help and provided his own force, in the form of a Colt Peacemaker. He shot and killed Soapy Smith, claiming self-defense, and Pantages has been beholden to him ever since."

"How'd Pantages hear about Zarenko and Ivanovich being married?"

"I'm getting to that," Sylvie said, sitting down in the reclining chair while Alan stood nearby. She stretched out, put her feet up on an orange crate, a poor substitute for an ottoman, and crossed her legs slowly. "Pantages ran afoul of the law with an underage girl about ten years back, long before I met Claude. He'd been convicted of statutory rape and fought it on appeal. A shrewd businessman would have cut his losses, bribed a judge for early release, and kept his fortune intact, but not Pantages. He had a reputation and honor he felt he needed to recover. So he fought long and hard on appeal and eventually prevailed. While doing so his business suffered horribly, and he spent all his money on attorney fees. Deep in hock, he sold his theaters to the new kid in town, Nikolai Ivanovich."

"How many theaters."

"Five of Seattle's best, I'm told."

"That must've taken some serious cash for that kind of real estate, despite it being the Depression," said Alan.

"I imagine so, but I think Claude would've helped Pantages financially, if he'd known about the troubles, but he had his own legal problems in California at the time and might have been *unavailable*. Long before I met him, Claude spent time in prison for a statutory rape charge of his own, he spent time hiding out from G-men for rum running, he spent time running from angry husbands, he spent time shacked up with Hollywood celebrities, and he spent time unavailable, shacked up with some rich patron somewhere else, possibly in Mexico. He needed a manager to tap his potential and keep him pointed in the right direction, finding his business compass so to speak."

"And you're the one who's done that?"

Sylvie nodded. "Claude has unbelievable earning

potential, largely untapped till now. His box office take on this tour is phenomenal, and then he'll supplement it when we're done by catering to the stars and their private needs."

"Before I take my seat, I wanted to know about your intermissions. Do you take them?"

"Of course we do. The theater wants to make money selling popcorn and bonbons, but Claude doesn't like vendors roaming the aisle during his act, so he takes a fifteen minute break during the show, about an hour and ten minutes into it."

"Is that what happened last night?"

Sylvie nodded.

"How about the night of the prediction?"

"We'd barely gotten started," said Sylvie, glancing away. "Most unusual. We had to mop up a water spill and do some other tidying up, so that one ran to about twenty-five minutes. Because of that we didn't take one later, because people have babysitters and need to get home."

"Your business skills are incredible," said Alan. "How'd you learn so much while you're still so young?"

"Hard knocks and experience. Probably the same as you and your detective work. How'd you get into something so rough and tumble while so young?"

"How about we talk about it after the show, over a drink or coffee? Can you get away for that?"

"Can I date you, or am I Claude's girl? Is that what you're asking?"

"That's what I'm asking."

* * *

"He's quite good," whispered Vera, leaning slightly closer to Alan, forty-five minutes into the show.

"You have a thought how he does it?" asked Alan.

Vera shook her head. "Not yet."

"I've got a theory," said Alan, "but then I saw things backstage that helped."

Vera nodded but didn't encourage Alan to go further.

The audience applauded as yet one more from their ranks returned to her seat, thrilled to tears with the message Alexander brought her from beyond the grave. Stepping back onto the carpet and spreading his slippered feet evenly, the seer held another white envelope to his head, touching the area above his brow he had referred to as his inner eye. After a brief second, he twitched spasmodically and stepped off the carpet, his feet scuffing quietly as he moved robotically forward on the apron of the stage, his eyes still closed. After a moment the eye lids rose half way, revealing only the whites of Alexander's eyes.

"I warn you that we are not done with you yet, vile murderer!" Alexander screeched in a high-pitched voice with a Russian accent.

Vera grabbed Alan's hand, and he responded quickly, squeezing it tight. "What the hell?" she whispered.

"Pavel Medvedev defiled us, and so he's been defiled and his face melted away," said the voice in Alexander. "You escaped in your uniform and don't think we will find you—but we will, traitor. We trusted you, false magician and betrayer! A bullet shall find you on stage before the week is out."

Alexander's eyes closed and then his head fell forward to his chest, as if he'd fallen asleep in a comfortable chair, rather than standing on a stage in front of 2,700 people, all shocked into silence. After a hushed moment he shook his head and gazed out into the audience, his brow furrowed, as if puzzled. He inhaled deeply, back-pedaled to the carpet, and rubbed his temples, while touching his turban near the ears.

"It appears we've been visited again by Anna," said

Alexander. "I wish she would do me a favor and schedule an appointment first."

The audience chuckled nervously.

"I have time in the afternoon that's available. Can someone in the audience tell me what she had to say?"

The woman Alan had seen earlier in the dressing room with Sylvie suddenly stood up.

"Yes, you," Alexander said while indicating the woman with an outstretched hand, palm held upward.

"Another prophecy," she said. "This one involving a 'false magician' and a lethal bullet before the week is out."

Alexander tugged on his chin, as if stroking a non-existent goatee. "Fortunately for me, I'm a seer and not a magician—and firearms and bullets are not a part of my act.

"Well, ladies and gentlemen," Alexander continued, "this is a little early, but since it's my show and I'm in charge, I vote we take our intermission now, and I will see you all again in twenty minutes. In the meantime, please enjoy the refreshments in the lobby."

Alexander bowed to enthusiastic applause and disappeared through the curtain. As the applause died down, people began chatting among themselves, while many got up and headed toward the lobby.

Ben leaned forward in his seat, and Alan did too, making a small huddle around Vera in the front row.

"She's with the act," said Alan, and so is the guy seated next to her. I saw them backstage."

"They're plants," said Vera, with Ben nodding in agreement. "Almost every act has trained actors in the audience. They lead the applause and get the crowd going, while also providing security. They act as foils and volunteer early on, if the crowd needs warming up, but something tells me this caught everyone by surprise. Alexander's confusion doesn't play well to a large crowd, because his persona is to always be in control—so because of the bad timing and catching them unprepared, it actually adds to the authenticity of it."

"Medvedev?" asked Alan. "I thought I asked Alexander if he knew a Medved. Did the voice stutter? It didn't sound that way, and I don't believe I mentioned a first name at all."

"You didn't," said Vera, glancing at Ben, who also confirmed what Alan thought.

"So how in the world did 'Anna' get 'Pavel'?" asked Alan.

"And did she or he mishear you say Medved?" asked Ben.

They all sat silently for a moment, while the chatter in the theater continued to grow louder.

"The voice and accent?" Alan asked Vera.

"Creepy!" said Vera. "I've never heard a man do such a good job capturing a woman's voice. I've heard plenty of men speaking or singing in falsetto, and that's like a cheap imitation to a woman's voice. This sounded real, and I thought Russian—like Tasha Zarenko's neck of the woods, but a touch more English, more formal."

"Speaking of Zarenko," said Alan. "I've got to catch you up on what Sylvie tells me about her and Ivanovich being married."

13

◇◇◇

Alan met Sylvie backstage at the Orpheum Theater and they left through the rear door, walking the two blocks to El Gaucho's Hunt Club, where they had their choice of either a late night dinner or early breakfast, but they hadn't yet decided. The place filled in the late evenings with theater performers and wait staff from downtown hotels and cocktail lounges, seeking the companionship of their own kind, as well as enjoying the service and entertainment of waiters, who had their own following. Dressed in snug vests and trousers, the male waiters brought flaming skewers of meat for diners to select from, while other waiters performed tableside magic with bottled gas and flaming dishes, putting the finishing touches on desserts like cherries jubilee. Most patrons enjoyed the show put on for newer customers, while opting for the hearty Hunter's Breakfast, with a petite filet mignon, pork cutlet, sausage, hash browns, and eggs. That's what Sylvie decided on, and Alan went with it.

"Big appetite?" asked Alan.

"Don't worry, I'll pay my way."

Alan patted her arm reassuringly as it rested on the table. "It's not that at all. I've brought plenty of money and would like to treat. I'm just not used to people ordering what they really want to eat. People are usually too polite or watching their calories."

"I burn it off with nervous energy and worry," said Sylvie, "but I imagine at some point I'll slow down."

"You'd fit right in at my house," said Alan. "Two brothers and a sister, and we're all big eaters, especially the boys. My father used to say we had hollow legs and stored food there."

"'Used to say,'" said Sylvie. "I gather he's no longer with us."

Alan lowered his eyes and shook his head. "Gone too soon, but he taught me enough to get me started as a private detective. Wish he were here, though."

Sylvie stroked Alan's arm and waved down a waiter at the same time. "Two martinis, straight up with olives, if you please."

"Thank you," said Alan. "That's how I like mine."

"Oh those are for me," said Sylvie with a straight face. "You'll have to order your own."

Alan glanced about to see if he could recall the waiter, already out of range, but no luck. He raised his arm to get the attention of one serving a table nearby, but Sylvie grabbed his hand, squeezed it tight, and pulled it into her lap. "I'm kidding, boy detective. Didn't you have a clue?"

Alan leaned back and eyed Sylvie as best he could, while sitting in the booth. "Normally those would be fighting words, lady, but I got a feeling you'd come out on top, sitting on my chest, pummeling my noggin."

"That's only because you're a gentleman and wouldn't fight back."

"How do you know that?"

"I have a sense about people. I can read them. I see you as tough as nails when you have to be, but I bet you're a

124

pushover when it comes to love."

"That's rather insightful. Is that why the show is doing so well now, because of you?"

"I'm not the front man on the stage who has the charisma to pack a house, but I've got a sense for timing and know what works. You can't teach or train someone to replace Claude, and that also applies to me. We see those skills in each other."

The waiter stopped in front of the table, bent forward while delivering the drinks, and bowed his head formally. "Your breakfast will be here shortly, would there be anything else?"

"Two more of these," said Alan, indicating the martinis with his hand.

"Of course, sir," said the waiter, before quickly walking away.

"So your plan is obvious now, detective. You're going to ply me with liquor for... for what... my affections or information?"

"Hopefully both."

"What haven't I told you already?"

"I don't know or care at the moment," he said, while toasting Sylvie and taking a sip.

"This is nice. Quality gin, I'd say."

"Agreed," said Sylvie, sighing and letting her shoulders droop for a moment.

"How about tonight's prediction," said Alan. "Why don't we start there?"

"Good as place as any, but I have absolutely no idea where Claude got that. Another bolt out of the blue, and this one I didn't see, feel, or hear coming."

"Did you see, feel, or hear the last one?"

"Proprietary information, detective, but since most people saw it, I'll go along with the bolt. And in that same sense of seeing things, neither I nor anyone else saw this one tonight. First thing I know is Claude's babbling in Anna's voice, at least that's what he's calling it now."

"And he's never done that before?"

Sylvie shook her head.

"Never spoken in a woman's voice before?"

Staring straight ahead, Sylvie shook her head again. Alan canted his head sideways and stared into her eyes. "Unless you can tell me anything about who might be shooting somebody on stage this week, I think my detective questions are out of our way."

"Only act that still has shooting on stage is Wang Tao Chia's, down at The Moore. His signature act is to find a couple of soldiers in the audience and have them load a pair of muzzle loaders up on stage. Then two Chinese soldiers of some kind shoot him in front of everyone."

"Anna's man in uniform... maybe. That could be American soldiers or Chinese, couldn't it? Why does he have soldiers load the guns and not regular Joes?"

"I'm not sure. Wang Tao only speaks through his pretty little interpreter. She says he feels that Marines are better with rifles and understand safety, which means less risk."

"Seriously? He specifies Marines over soldiers?"

"I'm sure he takes whatever he can get, but he may have one that is the same every night, whether it's a soldier or Marine, who's likely on the payroll."

"Why a muzzle loader? Seems like that would be as unreliable as hell."

"I think it's the only way he can assure the audience the gun's really loaded—instead of slipping in a blank cartridge, which would be easy enough to palm. The musket makes a big bang and shoots out a large puff of smoke. More theatrical that way."

"Of course it is," Alan said, rolling his eyes. "So unless

you know what's behind these premonitions and who barbecued the guy in the coffin—old what's his name..."

"Anna had a different name for the man, didn't she?" Sylvie asked.

"You noticed that too."

"I hadn't really thought about it when she said it, but I think she gave him a first name, starting with a 'P.'"

"That's what I thought I heard," said Alan.

"Like Pablo, but not Spanish, more like it had a 'V' in it."

Alan nodded.

"Sort of like 'Medved,' like you said but only longer, like it had another syllable."

"That's right," said Alan. "I thought I'd heard the voice say 'Pavel Medvedev.' Does that mean anything to you?"

"Not a clue."

Alan took another sip of his drink. "Afraid of that..."

"Any word on Frederic? Has he shown his sorry face anywhere? A hospital or private sanitarium?"

"Not a peep, and so ends our round of no-holds-barred questioning for the night."

"Good, because you play rough, but I'm not talking to you anymore, unless you're going to give me the third degree."

"What? You say you want the third degree?"

"You have handcuffs, detective, don't you?"

"I'm a private detective. So I'm not normally in the arresting business. That's more Ben's specialty than mine, but I can scrounge up a pair from the car, if you'd like?"

"We'd need to first make sure you have a key that works, so you can get loose later."

"Me get loose?"

"Sure...unless you want to wake up with me in your arms and the sun in your eyes..."

Alan sat in their regular booth at the Five Point Café at
Fifth and Denny, reading the paper while he waited for Ben
and Vera. Given how his evening turned out last night, he
expected that it would've been him dragging himself in late
for breakfast, instead of it being the other way around. A
few steps ahead of Vera, Ben stopped to hold the door for
her. Alan gave them both a curious look as they walked his
way. He slid over and made room for Vera.

"Late night?" Alan asked, trying to play it nonchalant.

"Cards and vodka," said Ben. "The girls know every
game and every trick. Don't play them for money. I might
have to file Chapter Eleven later today."

"Tasha's girls?" asked Alan.

Vera nodded. "We figured you'd be busy last night, so
Ben came up and helped me entertain my company. Besides
eating me out of house and home, they're eager to collect
their things from the theater and get back on the road. They
don't like spending too much time in one place without an
income stream."

"They were all but out of their clothes last night," said
Ben.

"What they have is in the laundry," said Vera, "and they

don't mind at all showing what they've got."

"I'll say," said Ben.

Alan arched his brow and smiled, following the conversation.

"The problem is," Vera continued, "that they've drunk all of my booze. But on the plus side, they're wonderful cooks. I've had some amazing meals with them. Today, they're fixing piroshky, which I adore, especially fresh. So I'm going to eat light today. My metabolism doesn't run as high as theirs does, especially since I'm not shaking my bottom anymore."

Alan knew Vera wanted him to have a visual image of her doing that, and her strategy seemed to be working. She knew how to keep him thinking about her.

"Will there be extra piroshky?" asked Ben. "Marvelous what they cooked up last night."

"I'm sure there will be. I'll save you both some," she said, turning toward Alan. "And how did things go with Sylvie last night? Are you two engaged yet?"

Alan raised his hand and scratched at his nose as he laughed, stalling for time. "Things were fine. Fine indeed."

Vera tilted her head back and nodded knowingly. "I'm glad things were *fine*. That's how an evening with a pretty girl should turn out. It should be *fine*."

"She's actually a lot like you in many ways," said Alan, giving Vera his best smile.

"I hope not," said Vera. "That's a tough road no one should have to endure. If she is, then I'd really have to worry about you."

"Ben, are you going to bail me out on this?" Alan asked, forcing a smile.

Judy the waitress appeared at the table with two cups of coffee, while carrying laminated menus under her arm. "You don't need these, do you?" she said with a nod toward

130

the menus.

Ben shook his head and ordered the corned beef hash, while Vera went with a maple bar.

As Judy left with the order, Ben grinned at Alan. "I know better than to wade in when you two are going at it. Sorry, Champ, but you're on your own this round. No tag-teaming for the main event today."

"The long and the short of it is that last night's prediction caught her by surprise," said Alan, "probably as much her as it did us. I tried prompting her with variations of Medved's name, and she didn't have it locked in all that well. She certainly didn't know the first name."

"You believe her?" asked Vera.

Alan nodded. "I do. She's definitely the brains behind Alexander's success, and she told me he got his start way back in Alaska with Pantages, the guy who used to own these theaters. Like Billy the Kid, Alexander up and shot Soapy Smith, and it sounds like more of the gang over a week's period. With no law in town, he got off claiming self-defense, although it could have been the town overwhelmingly appreciated him killing Smith. In the process, Alexander recovered what Smith stole from Pantages and others. The grubstake likely helped Pantages get his start. So when Alexander eventually took to the stage, Pantages helped him along and gave him favorable bookings, up and down the West Coast. Alexander had conman talent, but as soon as he got a few bucks in the bank, he'd run off with another woman, or two, or three, often all at the same time. He'd get back on stage only when he ran out of money. Sylvie's the one who got him to focus on his show and amass his fortune—and hers too, I imagine."

"Anything else?" asked Ben.

"I asked her about a stage act with a shooting in it, and the only one she can think of is Wang Tao Chia, who's playing at the Moore this week. He catches a shot from a muzzle loader and spits out the round—or something close to that."

"A muzzle loader?" asked Vera.

"I asked her that, too," said Alan. "Seems it's more theatrical that way. The audience sees a guy in uniform loading it and shooting."

"'Uniform' is part of the prediction," said Ben.

"This could be a good fit," said Vera. "Looks like we'll have to check it out tonight, if tickets are still available."

"I'll stop by their box office when we leave here," said Ben.

"I have some news, too," said Vera, "but don't ask me about my connection, Ben, or how I came by this, okay?"

Ben glanced to Alan and then back to Vera and nodded. "The Champ knows?"

"It's a source we've sworn to protect. Neither of us can acknowledge it without permission, which we don't have."

"I get it," said Ben, "and I'm not offended. I don't figure I'm entitled to know everything you two are up to, and Chief Ketchum likes it that way. There's a certain deniability he takes comfort in. He told me not to crowd you on things like this, or your searches, or your talents for physical persuasion, which I understand can get very rough at times. The Chief says you play for the right team, and that's what matters to him, so that what works for me too."

"You're such a good sport, Ben," said Vera, patting his hand. "Thank you for that."

Ben smiled his thanks.

"The source we have would be very interested in this matter if our dead man turns out to be Pavel S. Medvedev, a Russian national believed to have slipped through our notoriously porous northern border, possibly through Canada near Lake Michigan. Pavel could actually be

Mikhail, his brother, but whichever one it is doesn't matter all that much, because the FBI wants them both. They're considered 'persons of interest,' and that's all my source would tell me."

"So we don't know what exactly they're wanted for?" asked Alan. "Is that right?"

"The detainer would probably read: Entering the Country Illegally, but the real story is apparently on a need-to-know basis, and our need-to-know hasn't been met yet. We identify him, and they might feel we have the need-to-know."

"Real friendly group your source," said Ben.

"I've got a sneaking suspicion that Alexander and Anna are onto something," said Alan, "but what, and how, I don't know. I'm not seeing a connection."

"I think you're right," said Ben. "What are the odds of this being a coincidence? You both know how I don't believe in them."

"Whether it's Pavel Medvedev, Frederic St. Laurent, or someone else for that matter, this is a homicide, right?" asked Alan.

"That's correct," said Ben.

"Can your department run an all points bulletin on St. Laurent and Pavel, since we still don't know which one is dead and which is missing?" asked Alan.

"That's not normally how it's done," said Ben, "but your logic is good. We like to know who we are after and have to be able to articulate why, because of liability issues. The department doesn't like to take the scatter gun approach and round up 'the usual suspects'. The ACLU gets their collective panties in a bunch when we do anything close to that. One of them is likely the deceased, so we're not going to be ruining his reputation, the other is likely our suspect—so his reputation is toast anyway. It's not likely he'll be able to come back and sue me and the chief."

"So what do you think, Ben?" asked Vera. "Can it be done?"

"Let's head from here to the Paramount," said Ben. "We'll collect flyers, programs, and whatever they've got, and I'll hit the downtown roll calls with them. While we're there we can re-examine the stage and collect Zarenko's belongings from the dressing room, so we can eventually return their property to them."

"And they can hit the road and make a living," said Vera. "But are you sure you want to see them gone?"

"I'm planning to put their belongings—or most of them anyway—in the Police Property Room for safekeeping. I'd just as soon everyone close to the murder stayed in town until we can sort out who didn't do it and work our way to who did."

"That makes perfect sense," said Vera, "but I'm not sure how long I want to play hostess to them."

"Why don't you rent them one of your apartment units on a short term?" said Alan. "Do you have one available?"

"I don't," said Vera. "I'm a happy landlord at the moment, and they've always got their place back at the Paramount Apartments. How long before they can go back there? If someone were trying to kill them, they must've read the papers by now and have seen that they didn't perish in the fire."

"Actually, we don't have any reason to believe they were targeted," said Ben, "but I think once they get to their apartment and start collecting their clothing, they're going to work their way to the railroad station soon enough. I'd like to keep them around at least one more day. Besides, I'd love another night of pinochle, if you're up to it? And I'll bring the vodka this time, replenish your supply."

Vera glanced sideways at Alan with a hint of a smile.

"If there's an invitation in your smile, I'd love to join in," said Alan.

"Really?" asked Vera. "I'm sure the ladies would love to see you again and say goodbye. It might also give your wrists a chance to heal from the handcuff marks."

Alan reflexively grabbed for his wrist but then stopped. He strummed his fingers on the table, smirked, and playfully rapped the back of his hand against Vera's shoulder. "You're an evil woman, Vera."

"Yes, I know, but you love me anyway, don't you."

Behind the Paramount Theater Ben unlatched the police padlock on the rear stage door and held it wide for Vera and Alan to enter. They'd brought their own flashlights but didn't need them at the moment. The chain and lock St. Laurent had bolted the door with on the inside lay in a pile near the door, apparently removed by the fire department when securing the scene. The trio climbed the flight to the back of the stage and dressing rooms.

"Let's start with the props and we'll walk you through what we saw the last time we were here," said Ben to Vera.

Ben switched his flashlight on and pointed it at the open casket. Alan caught himself checking for the body, although he knew the coroner had removed it the day of its discovery. Ben pointed out the release mechanisms for the coffin's escape door.

Vera shook her head but then nodded, working something out internally. "I don't think that there's any way that two guys could lift a dead body and stuff it inside the coffin post mortem, which obviously means the Champ and I must have witnessed the murder, which isn't exactly a first for us, but let's not go there."

"That's how I figure it," said Ben.

Vera glanced around the stage, at the second coffin on the floor in which Yvette had been trapped, shoved against a wall. "Has anything been moved or removed from the scene since you were here last?" she asked.

Alan shrugged and checked with Ben, who did the same. "Not so we've noticed," he said, "but I don't think we can be sure."

"I can't figure out the need for the magician to have Yvette hide in another coffin after she escaped the first one," said Vera. "What purpose did that serve?"

"Other than to keep her from watching the rest of the act... " said Alan.

"Possibly, but that's about all I can get out of it," said Vera. "And then I suppose if you want to have her die in the fire, you push the box against the wall."

"Makes me wonder if she knows something the killer didn't want her sharing with us," said Alan.

"That or he wanted to tie up his loose ends," said Ben, "or throw us off track."

"So what's this Otis Elevator device look like?" asked Ben.

Vera shook her head. "It's been awhile since I've seen one, but I'm not seeing anything that looks familiar."

Alan put a lone finger up in front of his mouth, giving the quiet sign. "Did you hear something?"

Ben and Vera shook their heads. "Like what?" she asked.

"Animal sounds and movement."

"If it's rats," said Vera, "I hate goddamn rats!"

"Vera?" said Alan, still holding the quiet sign while he softly crossed the stage.

Vera picked up a sword from near the coffin and felt the blade's edge. "This is as dull as a Herbert Hoover speech, but I can club rats to death with it," she whispered.

Alan stopped in front of a collapsible stand with a black cloth draped over it. He nodded, grinned, and pulled the cloth off quickly. "Aha!"

A pair of doves cooed inside the cage that Yvette had carried two nights before, while a third one sat on a nearby perch listless.

"Nice trick!" said Ben, clasping Alan by the shoulder. "I didn't know you'd taken up magic."

"These were part of St. Laurent's act," said Alan. "Yvette carried the cage while Frederic caught the birds."

"Or so it seemed," said Vera. "They haven't had food or water in nearly forty hours, the poor darlings. I'd forgotten all about them."

"Apparently so have Yvette and St. Laurent," said Ben. "Either that or they thought they'd all been killed during the smoke and fire."

"There's bird seed on the cage floor and small puddles of water," said Alan. "Some of the nozzle spray must have worked its way through their night drape. Lucky fellows!"

"I'd say two boys and a girl," said Ben.

"How can you tell?" asked Vera. "You can't see their equipment, Ben. So do the boy birds fart all the time and spit on the sidewalk, while the girls polish their beak and nails?"

Ben grinned and shook his head. "The girl's flitting her wings, and one of the fellas is bowing and cooing to her, as if he's expecting applause for his recent performance."

"They're love birds, and they've enjoyed their privacy these past two days." said Vera.

"These two have, but I'm not so sure about the third. Maybe that's why he's tired. I understand you can only watch so much porn before you're exhausted and get tired of it. Isn't that right, Champ?"

Alan laughed. "Ouch!"

"They'll be needing twigs for nest building," said Ben. "Apparently the other fella is the cuckold—or it might be that he's not interested. Maybe he's older and out of her range."

"You've been around birds, Ben?"

"I've had parakeets. Few years back, and for the record, even small birds can whoop doves' tail feathers because their skin is thin and their beaks soft. A smaller bird with a hooked beak can tear these guys up."

"Soft beaks won't get you far," said Vera, smiling. "You're always better off with a stiff one."

Alan laughed, while Ben shook his head. "I'm not touching that," he said.

"Some other time you'll have to tell me more about your birds," said Vera.

"I'd like to hear more about the bird porn," said Alan, "but that can wait for another time also..."

*   *   *

Vera led the way inside the dressing room. "This is just my hunch, but this looks exactly like the girls stepped out for a cigarette break and planned on coming right back. What is it we're looking for, Ben?"

"Matter out of place is always a good place to start," said Ben, "and then anything that might possibly link someone in here to the fire, to Pavel Medvedev, or to St. Laurent—or a motive."

"Knowing the girls now, I feel like I'm invading their privacy," said Vera, staring at an open suitcase. "When I worked we were all very close and looked out for each other. I can't help think I'm breaking a sacred trust."

"Do you want to search St. Laurent's dressing room, while the Champ and I finish up in here?"

"Yeah," Vera said, nodding thoughtfully. "That might speed up the process too. Are you coming with me Champ, or are you going to stay here and sift through the girls' panties and bras?"

"I thought I'd help Ben."

Vera stopped at the door and looked back. "I guess you can be glad they don't use a boa constrictor in their act. You'd hate to find that hidden in a suitcase unannounced."

"Wait!" said Alan. "They have a snake or not?"

"I don't think so. Girls with those usually make a big production out of it. It's something phallic about it that the guys like to see them playing with."

"Not me," said Alan. "If I see beady eyes, the Colt's coming out and there will be gun play...a whole magazine's worth."

"Just remember the poor snake is unarmed," Vera teased.

"I'm not going to frisk him," said Alan. "Tricky bastard got us tossed out of the Garden of Eden. I'll dust him purely to revenge all mankind."

As Vera walked away, Ben patted Alan on the shoulder. "You two are better entertainment than anything on radio. What'd you do to provoke her this time?"

"Doesn't have to be anything," said Alan. "Sometimes she just likes to push my buttons."

"And you love it when she does... "

"Yes, I do."

"She wants you with her, you know. I don't think she's comfortable with you digging through the girls' stuff either."

"I know that," Alan said, staring blankly at a full wardrobe with something dark, long, and fluffy hanging out the bottom and touching the floor. "I'm going to make her wait, and then I'm going to attack and wrap this feather boa around her neck."

"Oh yeah," said Ben with a wry smile. "She'll love that."

Alan tugged the boa out from the wardrobe and stretched it out to its full length. "Who made these famous? Tallulah Bankhead?"

"Isadora Duncan, America's most famous exile."

"We kicked her out of the country, how come?"

"For her pro-Soviet sympathies. If that's not enough to raise your curiosity, there are plenty who doubt the official version of her death."

"Didn't her scarf get wrapped around a wheel spoke of her car and break her neck."

Ben nodded. "That's the official version."

"What's the unofficial version?"

"Angry monarchists loyal to the royal family caught up with her and staged the accident."

"Seriously?" asked Alan.

"In our country we have a long history of political shame: name calling, libel, slander, poll taxes on the poor, ballot box stuffing with the names of the deceased, but no one here gets particularly outraged by it all. On the other hand, foreign countries, where liberty and freedom are mere concepts for the philosophical, they resort to deadly violence, assassinations of whole families, and coup d'états by generals and jealous rivals. An ideologue from here can't wander over to Europe or Russia and start preaching their western idea of politics. Even your friend Machiavelli took his lumps for telling others what to do. What he said mattered to those people and their religious leaders."

Alan scrunched the boa into a ball and shoved it back into the wardrobe. As he headed for the door, Ben stopped him, nodding his head towards a packet of photographs in his hand.

"Have you ever seen pictures of the Romanovs?" he asked.

Alan shook his head.

Ben handed him a five-by-seven, and then another and another. "I think you're seeing them right now."

Ben held up an eight-by-ten to the light. "These are amazing," he said. "Looks like they were lifted from the royal family's personal collection."

"How in the world would somebody come up with these?" asked Alan.

"I have no idea," said Ben, "but Zarenko must have forty-five or fifty of them here. And these look like candids, taken by the royal photographer for the personal use of the family—not the official studio portraits they make for the public. These have got to be very valuable to collectors."

"What a beautiful family," said Alan. "Past tense now, and that makes it a crying shame."

Ben nodded and exhaled loudly as he tapped one picture against the stack of others, lost in thought. "A damn shame what they did to that family. They herded them together in the basement where they were keeping them in the Urals, told them they needed to take a picture to prove they were still alive, and then they snuck in a firing squad and executed them viciously. When the shooting didn't work as planned, they bayoneted the survivors, shot others in the head, and burned and buried their bodies, but they made a mess of the burial too. The Bolsheviks kept the killing of the daughters under wraps for years, lying to the people that they were still alive but scattered around Russia, Europe, and China, which led to imposters popping up in several places, all over the world."

"Who's still alive?" asked Vera, wandering back into the room.

Alan handed her a small stack of the photographs he had already looked through.

"The Romanovs!" said Vera.

"Where'd you find these?"

"Madam Zarenko's suitcase," said Ben.

"Why would she have these here, and not in her room?" asked Vera.

"I don't know," said Ben.

"Who's the big guy with the beard and the priest robes?" asked Alan. "Doesn't seem like part of the royal family, but he shows up in many of these pictures."

"Grigori Rasputin," said Ben. "The spiritual advisor, healer, hypnotist, and mystic for the Russian royal family. There're slurs that he exerted more influence than a man should on Alexandra, the late tsarina. Personally, from what I've read, I think the Bolsheviks were doing all they could to discredit the Romanovs while drumming up support for their revolution and what they were doing."

"I know next to nothing about Russian history," said Alan, "so...what happened to Rasputin?"

"He'd already been assassinated by the end of 1916," said Vera, "by other nobles, relatives of the Romanovs, worried about his influence over the royal family and the tsar's decision making processes. They questioned the way the tsar ran the war and Russia with that dubious kind of guidance, and critics didn't like it that the powerful mystic monk came from peasant stock. As Ben said, the sexual rumors involving Tsarina Alexandra didn't help the family's position as the ruling monarchs. Rasputin gained favor with Tsar Nicholas by 'curing' the heir Alexei of hemophilia, using hypnotism or mysticism of some kind. Rasputin also claimed he could predict the future, and with the tsar's blessing, he had complete access to the throne and all the bedrooms, which raised more fear."

"That sounds shaky," said Alan.

"Adds to the concern about the tsar's judgment," said Ben. So with Rasputin's implied divinity and his influence over the court, he sold political offices to friends and admirers, which added to the shabby ineptness of it all. So a group of nobles decided to put an end to Rasputin, with the tsar away leading Russian troops on the Eastern Front. A prince and a grand duke got together with others and tried to kill the priest in secret. Many foes of Rasputin complained about his voracious appetite for sex and liquor. Rumor had it that when not seducing the tsarina, he and she conspired together to broker a shady treaty with Germany, her country of birth, to end the war in its favor."

"Seriously?" asked Alan.

"It gets more complicated than that," said Ben. "Although German by birth, she's the second granddaughter of Queen Victoria. It's believed the hemophilia that threatened the Russian throne came from Queen Vickie."

Vera nodded in concurrence and stopped to stare closely at a picture of a girl sitting almost on Rasputin's lap. "She's much darker than the Romanovs," said Vera. "I wonder who she is?"

"Do you remember the names of the girls?" asked Ben.

Vera shook her head slowly. "Other than Grand Duchess Anastasia, not really. I'd have to think about it for a minute, but they'll come to me. At any rate, the assassins poisoned Rasputin, but it had no immediate effect—so they shot him three times, including once at point blank. A visiting Englishman who'd joined them delivered the fatal shot."

"An Englishman?" asked Ben.

"So I've been told," said Vera. "Only the English rival the Russians when it comes to spying. They had a young noble, a military liaison who went to Oxford with a Russian prince named Felix, a reported bi-sexual married to Princess Irina, a beauty Rasputin wanted desperately to bed. England feared Rasputin might influence the tsarina and convince Russia to withdraw from the war, which would leave the Brits with a much bigger fight on the Western Front.

England needed Russia to help them keep Germany busy on two fronts. So the conspirators used the allure of Irina to draw Rasputin into the palace where they killed him—or started the process anyway. They intimated that the lonely princess had an interest in seeing the mystic for private counseling."

"You have a much better source of information than I do," said Ben.

Vera beamed a smile and shook her head. "Rasputin had been having headaches for months and predicted his own death. In the palace he refused the offer of wine and poisoned sweets, but while waiting for Irina, he got bored and indulged in the treats. But the poison didn't work as expected, at least not right away, so they worried he might survive until daylight, and then they wouldn't be able to dispose of his body without drawing notice. So they shot him in the back at close range to put a quick end to it all."

"After celebrating his death," Vera continued, "and while congratulating themselves on how bold and clever they'd been, one conspirator decided to check on the dearly departed. But Rasputin felt warm, and while being touched he batted an eye open. Startled into a panic, he got up and ran out of the house, running across the lawn, threatening to tell the tsarina. The nobles chased and shot him three times more. Then they took his dead body back to the palace, wrapped him in a rug, and finally threw him into the frozen Neva River, once they found a hole big enough to fit him through the ice.

"That's pretty gruesome," said Alan.

"It's not over yet," said Vera. "Police officials fished Rasputin out of the river two days later. The autopsy showed he had water in his lungs."

"He drowned?" asked Alan.

Vera nodded. "Appears so, but I'm no expert on whether

or not that's conclusive evidence of drowning. Devastated, the royal family had Rasputin's body buried on palace grounds, but over a year later, following the Revolution, the Bolsheviks dug up the body to cremate it so zealous fanatics wouldn't rally around it. During the burning process, Rasputin sat bolt upright in the fire, which shocked the hell out of everybody there."

"No kidding?" asked Alan.

"I'd heard that part of the story before," said Ben, "so I asked the Butterworth morticians about it. They told me that if you don't sever the tendons before cremating, the muscles contort and that kind of thing will happen, and it very well may have happened in St. Petersburg. There's also a rumor that the assassins cut off Rasputin's penis, kept it as a talisman, and that it holds magical powers of some kind, but I'm told by others that is purely legend."

"Keeping the penis or the magic powers?" asked Alan.

"Both...I'm hoping," said Ben.

"Good Lord, I hope so too," said Vera.

"So back to these pictures," said Alan. "What do you make of them?

Vera had them all in her hands and leafed through them slowly, one at a time. She flipped the one over with the girl on Rasputin's lap. Written in a mix of English and what appeared to be Russian were names penciled in. "Alexei, Maria, Anastasia, Tatiana, Olga, Grigori, and another Maria," said Vera. "Those are the names of the tsarevich, the grand duchesses, and Rasputin. I'm thinking the words in Russian explain who the girl is on Rasputin's lap."

"Sounds reasonable," said Ben.

Vera flipped over another photograph, a candid that included servants standing nearby the royals. Penciled on back were more names and more Russian. "This looks like it says 'Ekateringburg,'" said Vera. "Isn't that where the

Bolsheviks murdered them?"

"I'm not sure," said Ben, "but that sounds right."

"More Russian writing and names we've seen before, with additional ones of 'Anna Demidova,' 'Yeveg... something Botkin,' and 'Alexie Trupp.' I'm going to guess these people are part of the house staff," Vera said, flipping the picture over and back again, lining up names with the photographs, "and this might have been the place of their last stand, before they were killed. If that's true, how in the world would Tasha have come up with these?'

"I suppose we're going to have to ask her," said Alan.

"So what did you find in St. Laurent's dressing room?" asked Ben.

Vera shrugged her shoulders. "Nothing remarkable, which is rather remarkable in itself. It could be that he and Yvette did all their makeup and dressing upstairs in their room, which is nearby enough to be handy, but I didn't find much more than a top hat, gloves, basic make-up, and brushes in there."

The only seats available in The Moore Theater for Wang

Tao Chia's magic act were underneath the balcony, main floor. While purchasing their tickets, the trio spotted Nikolai Ivanovich in a tuxedo and top hat, sliding through the crowd.

"What are you staring at?" Vera asked Alan.

"Nikolai Ivanovich."

"This time without the beard," said Vera. "You still sore at him?"

Alan exhaled and nodded. "Curious to know if he leaves a slime trail behind him like other slugs."

"I understand that slugs are one of the state's symbols," said Ben. "He could be a protected species."

"They are not a state symbol," said Vera. "That's an urban legend. Honestly, you two. I can't take you anywhere."

Vera led the way, and the men followed, stopping for popcorn and soda along the way. "Let me indulge my butter and salt craving," she said. "I didn't have a chance to eat earlier, and I used to eat a ton of popcorn back in the day."

They worked their way through the late arriving crowd, and an usher pointed them to seats just inside the door.

"Not my favorite view back here," said Vera, "but there are

no pillars and the theater is still a showcase. The Orpheum Circuit bought this in the twenties for their vaudeville shows. They staged all their premier acts here, from across the country, until they opened the new Orpheum on Fifth. Then they intentionally downgraded this one, removing the luxury boxes that jutted out from the sides, near the stage."

"I like the unobstructed view you can get from here," said Ben. "Every old theater I've ever been in you had to deal with the support pillars."

"Groundbreaking for its time," said Vera, "but behind its time racially. The top tier has a separate outside entrance, giving 'colored' people their own entrance and seating, but I think the management has stopped that practice. The Coliseum had one of those too."

"One of the reasons I like living here," said Ben, "is Seattle doesn't have all the hang-ups common to other parts of the country—or at least not to the same degree."

"Amen to that," said Vera.

"So what's the story on Wang Tao Chia?" Ben asked Alan. "What did Sylvie tell you?"

"His signature act is where a firing squad of Boxer revolutionaries shoot at him with old fashioned muskets, but he manages to catch the lead using a Chinese plate as a shield," said Alan. "The plate and the trick has something to do with the origination of the Boxer cult. They claimed to be impervious to foreign bullets, especially British, so his using a piece of china is a form of defiance, showing how he's protected by a common dish from their bullets.

"I thought shooting acts were banned," said Vera. "There've been a number of magicians wounded or killed over the years. I think the numbers are in the teens."

"The train wreck syndrome," said Ben. "People want to see tragedy involving others. It somehow makes them feel more alive."

"Other than his signature act, I don't know much about what he does," said Alan. "He reportedly doesn't speak English, except to say, 'Much good,' when he's pleased. So his assistants interpret for him, but since he spent time in a British Crown colony, Sylvie figures he should be able to speak a little English."

"Sylvie sounds like a clever girl," said Vera. "And she said he uses an interpreter? My bet is that the interpreter will be a she, and she will have visible assets, as well as responsibilities other than just speaking for him."

"Another Yvette?" asked Alan.

Vera nodded as she thought. "More like Yvette and Sylvie combined, with a stronger stage presence, like that of a director during opera rehearsals. While Chia's busy working his tricks, she can coach him as well as distract us when necessary."

"So she'll be another looker?" asked Ben. "That will make our taxing surveillance much easier."

"Honestly, you guys," said Vera. "You can count on the looks. Sex sells, but that's not a bad thing. I certainly took advantage of that and made a living for years. And if the women in the audience are honest with themselves, they'll admit they love seeing the naked female form. After all, how many statues do you see of naked men? Two? Rodin's *The Thinker* and Michelangelo's *David*. Maybe a few more, but you see countless ones of women, and that's not a bad thing. It sets a standard of beauty and women want to see how they measure up."

"We are in total agreement," said Ben. "But I have seen a few more statues of males in Rome, fine specimens of male anatomy, except some pope had their penises chiseled off, which took away from the artwork."

Alan grinned. "That had to hurt."

Vera playfully slapped Alan's upper arm. He leaned back and started to weave his hand along her armrest, intertwining it with hers, but she squeezed it with her arm against her body, flicked his hand, shooing it away, while shaking her head without looking at him. Not the time or place for that.

The orchestra struck up a few bars of fanfare, as the dapper Nikolai Ivanovich strutted across the apron to the front of the stage. The large spotlight caught and followed him, while the audience applauded politely.

"Why is he here tonight?" Alan asked Vera. "Is he cashing in on the free publicity that Alexander gave him?"

"I don't know," said Vera. "That backfired on him last time."

"Maybe he likes playing with fire," said Ben.

"At least we're close to an exit this time," said Vera.

Ivanovich thanked the crowd, introduced himself. "Welcome to The Moore Theater," he said. "For tonight, we are bringing you exotic entertainment from the Orient. It's a bit unusual for us in that the magician doesn't speak more than a word or two of English. We can't provide you with subtitles, but we can avail ourselves of the services of a pretty young China doll, who will serve as our interpreter."

"Ladies and gentlemen," Ivanovich continued, "may I present to you from Peking, China, Liu Yang!"

The crowd applauded enthusiastically as the curtains opened part way. Ivanovich backed out of the light and quietly exited the stage as a woman in brightly colored silks emerged into the spotlight.

Vera nudged Alan playfully and smirked. "I told you she'd be pretty—and all dolled up for you."

The small woman shuffled to the front of the stage apron, opening and closing a delicate fan in front of her face, taking mincing steps, as if her feet had been broken and bound while in her youth. Asian music from the orchestra pit accompanied her gliding shuffle, the music rich with plinking strings, shaking cymbals, and finally a gong.

"Sounds like they brought their own instruments," said Ben.

"I imagine it would be hard for the local orchestra to fake it for very long," said Vera.

The woman stopped in front of the closed curtain and bowed obsequiously, as if she wanted to hide behind the fan. Her face painted in the fashion of Chinese opera characters, the features carefully drawn over white makeup with a pink tint to it. She had arched eyebrows that pulled her eyes upward into a mild slant, while tiny cupid bow lips below a small nose served as the bright focal point on her youthful face. Her opal blue headdress, festooned with colored glass beads and bright decorations stuck out exotically, shaking and bobbing as she moved, while her matching robe swept elegantly across the stage.

"I am Liu Yang," said the woman when the applause subsided, her voice clear but halting, as if English were not her preferred language. She followed by setting the ground rules, explaining the need for her to interpret for Wang Tao Chia. Her narration told that his origins were actually Manchurian, from the north of China, which meant he spoke a dialect not common to the majority of local Chinese immigrants, should there be Cantonese speakers in the audience. Wang Tao supported the embattled British Crown during the Rebellion, while he expressed disdain for the Chinese Nationalist Boxers, who pursued him with vengeance, wanting him dead because of his pro-Western loyalties. She reminded the audience that members of the Righteous Harmony Society had killed European missionaries in Peking during the turn of the century uprising.

Wang Tao had recently arrived in America after publicly disgracing wizarding rival, Chin Ling Foo, who forfeited 1,000 pounds rather than duel Wang Tao on stage with feats of magic. Each had claimed the other a fake and imposter until that point, and following the showdown, which didn't occur, the press "rightfully acknowledged" Wang Tao Chia as the greatest magician alive. As Liu Yang spoke, the curtain continued to slowly pull back on a darkened stage. Faintly visible, an arched bridge, curved boughs, and roof rafters came into view, as if the audience were entering a Chinese village depicted on a porcelain plate. A muscular, bare-chested man struck a huge gong, which soon disappeared, being raised into the rafters. As the disc disappeared, a dim spot light slowly focused and brightened on the silhouette of an Asian man, hands on hips, standing in profile.

"Ladies and gentlemen," said Liu Yang, "I present to you the world renowned master of Chinese magic and mysticism, Wang Tao Chia."

From the orchestra pit, Chinese carnival music with pounding drums and clashing cymbals created a noisy cacophony that filled the theater, while on stage a dozen young Chinese men and women carrying streamers danced across the stage, chasing a Chinese dragon, with several human legs visible underneath, like a centipede, circling back and forth around the stage.

Wang Tao strutted bowlegged to the forefront, passing through the midst of the other performers, wearing a gold embroidered silk robe. As the magician stepped out of the darkness, into the light, his features became clearer, revealing that he, too, wore operatic makeup, with painted brows, heavy eyeliner, and a matching mustache, similar to what Groucho Marx wore in films. A long plaited queue hung down from beneath a silk and fur hat, dancing back and forth with every step he took.

Wang Tao bowed formally to the audience, and took the circular cap from his head and handed it to an assistant, revealing a head nearly shaved, save for a patch of hair in the back that grew long into the braided queue. He continued to make himself comfortable by taking off his colorful cape, twirling it around in front of him like a matador, back and forth, twisting it about to show the audience every facet of it. He stretched it out in front of him, fluffed it as if he were making a bed, and then laid it on the floor. While lowering the cape, it took on the shape of a large object, which hadn't been on the stage before. Wang Tao withdrew the magic carpet and revealed a large wooden tub, full to the brim with water and a white swan that flapped its wings and splashed about in the tub. Two assistants picked up the tub, gentled the swan, and carried it off the stage, while the audience applauded.

"He's quite entertaining," said Vera. "I've not seen that before."

"I haven't a clue as to how he did it," said Ben.

Without the gaudy robe, Wang Tao wore a loose peasant tunic over silk pants and plain slippers, in stark contrast to the brightly colored outfits of the assistants and stage extras. An assistant brought him a tray and bowed in front of him. From the tray, Wang Tao tore strips of red tissue paper, reducing it into dozens of tiny bits, and then he rolled and wadded the pieces into a single ball at his fingertips. He blew on the torn bits as if extinguishing a candle, and as he opened the bundle, ever so slowly, he revealed the pieces were whole again. He held the sheet so that all could see it in once piece, and then he let it float elegantly to the floor, like a miniature magic carpet he no longer needed.

Wang Tao displayed the skills of a master at pantomime, as well as magic. He had a flair for dramatizing every illusion with expressive gestures and well-practiced poses, conveying his thoughts with a crooked smile or cocked eyebrow, like when he stuffed his mouth with white cotton balls from a large glass beaker. After his cheeks filled and his eyes bulged wide, Wang Tao stuck the tips of his fingers in his mouth and began withdrawing silk scarves tied end-to-end, pulling out several yards of them, as attractive assistants followed him about and collected his cast offs. He bowed when he finished, and the assistants danced off the stage to loud applause.

Liu Yang stepped into the spotlight, wearing a less cumbersome outfit. She bowed appreciatively to the applause that greeted her. She had forsaken the headdress and formal attire from the previous century for something much lighter, which more closely resembled the silk harem pants Yvette had worn for St. Laurent. Liu Yang wore a short jacket over a bustier that covered her midriff, and her movements were more agile.

"For our next trick," said Liu Yang, "we have asked the theater's owner to join us on stage to assist us. We understand there are concerns about the portion of the show involving shooting, so we've asked Mr. Ivanovich to inspect our equipment to ease his fears and yours."

As Nikolai Ivanovich re-entered the stage and stood near Wang Tao, Liu Yang spun around and skipped across the stage and stood in front of a large target, with painted concentric circles on it. She stopped about two feet away from the target, while a second spotlight followed Wang Tao and Ivanovich to the other side of the stage, where they stopped next to a small cannon that resembled a harpoon launcher. Wang Tao held up a white rope attached to a large tipped arrow, which he presented to Ivanovich, who scowled doubtfully and crossed his arms in front. With Wang Tao nodding encouragement, Ivanovich unwound his arms and touched the arrow point. He quickly withdrew his fingers and rubbed them together, demonstrating the arrow's sharpness. Wang Tao then loaded the arrow and rope into the front of the cannon, down the barrel, tamping it in with a special ramrod. Satisfied with the loading and adjustment, he bowed to Ivanovich and then to Liu Yang, who dutifully covered her eyes with only her hands, while a musician in the pit began tapping out the press roll on a snare drum: firing squad music.

Wang Tao stepped behind the cannon and lowered the barrel to sight it in. Ivanovich stepped around toward the front of the cannon and with gestures indicated Liu Yang in front of the target across the stage. Wang Tao nodded that he understood and motioned for Ivanovich to come back and join him behind the cannon. Ivanovich again pointed at Liu Yang and made a waving motion, indicating she should move out of the way of the target. Wang Tao shook his head and placed his hands on his hips, indicating his satisfaction with the set up.

Ivanovich stretched his neck, shook his head slowly, and stepped behind Wang Tao, out of the spotlight. Wang Tao stood erect, nodded at the audience a final time and tugged on a lanyard connected to a trigger device. Black powder flashed from the barrel of the cannon as it banged, and sent the loaded charge across the stage, where it passed through Liu Yang's midsection, impaling itself into the target behind her. Liu Yang let out a sharp scream of surprise, which is exactly how the audience reacted, seeing the rope threaded through her body and the base of the arrow sticking out the target behind her.

Ivanovich stepped back into the spotlight, scowling angrily as Wang Tao crossed the stage, his swagger a little less confident than before. When he reached Liu Yang, still covering her eyes, he leaned close to her ear and whispered something. She lowered her hands, opened her eyes in surprise, and tugged at the white rope passing through her midsection. Chia took the rope from Liu Yang and tugged it back and forth through her body, demonstrating that it had passed through her completely. He unlatched the rope from the arrow base and pulled it free, out the front of her body, and let it fall to the stage floor, where assistants hurriedly coiled it up and carried it away. Now free of the rope, Liu Yang smiled, bowed, to the audience, and skipped off stage as the curtain closed, while the audience applauded enthusiastically.

Ivanovich stepped through the curtain as it closed around him. "One moment, if you please, while the amazing Wang Tao Chia and his company prepare the stage for their next illusions."

The orchestra segued from playing Oriental music to contemporary western, as Ivanovich disappeared, stepping through the closed curtain.

"Bravo," said Vera. "I totally didn't expect that."

"Have you ever seen anything like that before?" Alan asked Ben.

Ben shook his head. "It seems on the dangerous side, if you ask me."

"Yet you felt safe wrestling behemoths trying to snap your head off?" said Vera.

"Most of the time—and that's my point. Even as well-rehearsed and scripted as we were, accidents happened and a nose got broken...or an arm. But if an accident happens when you're playing with firearms, it's nearly always fatal."

"We didn't have those kinds of accidents in burlesque," said Vera. "Occasionally a dancer dropped her fan or a G-string broke, but no lives were lost on stage."

"Your G-string broke?" asked Alan.

"Just checking to see if you were paying attention,

Champ."

"Dang," said Alan. "I'm going to be thinking about that all night, now."

After a moment, the orchestra struck up again, but the tone of the music shifted to something darker, still Asian but more somber than before. The burgundy felt curtain pulled open to reveal an interior silk screen with a large green and gold dragon emblazoned with red eyes. The size of the silk screen obscured much of the stage behind it. Chinese drummers on stage picked up the orchestra's foreboding march and continued with it, marching in step, lights shining more brightly to reveal them as Chinese soldiers in leather and brass plated armor, coursing through an East Asian archway toward the audience. Two in their midst carried long, antique rifles, pressed against their shoulders and pointing into the air. The soldiers stopped their march and spread out as additional performers passed through the same archway carrying a single seated palanquin between two men, with ornately carved details in gold and black. The men set the palanquin down, and one of them held the door open, as Wang Tao climbed out, wearing an elaborate headpiece and the quilted robe of a Chinese warrior, conspicuously different from the soldiers, the dreaded Chinese Boxers. Wang Tao took on the somber expression of an unhappy man lost in thought over his foreboding future.

"Ladies and gentlemen," said Liu Yang, standing to the right of the stage in the shadows, "if you please... Wang Tao will now demonstrate for you how the Boxers condemned him to die during the rebellion, before executing him by firing squad. But Wang Tao will recreate for you tonight how he defied their bullets, and he will do it again for you just as he did in Peking many years ago."

Wang Tao took several steps back as Liu Yang took

several toward the center of the stage, moving up to the edge of the apron. "Two gentlemen who know something about old guns, come to the stage please. Two men who have loaded bullets and are willing to assist. Do we have American soldiers who are willing to help?"

Liu Yang looked across the klieg lights, holding a hand over her eyes to shield the glare. A man in an olive drab uniform with breeches and brown riding boots stood up, as did an older man wearing a lighter colored uniform with breeches and spats, holding a crumpled slouch hat. Liu Yang pointed at both of the men and waved them forward, encouraging them to approach the stage. The younger of the two handed his hat to a woman sitting next to him and whispered something to her, while the older man put his hat on, pressed his shoulders back, and marched gracefully toward the stage.

"Very good," said Liu Yang, "or as Wang Tao prefers, 'Much good.' We don't always have soldiers in the audience to draw from."

Both men climbed the steps to the stage and met Liu Yang in the middle, where the older man removed a thick riding glove to shake hands, while the younger man conspicuously checked out the old soldier's uniform, from head to toe, before shrugging toward the audience, as if never before having seen the type of outfit the Teddy Roosevelt Roughrider wore.

Please introduce yourselves to the audience.

"Sergeant Daniel Oliver from Fort Lawton," said the younger man in a strong voice.

The audience applauded politely as Liu Yang smiled up at the gray bearded older man wearing spectacles and in need of an upper denture plate.

"I am Captain Quentin Black of the United States Volunteers. One of the last men standing from Teddy's

Roughriders. I fought alongside him on San Juan Hill, back in '98."

The audience applauded enthusiastically, with a few older souls shouting "Bravo" for the aging captain, who nodded and saluted back to them.

Although the younger sergeant had already shaken the man's hand once, he again approached the senior captain and shook it again and patted him affectionately on the shoulder.

"Much good," said Liu Yang, "and now if Nikolai Ivanovich would be so willing, I would like him to assist us again, this time with the marking of the bullets, if you please."

The audience applauded as Ivanovich came out from the wings and joined Liu Yang and the soldiers at the middle of the stage.

"Have you ever loaded one of these before?" asked Liu Yang as the Chinese soldiers handed their muskets over to Sergeant Oliver and Captain Black.

Oliver shook his head, while Black slowly nodded his, as if recalling an ancient memory. "It's been fifty years or more, but yes, I have loaded and fired one of these before."

"Much good," said Liu Yang, turning back to acknowledge Wang Tao, still standing in the shadows. "Then we know we have someone here to make sure we are doing it right."

A small assistant brought a tray out and stopped in front of the two soldiers.

"Now please select two bullets from the box on the tray and mark them with the stylus," said Liu Yang.

Each soldier took turns scratching their initials into the soft lead of a bullet about the size of a marble. When completed, they dropped the bullets into a small cup.

Another assistant brought a second tray and stopped next to the first. On it sat a tin painted with the word "Gunpowder."

"Is it real gunpowder?" asked Liu Yang, as she used a small spoon to dip out some of it and hold it close to the soldiers.

Each man leaned forward and sniffed at the powder, nodding their heads in turn. Liu Yang shook the spoonful into a shallow pan, stepped away from the group, and extended her arm away from her body. Another assistant struck a wooden match and handed it to her. The powder in the pan exploded instantly with a white flash, leaving an acrid smell.

"Yes, real powder," said Liu Yang. "I should know, because we are Chinese, and after all, we invented it."

With Ivanovich holding the barrels of the rifles upward, less than a foot apart, the two soldiers watched closely as Liu Yang poured a charge of gunpowder into each barrel, followed by pushing in a cotton wad with her fingertip. The soldiers removed the ramrods from beneath the barrels, inserted the blunt ends into the barrels, and tamped down the charge and wadding.

"Most good," said Liu Yang. "You did that as if you are old pros."

Liu Yang then rolled the marked bullets from the cup, held them in the air so the audience could see, and tapped them into the tip of the barrels of the muskets in front of the two soldiers. She followed this step by adding more cotton wadding on top of the bullets. The soldiers again used the ramrods to tamp down the bullets and wadding. As soon as she finished, an assistant took the ramrods from the soldiers, set them aside, while the participants huddled around the muskets as Liu Yang positioned percussion caps onto the firing mechanisms connecting to the barrels of the muskets.

"Gentlemen, are the rifles ready to fire?" asked Liu Yang.

"Locked and loaded," said the younger of the two soldiers, giving his musket a final once over, before passing it along to a Boxer soldier standing nearby.

Captain Black picked up his musket, tossing it over in his hands and inspecting each side, before drawing the firing mechanism up to his eye for a close inspection. "Most curious," he said, shouldering the stock and swinging the barrel around the stage, drawing near to Ivanovich, who had just turned back around to face him. "Conspirators and saboteurs!" he shouted. "Watch your flank, men—"

Sergeant Oliver caught the barrel with an open hand and redirected it firmly toward the rafters. "Careful, sir!"

Captain Black paused, as if startled from reverie and now found himself busy catching up on the happenings around him. He eased his grip on the rifle and nodded to the other soldier, allowing him to take it from him.

"Right you are, Sergeant. Safety first."

The sergeant flashed a painful grin and took the musket from Captain Black, passing it on to Ivanovich, whose eyes were wide, face pallid. He kept a hooded eye on Black while turning sideways and passing the loaded weapon to another one of the Boxers.

"Thank you, gentlemen," said Liu Yang, "and if you would please stand to the side, we will need you to verify in a minute that your bullets were the ones fired during the execution. For the rest of you, we will need you to be silent for a moment and watch closely. Watch, everyone."

The two soldiers moved to the left of the stage apron, all the way over to where the curtain disappeared behind the wall. Captain Black shook his head as they walked and whispered something to Sergeant Oliver. Across the stage, the spotlight focused again on Wang Tao who stepped a few paces backward, to the audience's right, stopping a few feet inside the curtain at the front of the stage, making himself visible to the entire theater. An assistant tied a blindfold around Wang Tao's face and handed him a blue and white porcelain plate, which he grasped tightly with both hands, holding it in front of his chest, as if it were a bulletproof shield, a talisman that would protect him.

The orchestra played a dirge which seemed a blend of sorrowful English and Chinese instrumentation. The two Boxers with the long rifles, shouldered their weapons, fell into formation with the others, and marched to the left side of the stage, where they fell out and stood together, shoulder to shoulder, facing Wang Tao across the distance of the stage, while the remaining Boxers tightened their formation and moved to the back and out of the lights.

The music in the orchestra pit stopped, and an assistant on stage began the drum roll, as the leader of the contingent of Boxers marched to the center of the stage, taking exaggerated steps like the drum major leading a band. He stopped in the middle, halfway between Wang Tao and the marksmen—but well back of the firing line. He drew his sword, raised it over his head, and said something in Chinese. As he did, the drummer stopped and the theater went completely silent. The marksmen crouched into position, raised their muskets to their shoulders and supported the barrels with opposite arms as they took aim on Wang Tao. The leader gave another command, and the Boxers cocked the hammers back on their muskets. After a seemingly endless period of silence, with no sounds at all coming from the stage or audience, the leader barked something irritably in Chinese and dropped his sword sharply.

CRACK! CRACK! The two muskets fired in near unison. The weapons recoiled sharply, one more so than the other, as the black powder flashed brightly from them, the roar of the muskets ringing throughout the theater, drawing gasps from most everyone in the theater.

To the right of the stage, Wang Tao thrust the plate forward to catch the round, lead balls, but this time the always impervious plate exploded in his hand, scattering broken shards to the floor. Stunned, Wang Tao reeled backward, and twisted to his side. His shoulders arched and he dropped what little remained of the plate, while his assistants watched horrified, mouths agape and eyes wide, as the hole in the front of Wang Tao's silk tunic began to ooze blood.

Wang Tao slumped to the floor as if his legs had been swept out from under him. "Oh, my God!" he said, pulling the blindfold off. "Something's happened. Draw the curtain!"

Vera clasped Alan by the wrist. "Oh my word!" she said. "Another one."

"Right in front of us," Alan said, wrapping his fingers through hers.

Liu Yang ran from the wings and slid to a stop on her knees in front of the prostrate magician, whose eyes remained barely open. Other assistants and stagehands joined Liu Yang at Wang Tao's side, huddling around their fallen warrior. Behind them the stage manager dressed as a Boxer issued orders in Chinese. The curtain hastily drew closed. Instantaneously, the movie screen began descending in front of the drawn curtain. Instead of waiting for it to drop to its full length the projectionist began showing a newsreel with war footage of Japan's invasion of Manchuria. The screen soon filled with explosions and marching soldiers, the accompanying sound late in catching up to the black and white action.

People stood up and began chatting excitedly, gathering their personal items, making ready to leave, but they didn't leave. Most remained poised in front of their seats, spectators staring up at the stage, as if waiting for someone to tell them what they had seen had not really happened, but no one came out to explain or to tell them what they needed to do next.

A few moments later, Ivanovich stepped around the curtain and stopped at the edge of the apron. "Is there a doctor in the house?" he asked. "Please, we need a doctor to the stage right away."

The audience quieted down completely, while some in attendance repeated the request, passing it up the aisles, which only now began to fill with patrons getting ready to leave.

"I'm a doctor," a gentleman on the main floor called out, now standing next to his seated wife and another couple. People in the aisle nearby him stepped aside, making room for him to reach the stage.

Ben leaned close to Vera and Alan. "I'll call this in, order up an ambulance, and then I'd like to examine those rifles before anyone walks off and wants to clean them. We'll also need to interview everyone who touched them. Don't let the Army sergeant and captain wander away, would you, please?"

◇◇

Working through the crowd, now heading towards the exits, took a concerted effort from Alan and Vera. When they reached the stage they found Sergeant Oliver in the spot they had last seen him, squatting down on a knee to comfort his pensive wife, standing in front, below the stage.

Alan took out his badge, showed it to the Sergeant and his wife and made the introductions. "We work with the police," he said. "Detective Ben Kearney will be here in a moment, as soon as he calls this in to headquarters."

Oliver nodded his understanding.

"Where's Captain Black?" asked Vera.

"He went to check on the magician," said Oliver. "He said he'd dressed battlefield wounds during the war. Told me to hold the fort for him, and then he went through the side there, behind the curtain."

"I'll see how they're doing," said Vera to Alan. "I know a thing or two about battlefield wounds."

"I've got the stitches to prove it," said Alan.

"You be our anchor and wait with the sergeant here," said Vera, "otherwise we're going to end up scattered all over the theater." She stepped behind the curtain, following the path Captain Black had taken.

"Do you think it's something the captain or I did wrong?" asked Sgt. Oliver.

Alan shook his head. "We have no way of knowing until we examine the muskets," he said.

"Those barrels have rifling," said Oliver, "so in the Army we'd call them rifles."

"The words aren't interchangeable?" asked Alan.

Oliver shook his head, lost in thought. "Not necessarily. Muskets were primitive and terribly inaccurate, but then they came up with rifling in the last century. The best shooters got to use those and stand farther away, firing at single targets instead of closely packed groups, and of course the rifling made them better shots. There's no longer a need to stand fifty feet apart and see who could reload the fastest. Everything's got rifling now."

"I didn't know that," Alan said, giving Ben a courtesy wave as he came down the left center aisle. "Would these rifles be accurate then?"

"Probably so," said Oliver, "at least on the first volley, but after that there's too much flash and smoke with black powder."

"Do you know much about these and how they work?" asked Alan, "like how to load them and break them down?"

"I worked in the armory as a private for a few years. I can probably figure them out."

Ben climbed the steps to the stage. "Chief Ketchum's on his way from home. Should be here in half an hour."

"Does he think we have a murderous crime wave brewing?" asked Alan.

"He's more interested in seeing Vera than anything else, but he'd like a briefing on what we've got."

"Of course he wants to see Vera," said Alan, and then

he introduced Ben to Sergeant Oliver and his wife. "The sergeant has worked in the armory and thinks he could break down the weapons for us."

"Excellent," said Ben. "We can do that right after we gather up the participants and key witnesses."

"Vera went backstage to check on Captain Black. He told Sergeant Oliver he knew a thing or two about battlefield injuries."

Behind them, the newsreel showing on the screen came to a stop. An electric whirring noise followed a loud clicking sound, and the movie screen began rising to the top of the stage.

"That's good," said Ben. "As more people leave I'll want that curtain opened again for easier access."

Just as he said that, Vera pulled the curtain open in the middle and stepped through, the smile gone from her face, carrying the two rifles in her arms. "Black didn't show up here," she said, "or if he did he kept right on going."

"How's our magician doing?" Ben asked.

Vera shook her head and glanced toward Sergeant Oliver, as if to apologize. "It's not official yet, but if the bullet didn't hit his heart, it passed right next to it. Everything inside there is a vital organ."

"Did you say 'bullet,' as in singular?" asked Ben.

"That's right," said Vera. "He has only one wound, but it's severe."

"Any indication where the other bullet went?" asked Ben.

"I don't mean to intrude," said Sergeant Oliver, "but we've had occasions on the range during competition where some of the soldiers will dump a round into the brush, on purpose, rather than risking a poor shot."

"Both rifles looked on target from where we sat," said Ben, "but if needs be, we'll search around the backdrop for a bullet hole."

"So did they just let you walk off with their rifles?" Alan asked Vera.

Vera nodded. "Nobody wanted anything to do with them. The shooters are quite upset, and you can imagine everyone else is worried too. One of the men has black soot on his face. I'd say he held the rifle that bucked heavily. Maybe it had a double charge."

"Do we know which rifle he held?" asked Ben.

"He doesn't speak English," said Vera, resting the butts of the guns on the floor, "and the muskets pretty much look the same to me."

"How's Liu Yang doing?" asked Ben.

"Not well," said Vera. "She'll probably ride to the hospital in the ambulance with Wang Tao, so we won't be able to interview her until after the pronouncement's been made and she's had a good cry."

"It's that serious?" asked the sergeant's wife, chewing on her lower lip.

"I'm afraid so," said Vera. "I think the doctor's giving it his best, but there's not much he can do here, and the blood loss is great."

"The sergeant here has worked in the armory and thinks he can break these down so we can see what happened," said Alan.

"I've not worked on muskets before," said Oliver, "but I can give you my seat of the pants opinion."

"I'd greatly appreciate that," said Ben. "We don't know if this is some kind of accident or a strange coincidence, but it could be murder we're looking at here. I'd like a better feel which way we're leaning when the Chief of Detectives gets here."

"Am I a suspect?" asked Oliver.

"Not at this time," said Ben shaking his head, "but you

raise a good point. We probably shouldn't let you handle the firearms until that's determined for certain, but we can have you supervise us, look over our shoulders and suggest how we would take these apart to clean and inspect them."

"I can do that," said Oliver.

"Just what we need," said Ben. "Now if you'll excuse me a moment, I'll round up the stage manager, the shooters, get these curtains opened, and line up all the people we'll need to interview. Vera, if you don't mind, would you handle the interviews, while the Champ and I see how much gun oil we can get on our good clothes?"

*   *   *

Ben had ordered up a wooden table and a table cloth as a work surface. The house handyman brought them and set them up, after the ambulance crew left with Wang Tao and Liu Yang for the hospital. The show manager, who went by the name Li Yong, brought a cleaning kit along with him, but his English skills were marginal at best. The two shooters stood behind him, heads hung low. Alan set the rifles on top of the table, with the barrels pointed toward a sidewall. Ben stood over one musket and Alan the other.

"First thing I recommend," said Sergeant Oliver, "is to inspect the weapons for obvious signs of wear on the exterior. These have hammers that strike extended pins that hold firing caps. There should be a small amount of black residue around the head of the hammer."

"Check," said Ben.

"Check," said Alan.

"Now without touching the firing mechanisms or looking down the barrels, inspect the exterior surface, noting where you see residue or wear."

"The ramrod chamber on this one has a large amount of burnt residue and wear to it," said Ben.

Alan looked at the rifle Ben held and compared it to his.

171

"Mine also shows wear and residue."

"May I?" asked Sergeant Oliver as he leaned in close and glanced at the muzzles. "I think there's something wrong with both of these weapons. The one you're holding," he said to Ben, "doesn't appear to have discharged its round. There's not enough residue around the barrel tip for that to have happened, and yours," he said to Alan, "might have fired its round, because it has residue where it should, but I wouldn't bank on it. So to be sure, I recommend we probe the barrels with a bullet puller. Probably should do that to both weapons to be sure."

Ben addressed Li Yong, a Chinese man in his mid-forties wearing a Boxer's uniform. He had been the one who dropped the sword, signaling the two shooters to fire at Wang Tao. "Who cleans the guns after the show?" he asked.

Lee thought for a long moment and then finally said, "Liu Yang is only one who handles those."

"Nobody else, ever?" asked Ben.

The manager shook his head.

"What's going on with the ramrod sleeves?" asked Ben.

The manager frowned, as if unsure, and then he retrieved the ramrods from the back on the stage and brought them to the table.

Ben picked them up one at a time and examined them, while Alan and Sergeant Oliver looked on. "This is curious," said Ben. "Given the amount of residue around the sleeves, you'd think that the ramrods would have some of that on them too."

"Unless they're always left out of the rifles during the execution..." said Alan.

"And why would they do that, Champ?—I know where you're going with this, by the way."

"I'll know more when we find out what's down those

172

barrels. Right now, I'm suspecting one of them still has a full charge, and that will explain why Wang Tao has but the one wound."

"You gentlemen are brilliant," said Oliver. "You suspect the weapons have been altered, and you would like me to show you how that might be done."

"Exactly," said Ben.

"First we unload," said Oliver, "following a proper procedure just to be sure. Do either of you have much experience with guns?"

"Not all that much," said Ben.

"My dad taught me how to use and care for them," said Alan, "but I've never handled one like this before."

"Alright then," said Oliver. "You can serve as our trainee."

"I'm good with that," said Alan.

"Pick up the round wooden bullet starter," Oliver said, pointing to an object on the table, "and attach the wooden rods with the brass fittings, one at a time. Of the two end tips there, first use the one with the wire loop. Insert it into the barrel of the rifle."

Alan picked up the rifle in front of him and did as the sergeant instructed.

"The device you're using is known as the patch puller," said Oliver. "The cotton patch is the first thing we should encounter—if the barrel is still loaded."

Alan slowed the combined rods and spun the patch retriever around gently deep in the barrel. "I'm not feeling any resistance here," he said. "I think this one's shot its load."

Alan set the musket down and picked up the one Ben had worked on.

"While I'm thinking of it," Oliver said, "we can speed up the process if the houseman will fetch us four or five feet of very thin wire. The thinner the better."

"I've got a lamp cord I can strip and unthread for you," said the houseman.

"That should work," said the sergeant.

Alan sent the probe down the barrel of the second musket, comparing the length of the rod to how far down he'd gone in the first barrel. He slowed and began twisting the probe. "I've got something here."

Like a fishermen pulling in a trophy fish on a light line, Alan worked the rod out of the barrel. At the end of the brass tip a small swatch of gray and white cotton formed a knot.

"Not a very clean barrel," said Oliver. "I'd say that it's a bit dirty—but hasn't been fired. It's more likely the result of sloppy maintenance. So unscrew the end of the rod and replace the tip with the one that has the self-tapping screw on the end."

Alan did as instructed, and then he slid the rod down the barrel.

"Now spank the end of the round ball on the end sharply," said Oliver.

Alan did so and tamped the rod a few extra pats to make sure the screw would dig deep into the lead ball. Then he twisted the ball clockwise, shoving his weight into it. After a moment he exhaled and withdrew the rod, steadying the barrel and keeping the force even. He pulled the tip clear of the barrel, and it had a lead ball attached to the screw.

"We have a Bingo!" said Alan.

"Indeed we do," said Ben. "Are there initials on the ball?"

Alan left the screw impaled into the lead ball, but unscrewed the extractor tip from the rod. He held the ball close to his eye and spun it around slowly. "No marks at all."

"Let me see that," said Ben, reaching for the lead ball and extractor. He held it close to his eye and spun it around several times. "You're right. So what did she do with the marked ball?"

"Wait a second," said Alan, "I have an idea."

Alan stood up and crossed the stage to where Wang Tao stood and fell. A large pool of blood covered the floor and enveloped the broken shards from the plate he held. Alan squatted down on his haunches and picked through the large pieces of the china and nodded. He took a white handkerchief from his pocket, reached down and picked up two shiny lumps and wrapped them up. He returned to the work table, and wiped off the lead bullets.

"Here they are," said Alan, "and you'll see they have initials on them but no rifling marks—which means they were never fired through a gun. Liu Yang palmed these and passed them to another assistant on stage, who delivered them to Wang Tao before the shots were fired—probably when they blindfolded him. That way he could pretend to catch the bullets, and then later the soldiers would identify those as the bullets they had marked. So that means that since we all thought we saw both muskets being fired at Wang Tao—we were tricked by the illusion. And because this musket still had its charge with a near duplicate lead ball—there must have been separate charges already inside the ramrod sleeves to give the impression the weapons were fired."

Ben nodded.

"I agree," said Oliver. "The weapons have been altered."

"Is that what you want the wire for?" asked Ben.

While waiting for the houseman, the three Chinese dressed as Boxers passed out cigarettes between them, lit them with matches, and squatted down on their haunches, as if they were taking a smoke break in a rice paddy, while speaking in their language.

"I'm not happy with the way the interviewing is going," said Vera. "Nobody here speaks English except for the manager, and I don't think it's a good idea to let him control the information."

"We've got contacts in Chinatown," said Ben. "We can enlist their help tomorrow."

The houseman returned with a length of copper wire and a pair of pliers. He started to hand them to Sergeant Oliver, but Alan reached out and intercepted them.

"What next?" Alan asked the sergeant.

"Pull the hammer back to half-cocked," said Oliver, "and thread the wire into the nipple of the receiver connected to the barrel."

"Through the piece where the firing cap goes?" asked Alan.

"Exactly," said Oliver. "Probe gently. Don't force it. If it goes where I think it will, we'll have our answer."

Alan did as instructed and the thin wire bent easily and fed into the internal mechanism, first a foot, then two, then three, and then it poked out of the ramrod's metal sleeve.

"Voila!" said Ben.

"So what's happened," said Oliver, "is that a gunsmith or hack has rerouted the channel for the spark. It's supposed to ignite the barrel, but they've got it going to the ramrod sleeve, so they could fire a preloaded puff of black powder without a ball."

"The act is all an illusion," said Alan.

"That would mean that whoever handles the muskets has to unload the charges in the main barrels later at night," said Ben.

Alan nodded, following the train of thought. "And if they were sloppy about cleaning these, wouldn't that leave a trail of un-burnt powder that could ignite the main barrel?"

asked Alan.

"I'm not so sure about that," said Oliver. "I'll bet you the barrel's hole has been plugged. It could be the plug wore out because of the lousy cleaning job. Black powder is corrosive."

"What if someone were to stack the caps on the firing mechanism?" asked Alan. "Let's say they put two or three caps, one on top of the other. What would happen then?"

"That would be a much stronger ignition source than this old piece of metal could handle," said Oliver. "It would probably blast through any plug they had and ignite the wrong barrel."

"And leave blow back residue on the shooters face," Alan said, looking at the one shooter with soot covering the right side of his face.

"I think we have another Bingo," said Ben "And if someone deliberately put a second or third firing cap there, we indeed have another murder."

"We have another murder?" asked a voice at the front of the stage.

Alan glanced up from the muskets to see that Chief of Detectives Mike Ketchum had just arrived, his lanky frame ambling down the empty aisle toward the stage. Without thinking about it, Alan stood up to acknowledge the chief's presence. Ben did the same.

⋄⋄⋄

As soon as Sergeant Oliver and his wife left the theater, Ben gave Chief Ketchum a breakdown on what had happened before his arrival: the gravely wounded magician had been shot on his own behest by a gun that worked when it shouldn't have. Complicating the matter, one of the loaders of the rigged muskets—possibly the rifle that fired the fatal shot—had mysteriously disappeared without properly identifying himself or saying a word to the police.

"What do we know about this Captain Quentin Black who's gone missing?" asked Chief Ketchum.

"Next to nothing," said Ben.

"And you're pretty sure he might have packed a second firing cap onto this musket's firing mechanism?" asked Ketchum.

"Mere speculation at this point," said Ben. "We'd like to talk to him about it, though. See what he has to say."

"If he has half a brain," said Ketchum, lifting his foot up and planting it on an armrest, while leaning forward on an elbow, "he'd get himself an attorney who'd tell him to keep quiet while he sneered at us: 'Prove it.' And he'd be absolutely right. We'd have to prove it. Confessions don't stand alone in court nowadays, you know. They require supporting evidence to be upheld when challenged. People assume we still beat confessions out of the innocent, and of course you know that's not true."

Ketchum shook his head. "I'm sorry, I'm obviously preaching to the choir here. You lads already know this. So, tell me, what possible motive would Captain Black have for 'fixing' Mr. Chia's weapon so that it fired as everyone believed it should've in the first place? Did he aim to kill him, in a manner of speaking?"

"We don't know, Chief," said Ben.

"I'm wondering if he meant the bullet for someone else," said Alan.

"How so?" asked Ketchum, shifting his gaze to Alan. "Share your insight."

"Remember that the captain shouldered the weapon after loading it," Alan said to Ben, "and he pointed it at Ivanovich? He barked out something about traitors, while sounding like a senile old soldier, but fortunately Sergeant Oliver caught the barrel of his musket and pointed it toward the ceiling."

"That's right," said Ben, "he did."

"Who's Ivanovich?" asked Ketchum, lowering his foot and stretching his back, like a man needing a vigorous massage.

"Nikolai Ivanovich owns the theater," said Alan.

Ketchum didn't answer him, but instead turned to watch Vera cross the stage towards where they had gathered.

"Hello, gorgeous," he said. "You certainly made it worth my trip."

"Thank you, Michael, but I feel that I'm interrupting you here."

"The lads are briefing me on what happened tonight," said Ketchum, before glancing back to Alan. "I'm sorry, lad. You said something about Ivanovich owning the theater."

"Actually he owns several theaters, including The Paramount, the Palomar, the Coliseum, and the Moore," said Vera.

"The remnants of the Pantages properties," said Ketchum.

"He took advantage of the down market," said Vera.

"The market played a big part, there's no denying that," said Ketchum, "but I remember the owner's legal troubles. My detectives won a hard fought battle in court against Mr. Pantages for statutory rape, but despite the conviction, he wouldn't let it go. Claimed he had his honor to defend. So he poured all his resources into his defense. I still feel the Greek bought his way out of a dirty reputation, but then that's my opinion. I believed the girl, but money prevailed as always. That's not my idea of 'liberty and justice for all.'"

"I'm with you there," said Vera.

Ketchum pushed his fedora back on his head as he thought. "If I get this right, this homicide, whether it be accidental or murder, had been predicted by one Claude Alexander, the magician who claims he's the one 'who knows everything?'"

"That's correct," said Ben.

"And he also predicted the fire at the Paramount a couple of days ago, is that correct?" asked Ketchum.

"That's correct," said Ben, "but technically he didn't specify The Moore Theater for the shooting. We deduced it might happen here from the other clues we came up with. I don't mean that as a brag on how clever we are but to let you know we might not be absolutely accurate on our suspicions. There is room for coincidence, as much as I hate to admit that."

"And what's the story on these old muskets?" asked Ketchum, pointing to the two old rifles on the table. "What's next with them?"

"I think between us we've got it pretty well worked out, but we'll have the barrels taken apart in the crime lab, the mechanism inspected," said Ben, "to be sure. Our experts should be able to tell us how this thing had been reconfigured and what made it fire a deadly round tonight when it shouldn't have."

"I'd like you to find this Captain Black and have a word with him," said Ketchum. "Contact the Military Police attaché and see what their office can dig up on him from military records. Also get a sketch artist to come up with a drawing on Black that the beatmen can circulate around town, particularly the out of the way hotels. You got a good look at him, right?"

"Teddy Roosevelt," said Ben, while Alan added a nod of concurrence.

"Teddy the Roughrider?" asked Ketchum.

"Pretty dang close," said Vera. "He had on the uniform from the era but different glasses—and he's a bit thinner around the cheeks and the middle than the ex-President, but he could pass for his stunt double on a movie lot."

"Anything useful from the interviews?" Ketchum asked.

"No one speaks English here except their stage manager," said Vera, "and not very well at that. From what I gather, they all claim they don't know how the muskets do what they do. It's another one of those trade secrets that Wang Tao didn't reveal, even to his assistants."

"The one secret he finally revealed is that he speaks English," said Ben.

"The famous Wang Tao who never speaks without his interpreter?" asked Ketchum. "What did he say?"

"He said, 'Oh, my God! Something's happened,'" said Alan. "'Draw the curtain!'"

"In those few words I thought I detected a Brooklyn accent," said Vera.

"That's rather coherent for someone who doesn't speak the language," said Ketchum. "Now what about the actual shooters, the Chinese lads. Why didn't they aim high or off target? Why risk aiming directly at their breadwinner? Without him they'll be scrubbing charred woks at Tai Tung's."

"As near as I can tell," said Vera, "they believed in Wang Tao and his mastery over death. They actually thought he caught the bullets with the china plate. In order to make the trick work, they had to shoot on target."

Ketchum shook his head. "What a price to pay for fame. Unbelievable."

"Very sad," said Vera.

"How are you handling it, darling? This is the second murder in less than a week for you, plus all the trampled people at the Paramount, with you almost being one of them."

"I might be up for a scotch later, if that's what you're asking," said Vera, "but I can't stay long, I have house guests."

"That is what I'm asking," said Ketchum. "About time you and I catch up on things."

"I hate to be a party pooper," said Ben to Vera, "but we have a few questions we wanted to ask your houseguests about the pictures we found."

"Pictures?" asked Ketchum.

"Personal candid family shots of the Romanovs," said Ben, "not the official Royal Photographer kind that they released to the public, but the natural unposed kind that family members take of each other. They include Rasputin visiting the royal family."

"Why don't you go have your drink now," said Ben to Vera and the chief. "The Champ and I can run by the hospital and then meet up with you later at your place."

"Sure," said Vera nodding slowly, hooking her hand into the crook of Ketchum's arm. "Tasha and the girls will let you boys in, but they'll want to play cards."

"We'll be up for that," said Ben.

Vera and the chief turned to leave, but then she slowed to glance over her shoulder. "I won't be gone too long, and you two be careful—or before you know it they'll have talked you into strip poker."

Alan slid the Packard in next to the curb on a street off Madison, high atop First Hill, more popularly known as Pill Hill by the locals because of all the medical facilities, clinics, and doctors' offices. Ben led the way around back to the Emergency entrance of Columbus Hospital, where he flashed his badge at a nurse who glanced up stoically as they entered the building. Alan palmed his badge, holding it at the ready, but the nurse had already nodded and turned away to deal with something else on her desk. They followed the sound of a woman's crying. The unabated wailing took them to the first door on the right, where inside Liu Yang sat next to the table, her head lying on top of the sheet covering a body, from head to toe.

"I hate the hell out of dealing with people in grief," Ben whispered to Alan. "I can't help but absorb some of the pain they're going through—but time works against us if we wait. They're angry and hurting, and sometimes they're waiting for someone handy to drop by for them to lash out at, let their bitterness out."

Alan nodded, nothing to add.

"Excuse me ma'am," Ben said softly. "I'm Detective Kearney with the police department, and I need to ask you a few questions."

Liu Yang continued crying for another moment, paused to catch her breath, sniffed, and finally raised her head, inches off the sheet.

"I am not 'ma'am,' I am Liu Yang." She said. "Can't this wait? This is not a good time for us."

"I'm very sorry," said Ben, "I wish it could. There is no 'good time' for these interviews, and we have to gather as much information as we can right away, or we may lose evidence that will help us catch Wang Tao's killer."

"What you mean, 'killer?'" she asked, raising her head high enough to glance up at Ben and Alan.

The tears had caused the mascara and stage make up to run, aging Liu Yang and making her appear as if she'd had her eyes gouged out on stage in a Greek tragedy. Alan moistened a washcloth at the sink, wrung out the excess water, and handed it to her. She dabbed her eyes and stared at the grease paint stained cloth.

"Thank you for that. I must look a sight," she said, her English sounding much improved.

"You're fine," said Ben. "We're not here to judge you or take any pictures."

Liu Yang stood up. "I'm sorry, but I've got makeup in my eyes, and it's burning."

She stepped over to the sink, started the water running, and dabbed soap onto the washcloth.

"Aw shucks, this burns," she said, stomping her feet in frustration as she rubbed the wet cloth repeatedly over her eyes, while rinsing repeatedly.

"Ain't this the dickens?" she said, gazing into the mirror over the sink.

Ben and Alan caught the reflection and exchanged glances with each other. "You're not Chinese," said Alan.

"No," said Liu Yang, "I'm Hillbilly trash from Tennessee.

No sense hiding that any longer. That and a whole lot of other secrets are all going to come tumbling out now that Eugene's dead."

"Wait a second," said Ben. "Back up a bit. Would Eugene be the man lying on the table here?"

Liu Yang sighed and nodded. "That's right. None other than Eugene Roberts, Brooklyn, New York."

"Wang Tao is really Eugene Roberts?" asked Alan, making sure.

"Born and bred," said Liu Yang. "Via Scotland."

"Then what's your real name?" Alan asked.

"Luanne Bryant, Luanne Roberts—although we're not legally married, and Liu Yang. Take your pick. I've been called Liu Yang for nearly twenty years, I'll answer to that, but Eugene liked to bounce back and forth, particularly in Europe where no one knew him from before. On stage and in public people saw Wang Tao, but he liked to go out at night and often before the show, like the stories you hear of Presidents sneaking out of the White House and wandering about in disguise. He'd take the makeup off, put on a coat and tie, a mustache, and a hat, and go to clubs and smoke cigars. Only Li Yong, the stage manager knows he's not Chinese."

"What about speaking the language?" asked Alan. "Do you really speak Chinese?

"Dim sum, shumai, won ton, and how gow, are Chinese menu items I know. The rest has all been gibberish and whispers."

"But the whole world thinks you two are Chinese," said Alan.

"That's the beauty of magic," said Liu Yang. "It's all illusion, all good theater, and none of it a crime. We carried the illusion from the stage to real life, and no one knew."

Liu Yang rinsed and wrung out the cloth one more time,

approached the bed and reverently pulled down the sheet, exposing Wang Tao's painted face, his jaw slack, unmoving, his lifeless eyes staring straight ahead.

"It's all in the presentation," said Liu Yang. "The only prosthetics, if you want to call them that, is mortician's putty over the eyelids."

Liu Yang reached for Wang Tao's face.

"Wait a second," said Ben. "If you're thinking about removing his makeup, I can't let you do that right now."

"Why not?" she asked. "I don't want him buried looking like a caricature from the stage. That isn't who he is. It's a role he played. He's really a proper New York gentleman with Scottish ancestry."

"The coroner needs to examine his body, first, as is," said Ben. "He has to certify the cause of death before anything happens to the body. Once he's done that, then you and the morticians can clean him up as you see fit."

"I suppose you're right," she said.

"Sorry to be the bearer of bad news," said Ben, "but we also need to ask you about the muskets."

"Do you mind if I sit?" asked Liu Yang. "I'm suddenly exhausted."

Alan held the chair for her, and she plopped down wearily, no longer the small elfin character bouncing around on the stage.

"The guns were not my idea. 'Too risky,' I said. "At least twelve magicians we know of have been killed over the years while trying to catch bullets on stage—probably more we never heard about while learning how it's done—and what's that you said about this being a murder?"

"We'll get to that in a minute," said Ben. "First I'd like to know more about the trick, how it worked, and what you think went wrong."

"That's a loaded question—sorry, I didn't mean that to

be funny," she said closing her eyes for a long moment.

Alan and Ben waited her out.

"Eugene used to build props and create tricks for other magicians, before he became one himself. So he already had contacts within the business and knew a gunsmith in New York, who made the muskets and sold them to him."

Liu Yang lowered her head and shook it. "Now, talking to you, I'm remembering the magician's oath, and even though Eugene's gone now, that trick were talking about is worth thousands of dollars—well, to me anyway. I can't haul off and tell you how it works and still hope to sell it to another magician at premium price."

Ben rubbed the back of his neck, crossed his arms, and leaned against the wall. "This magician's oath is becoming a real pain in our investigation," he said. "I'm getting tired of it. Before we came up here, tonight, we emptied a lead ball out of one muzzle and discovered that the firing mechanism has a bypass that ignites the ramrod sleeve instead of the muzzle."

"We also found the marked slugs laying on the floor in the blood, mixed with the broken shards from the dish," said Alan.

Liu Yang stared intently as Ben talked, then at Alan, closing her eyes as soon as the men stopped talking. "Well, that's pretty much it in a nutshell," she said. "The gunsmith did all the fine metal work, very expensive, like buying a tiara at Tiffany's. Eugene and I were the only ones to handle the rifles off stage. We kept them under lock and key. We didn't trust our thieving assistants not to do what you did and figure how they worked. Next thing you know, they'd have sold that trick in a Hong Kong minute, ruined it all for us. So who are you going to tell?

"We're not planning on going public with it, if that's what you're asking, but the coroner's bound to call a public inquest, because this is most likely a murder—and then it'll become a matter of record."

"You can't imagine how badly other magicians have coveted our act," said Liu Yang. "None could figure out how we performed the trick. And none knew his secret identity. He fooled them all, and that makes him the greatest magician of all. They're so competitive they will hate him for it. None of them will want to admit they've been fooled. They'll be angry about it, so you can bet they'll dance on top of his grave as soon as he's in the ground."

"Who did the loading, who did the cleaning after the show?" asked Ben.

"I loaded the charges in the ramrod sleeves before the shows," said Liu Yang. "Eugene unloaded and cleaned up afterward."

"Every night?" asked Alan. "Thoroughly?"

"Not always thoroughly," said Liu Yang. "I could see that when I reloaded them before the next show. He likely had other things distracting him."

"Burnt powder residue around the sleeves," said Alan.

"I know," said Liu Yan. "But about it being a murder, how so? How do you figure?"

"Somebody stacked a second firing cap," said Alan, "maybe a third, like kids do with toy caps, either on the hammer or the strike. That made the spark strong enough to knock out the plug in the barrel and ignite the real charge. The question is who did it and why?"

"The police always suspect family," said Liu Yang. "Isn't that so?"

"It's as good a place to start as any," said Ben.

"And you suspect I did it because of jealousy," said Liu Yang, more of a statement than a question, "because of another woman."

Alan didn't see that coming, but he decided to take Ben's

lead and hold firm with his poker face, keeping silent.

"I know about his lover," said Liu Yang, "but I'm no fool. I'm a business woman first and foremost. Without Eugene, there's no show, there's no more income for me, and I'll soon fade into obscurity. People will remember Eugene as the glorious magician who had a Chinese or White assistant— old what's her name—a woman who didn't matter. Sure, I loathe him and his lover, but I'm not foolish enough to kill either one. Who told you about her, anyway?"

"We have our sources," said Ben. "You know we can't tell you that, but we're still unclear as to how long you knew about her? How'd you find out?

Liu Yang stood up, grabbed the sheet, holding it back. She stared at Wang Tao a long moment, hocked phlegm, and spat in his face. Then, as if nothing had happened, she pulled the sheet over Liu Yang's head and sat down again, her back to the corpse this time.

"Forgive me, but I no longer want to see him anymore than I have to."

Neither detective responded.

"He's had dalliances since the show went big in London, before we toured," she said, "and then he went wild when we hit the road, a sailor with a pretty girl in every port. I've always been Liu Yang, his assistant, his interpreter, and his confidant, but never good enough to be his wife. Now instead of meeting the local talent, he's brought one along with him from Los Angeles. Keeping her in a different hotel, hoping I wouldn't find out."

"Do you know where?" asked Ben.

Liu Yang glanced away and stared at the wall, taking a long moment to think. "The Sorrento Hotel, up on Madison."

"We know where it's at," said Alan. "Name and room number?"

"How's that going to help you?" asked Liu Yang.

"Like you said earlier," said Ben, "we start with those closest to the victim. Maybe she carries her own grudge."

"She's listed by her real name, Merle O'Brien, but you might recognize her as Merle Oberon."

"*Wuthering Heights*' Merle Oberon?" asked Alan. "The Hollywood actress?"

"That's her," said Liu Yang. "She's up here dodging gossip reporters who're asking questions about her mixed birth."

"Mixed birth?" asked Alan.

"She's Eurasian," said Liu Yang, stone face, a hint of disapproval in her tone.

"I think she's amazingly gorgeous," said Alan. "Whatever the combination, she turned out premium."

"Born in Calcutta to an Indian mother. Her father's believed to be Irish or English. No one knows for sure, and Merle keeps changing her stories."

"And now she's here in Seattle seeing Wang Tao?" asked Alan. "How did you find this out?"

"I had him followed," said Liu Yang.

"By whom?" asked Alan.

"Someone Nikolai Ivanovich sent over."

"You trusted Ivanovich with this?" asked Ben.

"I told him I had a blackmail problem," said Liu Yang. "The man he lined up for me only knew to follow Eugene Roberts, not Wang Tao. He assumed Eugene and the blackmailer were one in the same."

"I'm not sure this is important," said Ben, "but who ended up doing the leg work for you and when?"

"A Russian fresh off the boat named Mikhail Medved," said Liu Yang. "He spoke with a heavy accent. I had a lot of trouble understanding him."

"Mikhail Medved?" asked Ben, to be sure. "How did you

get hold of him? Where'd you meet?"

"In the theater after everyone else had left. I'm the one who puts the show to bed at night. I'm always the last to leave."

"How long ago?"

"About four days or so, a week or so after we got to town, the janitor at the theater handed me a telegraph message he'd found it on the floor near a waste basket. He didn't know if it had been dropped inadvertently or by whom. He gave it to me just in case it might be important."

"And it said what?" asked Ben.

"Something about a 'charming view of the bay from the top of the town,' and her looking forward to seeing him after *his* show."

"No hint at trouble between them," said Alan.

Liu Yang exhaled and shook her head.

"Did Eugene visit her every night after the show?" asked Ben. "Do you know if that had been his practice?"

"I believe so, but I'm not positive. My deal with Medved didn't include continued monitoring. I know Eugene saw her at the Sorrento is all, in a suite on the seventh floor."

"How do we find Medved, in case we want to talk to him?" asked Ben.

"You could ask Ivanovich," said Liu Yang, "but I'm not sure he'd give up that kind of connection to you, unless you had a lot of leverage over him."

Ben nodded at Alan, who grinned devilishly back at him.

"I can always bring persuasion if we think that's needed," said Alan.

Determining that the lead on Mikhail Medved couldn't wait
until morning, Ben and Alan decided to pay a visit to the
Paramount Apartments and see if the other Russians would
tell them which room belonged to him, and if he didn't have
a room there, where he might be found. Alan found parking
close to the Paramount Apartments. He glanced up at the
"Fire Closure" on the marquee as he crossed in front of the
Packard and stepped up onto the sidewalk. "That's sad,"
said Alan. "I hate to see it shuttered. I wonder how long it'll
be closed."

"This is still a tough time to put people out of work," said
Ben, "so I hate to see it too. But it could've been worse, both
in casualty and damage. My hat's off to the fire chief and
his assistant. I think they saved a lot of lives and property.
I think the theater will be up and running in less than two
months, but it'll be hell renegotiating contracts and start
dates with all of the scheduled acts. It'll be a nightmare for
the front office people who we never see."

Together they passed through the lobby of the apartment
annex and entered the elevator. "Start with Ivanovich first?"
asked Alan.

"Nah," said Ben, "I say we visit the hired help on the

fourth floor, and we save Ivanovich for last."

Alan pushed the button for four, and the elevator started with a slight lurch. It made up for the sharp acceleration by showing off its brakes, stopping abruptly at the fourth floor. Ben chuckled. "I'm all for automation, but nothing beats having little retired guys running these things. They develop a fine touch with practice and know how to smooth out the rides."

Alan nodded, waiting for the door to open. "Room 410 isn't it?"

"That's right," said Ben.

As they passed room 403, Ben suddenly stopped and raised his hand, making the quiet sign. Alan glanced back at the room's door, partially ajar, the room behind the door in the dark. Ben slid his hand inside his coat and pulled out his revolver, while Alan did the same with his Colt semi-automatic, bringing it to the high ready position. Each took a side of the door.

Ben taped on the door itself, striking it strongly enough to make it move further open with each knock. "Police," he said, keeping his voice low.

When the door had swung open a foot-and-a-half, Ben shoved it with authority, letting it swing in all the way to where it finally stopped abruptly. A strong waft of stale cigarette smoke escaped into the hallway. He pulled a flashlight out of his coat pocket, while Alan did the same.

"Seattle Police," he repeated, talking into the dark void.

Ben directed his flashlight near the base of the door at a dark spot on the carpet, now showing a deep red as the light glanced across it.

"We've got blood on the floor, partner," said Ben. "I'd say a lot of it."

Alan nodded.

"It's congealing," said Ben, "which mean it's had a lot of

time to set up."

Ben directed his light inside the door, shining it at the switch plate next to the frame. "Push buttons, no blood, which probably means daylight hours."

Ben examined a swatch of carpet inside the door and took a step in closer to the blood stain. He pulled the door toward him, leaned around and moved his flashlight beam back and forth at something on the floor. After a long moment he shined the light around the room.

"We've got a white male, D.O.A., face down on the carpet, several wounds to his back I'd wager. There's a long rifle next to the body with a bayonet attached. Otherwise the apartment seems empty of people, but we'll need to check. I'm going to turn on the overhead light with my pocket knife. But promise me you'll never do that, Champ. It's bad procedure."

"Sure, but why's that?"

"There's a theory we can get prints off of light switches, but I've never seen it happen—or heard of it, for that matter. Surface area's much too small if you ask me. I'll use my knife point, which is minimally intrusive, but if I slip with the blade, I'm in for a shock—quite literally."

Ben did as he told Alan he would, eventually turning on the light without getting shocked. With the better light from above, he stepped around the door and moved inside the room, stepping over the rifle and body. "Step where I step. Touch only what I touch."

Alan did as instructed, his eyes taking in as much information as possible. Other than a vodka bottle and an overfull ashtray on the table in the kitchenette, and the dead body on the floor, nothing else about the room seemed remarkable. Finding a safe spot to observe, he stopped to stare at the corpse on the floor, with slicked back hair on the sides, while the hair on top hung forward across the

197

face, the victim's nose mushed against the carpet.

"Brutal attack," Alan said. "The wounds to the back look like they came after death."

"Post mortem," said Ben. "Gratuitous violence. I'm counting eighteen puncture wounds, just on this side alone. Usually multiple wounds is a sign of rage, but then rage wounds would all be to the front so the victim would see it coming with the perpetrator seeing his face—at least in theory."

"What if there were a score to settle?" asked Alan. "The number of wounds might've been more important than where they were delivered on the body."

"That's a possibility. What have you got in mind?"

"I don't know. I'm sensing revenge as a motive, but I can't tell you why. Do you think this is our Mikhail Medved."

"I certainly do," said Ben. "As soon as we give the apartment a once over, I'll need to call Chief Ketchum and have the crime scene processed by a team of detectives, and then we can have this fella's countrymen confirm if it's him or not. That'll work better if we do it outside the room, like in the hallway on a gurney, when they're ready to haul him away."

"Why the old rifle with the bayonet?" asked Alan. "How many people keep those around? Did our perpetrator bring it with him?"

"This is a foreign cheapo, probably from the Great War, the kind you'd buy in a military surplus store on First Avenue for a couple dollars max. And then if you could find shells for it down at Warshall's, I doubt you could hit anything with it."

"Do you think he might have been shot before being bayoneted?"

"We won't know that until we roll him over, and the Homicide detectives should be the ones who do that. The more we do, the less kindly they're going to look at our help. Nobody, likes a grandstander, taking all the credit while they do all the work."

"But we want to solve these before there're more murders."

"Point well taken, Champ, if they are indeed connected. But again the more we do the less the other detectives will appreciate our help in the future, which we also have to consider."

"Vodka bottle on the table," said Alan.

"I caught that," said Ben.

"I haven't tracked Seattle's homicide history over the years," said Alan, "but it seems like it's always been miners, loggers, policemen, and prostitutes. Don't you find it odd that we've suddenly had more murders involving Russians than Fyodor Dostoyevsky had in *Crime and Punishment*?"

Ben stopped for a moment and creased a smile. "Vera likes how your brain works, always processing information, Champ, especially with what you've been reading, but I'm not seeing a connection to a Russian novel here, if that's what you're asking?"

"There isn't one," said Alan, "other than that these people have also come from St. Petersburg, Russia, and they're being murdered."

"How do you know about St. Petersburg?" asked Ben.

"Vera's contact told us the Medveds were from there, is all."

"We'll keep that out of the notes for now," said Ben, squatting down trying to get a better angle on the dead man's face.

"Do you see something on the carpet under his face?" asked Ben, "rolled up like a—"

"Like a note," said Alan. "I do. Under his hair."

"I'm going to do something else we're not supposed to,"

said Ben.

"I suspect you've got a reason then."

"Protocol for us now is that we first photograph everything in place; second, measure and log it in our reports; and third, we retrieve it."

Alan nodded. "We've been leaving all the reports to you."

"I'm fine with that, but I'm going to call these exigent circumstances," said Ben. "We need to know what that hell the note says. Sooner is much better than later."

"I'm with you there."

"Good, because this isn't going to be delicate. I'm going to pull the deceased's head up high enough for you to yank the note free from his mouth. Do you have any problem with that?"

"Not at all."

Ben reached from behind, slid his hand over the dead man's head and grabbed a handful of hair. As soon as he filled his grip he pulled back on the head, raising it about three inches from the carpet. Alan reached between the dangling locks and tugged the rolled paper from the corpse's lips, the paper resembling an empty straw. Ben released the man's head gently, pushing it close to where it had been a moment before. Alan handed Ben the still rolled note.

The big detective stood up, stepped over the body, and set the note down on the counter in the kitchenette. He rolled it open.

"Mikhail Medvedev. Unrepentant baby killer. Got what he gave."

"What do you make of this?" Ben asked under his breath.

"'Medvedev' is the full version of his name," said Alan. "We can be pretty sure this is our guy."

"Agreed," said Ben, "but who got to him and why? We

can bet that revenge is a motive, but revenge for what? And whose baby did he kill? When and where did it happen?"

"What doesn't work for the St. Petersburg connection is that I don't see any common link with his death to Liu Yang, Wang Tao, or Merle Oberon," said Alan. "At least not on the early go around."

"We're in for a long night," said Ben. "Oberon is one savvy lady. She has to be to keep the gossip column snoops from digging into her family's affairs. So I bet she pulls out of town before the ink is dry on the first newspaper of the morning."

"I'll use the payphone in the lobby to call Vera," said Alan. "Let her know we'll be running late."

<><><><><><><><><><><><><><><><><><><><><><><><><><><><><><><><><><><>

Alan nodded at the doorman, busy with another patron inside the Sorrento Hotel's lobby. He and Ben stopped at the front desk, badges in their palms and ready to bluff their way upstairs.

A night clerk wearing a vest and bow tie worked the desk with a woman assistant. Alan remembered the clerk's name from other visits. Friendly, smart, and discreet, Dennis stepped up to help. Ben flashed his badge, and Alan followed in kind.

"Detective Stewart," said Dennis, nodding towards Alan. "What brings you gentlemen here tonight?"

"It's our unfortunate duty," said Ben, "to deliver a death message to one of your guests. We hate to risk disturbing her, this late at night, but we're confident she'll appreciate knowing this information before reading it in the morning papers."

"This sounds serious,"

"She's a celebrity who may be traveling incognito," said Alan.

Dennis sucked in air and strummed his fingers delicately on the counter. "That could be tricky then."

"It's Merle Oberon, the actress," said Ben, "but she

might have a room on the seventh floor reserved under M. O'Brien."

"That's helpful," said Dennis as he flipped through occupancy cards in a file out of view. Alan had the distinct impression Dennis needed time to process the request, rather than refresh his memory to what room housed Miss Oberon.

After a moment, Dennis paused and glanced up.

"The privacy of our guests is of paramount importance to us," said Dennis, "but it seems your information is uncannily accurate."

"She's been here about a week," said Alan, "Usually has a nightly visitor who may stay until morning."

Dennis rolled his eyes heavenward as he listened. "At least one of you two already knows that we're not the morality police. It would be impossible to tell people who can and can't visit our guests, how long they can stay, and what they can or can't do while they're here."

"We're not interested in that part of her business," said Ben, "and you can see that we're not dragging a cameraman from *Hush! Hush!* magazine along with us."

"Alright then," said Dennis, "but I'll have to accompany you. If our guest doesn't answer her door, under no circumstances will I key it open for you."

"Unless she's screaming 'murder' or 'rape'," said Ben.

Dennis nodded. "Of course. That goes without saying."

Dennis palmed a key from underneath the desk, said something to his assistant, and walked into the back office, only to emerge a moment later from a side door that led to the lobby. He nodded for Alan and Ben to join him at the elevator, which they rode in silence to the seventh floor.

When the elevator door opened, Dennis led them across the hall and down to a room that would have a view overlooking the bay. The thought occurred to Alan that he might have spent the night inside here within the past year, but on that occasion the room's spectacular view went unnoticed.

Dennis stood in front of the room number, turned awkwardly, and knocked on the door.

"It's about time," growled a woman's voice inside the room. As footsteps approached the door, she spoke again. "Where the hell have you been?

The door opened with a jerk, and a smallish figure in a nightgown and robe stood framed by the door, gazing up at the taller men with puzzled eyes.

She clutched the loose hanging robe in front of her bosom. "Dennis, who the hell are these men?"

Ben tipped his fedora toward Miss Oberon, as did Alan, and he followed by bringing his badge up so she could see it. "We're with the police," he said, "and we're here to deliver some very unfortunate news to you. May we come in?"

"What kind of unfortunate news? Miss Oberon asked slowly.

"I'm afraid it's a death notice that you would prefer to take in private," said Ben. "Would you like Dennis to standby while we talk? I'm sure you'll have questions, and we may have the answers, some of them anyway. It could take a few minutes."

Miss Oberon stepped out of the way, and indicated with her head for them to enter. "Dennis, you don't have to wait. I'll call the front desk if there's something I need. They'll be able to find their own way out."

"Very well, madam," Dennis said, bowing as he closed the door behind him.

Miss Oberon sat down in an overstuffed chair and tugged a comforter into her lap. She canted her head towards the sofa and indicated with a nod that the detectives could also sit.

"Only one person knows I'm here," said Miss Oberon, "so it can't be him who's died, or you wouldn't be here—but then he's obviously the one whom I've been expecting for four hours. And there must be a reason he's not here. Is it Eugene?"

"I'm afraid, so," said Ben. "We only learned recently that you were staying here and thought we should inform you."

Miss Oberon stared straight ahead, past them and through the open blinds to the harbor below the city, enclosed partially by West Seattle in the background that had a ferry drawing past it on its way to Bremerton to the west. She buried her face into delicate hands and sobbed loudly, like a little girl abandoned to live on the streets.

Alan got up and went into the bathroom, where he moistened a soft washcloth under hot water. He rang it out and brought it to Miss Oberon, who took it and pressed it gently against her eyes as her sobs softened, accompanied by gulps for air. Alan felt the need to take her in his arms and hug her reassuringly, while telling her that everything would be alright, but he had no way of knowing if that were true. Maybe she'd lost the love of her life. He hovered nearby, wishing there were some way he could help her, rescue her from her sadness. He glanced at Ben who shook his head slightly, a signal Alan understood to mean that this might take a while and to be patient. Alan didn't envy Ben this part of his job, having to deliver death notices, while not getting caught up in the emotions of the moment. It must be tough being a real policeman.

"Tell me how it happened," said Miss Oberon. "I'm quite capable of listening."

"We both watched it," said Ben. "It happened on stage, right before our eyes."

"The infamous Boxers' Firing Squad," said Miss Oberon. "I told Eugene he didn't need to do that anymore, but the thrill of it had become an addiction for him. Defying death every night."

"It very well could be murder," said Ben. "We believe someone double stacked a firing cap, possibly on purpose. The hot charge ignited the barrel containing the charge and gun powder."

"I saw the trick years ago in London, and it scared me then," said Miss Oberon. "I refuse to watch the show anymore because of it."

"Of all the people in Seattle, we think you might be in the best position to help us," said Ben. "We're wondering what you can tell us about Eugene's relationship with Liu Yang? What did he tell you?"

"Presumptuous of you that Eugene and I are intimate," said Miss Oberon. "Before I tell you anything, I'd like you to tell me how you found me," said Miss Oberon, the sorrow replaced by anger.

"You know we aren't at liberty to divulge our sources," said Ben, "no one would ever talk to the police if we did. But I can assure you the source of information will not be talking to the newspapers about this."

"Must've been a private detective," said Miss Oberon. "Eugene worried all the time that someone might follow him. He feared ruthless competitors and blackmailers. He knew other magicians would pay dearly to discover that he led two lives. They also wanted to learn how his tricks worked, which he built himself."

"We live in dangerous times," said Ben, "but can we talk about Liu Yang?"

"Do you suspect her?" asked Miss Oberon.

"We need to be rigorous in gathering our information" said Ben, "and we thought you might be able to tell us more about her. Did Eugene worry about her or anyone else?"

"She's the one who loaded those rifles every day, isn't

she?" asked Miss Oberon.

"That's what we've been told," said Alan.

"She's the perfect place to start then, but if she killed him she's a terrible fool. It's him that people paid good money to see, not her. She's a very adequate box jumper but entirely replaceable, just like any other pair of shapely legs in the chorus line—there're plenty out there looking for their break. She didn't seem to understand that this is as good as it gets for her. She wanted more notice, bigger billing, wanted her name on the marquee with his, wanted more money, and she wanted more Eugene, as in him putting a big rock on her ring finger."

"Did she want that bad enough to kill for it?" asked Alan.

"That's my point," said Miss Oberon. "If she killed him, she killed the golden goose that laid her golden eggs."

"We know it doesn't make any sense," said Ben, "but murders often only make sense to those who commit them. Is there anybody else you know of who didn't like Eugene?"

"It's funny, but the only person I can think of right away is Laurence Olivier, from a few years back. Laurence is a racist who dislikes Asians, whether they're Chinese, Japanese, or Indian. He's not shy about telling people either. He refused to see Wang Tao's show because 'it stars a nasty little Chinese bugger,' but then later Laurence would play cards with Eugene—essentially the same man but without makeup—smoke his cigars, and drink his brandy because Eugene acted as the perfect Scottish gentleman, a man of substance, which he'd become by playing a Chinese man. Of course Eugene never let Laurence in on the joke."

"Mr. Olivier is not in Seattle, is he?" said Alan.

Miss Oberon shook her head and sniffed back a tear. She dabbed the warm cloth gently at her eyes. "No, he's not. I'd like to blame him, though, because he can be a nasty individual himself, but Laurence is not the murderer. And truthfully, Eugene didn't feel the sting of the slurs like a real Asian person would. Generally speaking, Eugene exploited the Caucasian belief that older Chinese males are inherently wiser, craftier, more spiritual, and more mystic than White males. He used this to his advantage to draw an audience willing to suspend their disbelief and believe he could actually perform magic before their very eyes."

"Agreed," said Ben, nodding.

"The opposite is true for Asian women, particularly Chinese," said Miss Oberon, "who are generally considered inferior intellectually and capable of performing only the most basic purposes in life, all subservient to the male, of course, which reinforces the mistaken belief that these women cannot be very bright or exceptional, collectively, and particularly as individuals. Ironically, Liu Yang falls into that category because of her success at playing her role so well, convincing people she is Chinese."

Ben and Alan waited to see if there were more.

Miss Oberon lowered the wet flannel and gazed at each of them. "Liu Yang is really White, isn't she? I'm afraid I don't know her real name."

"Luanne Bryant's her given name," said Alan. "Of course she also used Luanne Roberts."

"'Bryant' sounds familiar," said Miss Oberon, "now that you mention it. Perhaps Eugene told me it in passing."

"Did Eugene mention any problems with the theater owner, Nikolai Ivanovich?" asked Ben.

"He particularly didn't want Nikolai to see him as Eugene Roberts," said Miss Oberon.

"Why's that?" asked Ben.

"Before Eugene became Wang Tao, he sold the magic props he built to other magicians, and then he began putting together an act and performing under his own name, but he didn't do all that well starting out. It's so terribly hard to get noticed. So often fate plays a hand in who becomes a star. I'm probably a case in point on that topic. Then a promoter offered him a deal, if he could do what Ching Ling Foo had been doing in Europe at that same time. Eugene accepted his offer, and then the promoter billed him as Foo's biggest rival, who had come to Europe all the way from the outer reaches of Manchuria, and he booked him on a tour throughout the continent while he continued to hone his act and develop Wang Tao. Eugene met Ivanovich early on, before the transition. I think they met in Paris. He worried Nikolai might remember him and reveal his secret identity, which Eugene felt is the biggest legacy of his act. Despite twenty years as a headliner, Eugene felt his time in the limelight would be fleeting and that his talents were quite modest. Insecurity plagues many of us in the entertainment industry."

"How much did Eugene know about Ivanovich?" asked Alan. "Did he know his marital status or if he used another name?"

"Eugene said Ivanovich had a different name back then, which is nothing new to people in show business. I've obviously dealt that hand a time or two. Eugene called him Boris. The last name sounded like Solevad or something close to that, but definitely not Ivanovich. He believed that he and his wife were Russian émigrés who smuggled a fortune in jewels out of the country during the Revolution, but I don't think he mentioned her name."

"Having that kind of wealth would certainly help you get a start in the theater business," said Ben.

Alan parked on Tenth Avenue East, about a block from

Vera's apartment. "You don't think it's too late to pay a visit?" he asked Ben.

"Oh, it's too late alright," Ben said, "and there's no doubt we all need our beauty sleep, me more than others. But the problem with our witnesses is they're entirely too mobile. We can't afford to let them hit the rails before we talk to them. We'd play hell trying to track them down in another city. The department doesn't have nearly the money it takes to send us chasing after gypsies crossing borders."

Alan knocked on the door and then stepped slightly to the side, allowing the thicker jamb to protect him, like Ben had taught him. Ben smiled.

Vera opened the door, wearing a satin robe over something silky with a blush tone. She forced a smile through droopy eyes.

"Sorry to wake you," said Alan softly.

"Not a problem," said Vera, giving that smile her best effort. "This is one of the rare nights my guests went to bed ahead of me. So I took a short nap. Come in and I'll put on a kettle of water."

The two detectives followed Vera into the kitchen,

treading lightly. "We've got a lot to catch you up on," said Ben. "I suspect most of the details can wait until morning, but we need to talk to Madam Zarenko tonight."

"The Champ told me you found another murder victim," said Vera, while she filled the kettle with water at the sink. "Another Medved brother?"

"Bayoneted several times and maybe shot, too," said Alan. "The note sticking out of his mouth called him an 'unrepentant baby killer.' Said he 'got what he deserved.'"

"'Baby killer?'" asked Vera. "Didn't you tell me the other stagehands said something about a baby when talking about his brother, Pavel? Didn't he wake up in the night screaming 'Not the babushka!'"

"That's right," said Ben. "That's what they told us."

"I wonder if it's the same baby," said Vera. "At any rate I'm going to have to advise some friends that two from their *undesirables* list have shown up here in Seattle. I wonder if there're more in the area."

"Which baby did they kill, and how long ago?" asked Alan.

"How did you find his body?" asked Vera.

"Liu Yang told us that she'd hired Mikhail Medved to follow Wang Tao, who is in reality Eugene Roberts of Brooklyn, New York."

"Tao is not Chinese?" Vera asked. "Not even American Chinese?"

Ben and Alan both shook their heads.

Vera put the kettle on the stove, and a smile crept over her face as she thought. "Much good," she said. "He speaks just enough broken English so that you can't get a read on him, until he's shot, of course, and then he suddenly speaks Americanized English. Brooklyn English, no less. What a perfect dodge he ran."

"So while we're learning this," said Alan, "we find that

Liu Yang is really Luanne Bryant, who claims Hillbilly trash as a bloodline. She asked Ivanovich for a detective referral, and he gave her Mikhail Medved. Mikhail followed Eugene for her up to the Sorrento, where he had a love nest set up with Academy Award winning actress Merle Oberon."

"Merle Oberon's in town?" asked Vera.

"Under an assumed name, being very discreet," said Alan. "Turns out that Eugene also knew Ivanovich from his early days in the world of magic while getting his start in Europe. Says the name then might have been Boris Solevad, or something close to that."

"You boys have been busy," said Vera.

"I thought I heard talking," said a throaty woman's voice, entering the room.

"I'm sorry," said Ben, "did we wake you?"

"I'm not much of a sleeper," said Tasha. "My past seems to haunt me."

"We're having tea," said Vera. "Care to join us?"

"I'd love a cup, thank you."

"Your timing's good," said Ben, "because we have some updates you'd like to hear, as well as some snags you might be able to help us with."

"I'm listening," said Tasha.

Alan pulled out a black and white photograph from a photograph and laid it on the table in front of Tasha. "There are names written in pencil on the back," he said. "We were wondering if you could explain."

"You found my pictures?" asked Tasha. "I'm so glad they weren't destroyed in the fire."

"We found very rare pictures of the Russian royal family," said Ben. "We're not so sure who they belong to at the moment."

Tasha picked up the picture and flipped it over. "It has my name and my father's on it. Everyone else you see here is dead. I guess that makes them mine."

"And you were how old here?" asked Ben.

"Ten or twelve, maybe... I don't remember."

"How did you acquire it?" asked Ben, "and how did it end up in your dressing room? Why not keep it with your personal belongings in your hotel room?"

"Nikolai brought it to me before the show," said Tasha. "He thought it would mean more to me than him."

"And Nikolai had these because he's your ex-husband?" asked Ben.

"That is correct," said Tasha. "How did you know?"

Ben smiled benignly but didn't answer.

The hot water kettle began to whistle, and Vera removed it from the stove.

"Vera, if you don't mind," said Tasha, "I could use a shot of brandy in mine to help me sleep. I've got a feeling it's going to get rougher tonight before the sandman comes."

Vera nodded. "Certainly."

"How does this help your investigation?" asked Tasha. "Knowing about my private affairs, how does that help you with your murder?"

"The murders of these Russians seem to be revenge driven," said Alan.

"Murders? There's been more than one?" asked Tasha.

"So far, we believe we have Pavel Medved and possibly his brother Mikhail. We think Wang Tao's shooting could also be a murder, but were not sure of the connection, other than Mikhail Medved is the man who'd been following him. Nikolai recommended him to Wang Tao's jealous lover, Liu Yang."

"Sounds like a radio melodrama," said Tasha, "but are you sure the brothers' names are Medved, not Medvedev?"

"Actually, we're pretty sure Medvedev is correct," said Vera.

"So they shortened their names. Well, that's not all that unusual," said Tasha.

"Do you know them?" asked Vera.

Tasha sat back in the chair and stretched her legs out, while staring at her feet. "This is not something you would hear about in America, but for those of us who travel in different circles, Russian émigrés, we've heard the names of these braggarts who claimed to have killed the royal family. The Medvedev brothers are believed to be part of the bungling firing squad that assassinated the Romanovs."

"We found a note on one that called him a baby killer," said Ben.

"Tsarevich Alexei would have been thirteen," said Tasha, "not really a baby anymore. "Calling him babushka, or baby, would have been something his doting nurse would have called him, with his health being so fragile and all."

"Do you remember the nurse's name?" asked Vera.

"Anna Demidova," said Tasha. "These memories are so sad. They are what keeps me awake at night. How did these assassins die?"

"One died in the fire, trapped inside the casket on stage," said Ben. "He appears to also have been stabbed in the heart. The other bayoneted repeatedly and possibly shot."

"How exquisitely appropriate," said Tasha. "I apologize for this, but this brings a certain closure for me, which is long overdue."

"So, you're really Maria Rasputin?" asked Alan.

Tasha sipped her tea and then added a large dollop of honey to it. She nodded. "Until my father's murder in 1916, I had free access to the royal court. I dined with the grand duchesses. Most of these pictures, I took. That's why Nikolai finally returned them to me."

"And by 'Nikolai' you really mean 'Boris,'" said Alan, "isn't that right?"

"That's correct," said Tasha. "Boris Soloviev. After my father's brutal murder, the Holy Synod chose Boris as my father's successor. There had already been one assassin's attack on my father already, leaving him wounded. He knew people were jealous and that he had haters, like most great men. He predicted his death, saw it coming. During his melancholy he apparently endorsed Boris as heir should something happen to him. So the Synod followed his wishes and arranged the marriage on his behalf, for the good of Russia. I had little say in the matter. Boris had studied hypnotism, metaphysics, and tried his hand at séances, but he didn't have the spiritual gifts my father had. He could pretend with cleverness and sleight of hand, but that's not the same thing as having divine inspiration, like my father had. It became apparent to me that Boris in fact possesses no conscience. I should have listened to what my instincts were telling me and married the soldier."

"Divorced in Paris?" asked Alan.

"That's correct," nodded Tasha.

"Did Boris come from wealth?" asked Vera.

Tasha shook her head. "No, not wealthy."

"We have information that when you arrived in Paris you came with jewels and great wealth," said Alan.

Tasha cocked her head sideways and stared at him a moment. Alan didn't flinch. She turned towards Vera. "I would like to chase the tea with vodka, if you don't mind."

Vera took an unopened bottle from under her sink, opened the lid, and poured a healthy shot into a glass from the wash rack. She handed it to Tasha wordlessly.

Tasha took a large swig and smacked her lips. "I can see it's time to let the rest of the story out, but I don't want it repeated anywhere. Even my girls don't know what I'm about to tell you, and I want it kept that way. Is that understood?"

Nods came from around the room. "Understood," said Ben. "We only need to know enough to make sure we're on the right investigative track. Nobody's going to blab your life's story to the newspapers or put it on the radio."

Tasha gazed at Ben a moment, apparently weighing her decision before finally speaking. "Boris and I were in Ekaterinberg, across town from the Romanov family in 1918. The weather had been getting better, so it must have been late spring. We visited with the family at the Ipatiev home, which the Bolsheviks converted into what they called the House of Special Purpose. The rag tailed men guarding the family treated them vilely, as commoners, calling the tsar by his given name, Nicholas Romanov, as if he were a fellow on the street who owed them money. These cretins also drew pornographic pictures on the garden walls to shame the daughters, who were my friends. So Nicholas and Alexandra had great concerns for their family's safety. They knew these captors didn't have their best interests at heart. It seemed to me that Alexandra had a clearer sense of the real danger than Nicholas, and so she begged Boris to put together a band of White Russians, loyal to the tsar, to rescue the family from the Red Army. Boris told them that he didn't have those kinds of resources at his disposal. He said he couldn't easily put something like that together. It would take plenty of gold and jewelry to convince men to put aside their safety and risk their lives for the royal family. It would take coordination, weaponry, supplies, foreign currency, and transportation for them to flee to a safe harbor, which became the biggest problem of all."

"How so?" asked Vera.

"No country offered refuge to the family. Despite their bloodline, the ties to Germany and England, neither country would take them because of the war or worries about retaliation if they did. America refused to take them and congratulated the revolutionaries for 'throwing off the yoke of monarchy.' And if we were caught, we knew the Bolsheviks would execute everyone who had aided the family. The vengeance would have been most horrific, as an example to others."

Vera topped off Tasha's glass.

"Alexandra picked up a pillow she kept near her in the house and tore it open to show Boris the countless number of jewels she had sewn inside, an emperor's ransom. She urged Boris to take the pillow and all its contents. She said we were her only hope. So we left the house with the pillow full of desperation and left them with an empty promise we had little hope of keeping."

Tasha took a large sip of vodka and shuddered. "At first, Boris went through the motions, summoning officers he knew and relaying to them what Nicholas and Alexandra wanted. These brave men did not hesitate to risk their lives and put a plan together, but Boris began to have second thoughts. Maybe having all that jewelry corrupted whatever thread of humanity he might have once had. Before long, he imagined keeping the jewels and realized an opportunity to exploit the Romanovs and get more for himself. The tsar gave him a ring he wore all the time, sweetening the pot, so to speak. But Boris gambled with their lives, figuring the longer he took the more they would be willing to pay, and pay they did. But unbeknownst to Boris, the Czechoslovakian Legions were headed to Ekaterinberg. Their purpose had more to do with the Trans-Siberian Railway than rescuing the royal family, but the Red Army believed the Czechs were on their way to free the Romanovs and give the White Russians a champion. Lenin ordered the family executed, rather than risk the family being rescued and used to rally support for the opposition. So while Boris counted his wealth and dreamed of much more, the assassins gathered the family in a basement room, shot them, stabbed them, and burnt their bodies beyond recognition, before burying them in a pit, God knows where."

Vera sat down next to Tasha and held her hand. "That's awful."

"We're still not done," said Tasha, "and I need to finish this once and for all. I need to quit making excuses for Boris. He is not a good man."

"Very few people knew what had really happened to the royal family," Tasha continued. "The Bolsheviks tried to pretend to the rest of the world, even after their deaths, that the family members were still alive but scattered, while on the other hand they caught word that the officers had plotted a rescue attempt that never took place. That's how we found out that the orders to kill the family had come from Lenin, which scared us. Boris quickly turned the officers' names over to the Bolsheviks to save himself, and they were executed very horribly, but without their naming other conspirators, such as Boris and myself, who started it all."

Vera patted Tasha's hand.

"But still, there is more," Tasha went on. "After the horrible executions, other noble families were frantic to know where the grand duchesses might be hiding and if they were safe. So Boris saw another opportunity and recruited imposters for the daughters. We traveled around Europe and he passed the imposters off as the grand duchesses, fleecing well-meaning nobles of their wealth. I had to come to terms with the fact that I had married a grifter, not a worthy heir to my holy father."

"Remind me of the names of the grand duchesses," said Ben.

"Olga, the oldest, Tatiana, Marie, and Anastasia," said Tasha. "Technically, you were to address them as Imperial

219

Highnesses, but everyone referred to them as Grand Duchesses."

"It's a crying shame what happened to the Romanovs," said Alan, "and I have to tell you that it doesn't seem right that Boris—or Nikolai—is running around living in America, in the lap of luxury, spending loot stolen from the Romanovs like that."

"He squandered much of it in Paris," said Tasha. "Gambled a lot away, and then someone scammed him out of the bulk of it, or so he claims. If true, it might have been other Russian émigrés, but I doubt it involved blackmail. If it happened as he said, it was probably more a conman's scam of some kind he fell for. I think he changed his name to make it easier to move about Europe and enter this country, but not to dodge the shame. At any rate, he lost his theater holdings in Paris, dumped me, and moved here to start over."

"Where does Frederic St. Laurent fit in here, the magician?" asked Alan. "We know so little about him."

"I've been wondering that too," said Tasha. "I learned French in St. Petersburg, as did many of the noble families, except for the Romanovs. The tsarina didn't want the girls to have a French tutor. They could read French but not speak it. I never engaged Frederic in a discussion in French, but my ear tells me his French accented English has a Russian ring to it. I don't think he's really from France."

"My French is from Canada," said Vera, "and I would agree that his accent is a bit different."

"So who is he?" asked Ben. "And where is he? Why hasn't he turned up yet?"

"I have no idea, on either account," said Tasha. "I hadn't seen or heard from Nikolai until we got this offer to perform with Frederic St. Laurent, with guaranteed dates—at least according to Nikolai. I didn't even have a chance to really sit down with St. Laurent and ask him why he chose us to perform with him, and then once I met with Nikolai, I recognized him right away of course and forgot all about the other business."

"I'm sure you've heard the expression that 'this is such a small world'," Tasha continued. "Well, that's the first thing I thought. I didn't recognize Nikolai's new name, and he says he didn't recognize mine. Said he hadn't seen any of our publicity flyers, either. Still, our parting in Paris had not been pleasant, and he truly surprised me with these pictures. This is a kindness I didn't expect from him."

Alan reached inside his pocket and pulled out a folded piece of stationery and opened it. "We found this inside a police officer's tunic we believe belonged to St. Laurent. A transient found the coat in the alley, discarded outside the Paramount Theater. The note inside it reads: 'Filipp. We are in grave danger. Remember all in your prayers to the Holy Father. Anna.' Dated June 21, 1918."

Tasha's mouth sagged opened and she held out her hand toward the letter. Alan handed the stationery to her, and she read it over and over again, her eyes widening further with each pass. "This has to be from Anna Dimidova, but I'm not sure who Filipp would be."

"I've got this feeling that whatever's going on with these murders has something to do with the Romanovs," said Vera. "You add in Alexander channeling a Russian woman's voice he attributes as Anna, predicting the deaths we've had, and it points more and more to the story you've just told us. Maybe this Filipp is a relative. That would make sense to me."

"What's this about predictions?" asked Tasha. "I haven't heard about that before, but then I don't read your newspapers."

"Alexander Conlin, who bills himself as '*the man who*

knows,' sells out The Orpheum Theater every night. He predicted both of the murders while on stage," said Alan. "First, in a woman's voice, he predicted the fire at the Paramount. And you were at the theater, so you know it happened. Then we watched his act the following night, and he predicted another death on stage—a shooting death. We guessed that it might be at The Moore Theater, since they had an act involving firearms, and we were sitting in the audience when the shooting happened—just as predicted."

"Afterward, Alexander claimed to have no recollection of saying what we heard him say," said Vera, "and his voice changed while on stage to sound very much like a woman's. Very convincing. He—or she—spoke in both English and Russian, and when we asked Alexander later about whom he had channeled, he jokingly said, 'Anna,' but he didn't know why he picked that name. Said it popped into his head while talking with us."

As Vera spoke, Tasha's eyes widened, and her mouth went slack. "Do you think I could speak to Alexander?" she asked. "Perhaps if it is really Anna he's channeling, she might speak to me through him. I would recognize her voice and she, mine."

The three detectives exchanged glances, shrugged shoulders, and finally nodded their concurrence.

"We can ask for an interview," said Vera, "but there's no guarantee he'll grant one."

"How about if we arrange to have a reporter take a photograph of the meeting?" asked Alan. "The headline could say he's helping with the investigation into the deaths. That might encourage him to do it."

"No reporters," said Tasha, flatly.

"Alexander will want the publicity," said Alan. "He craves the attention, and maybe we could get the reporter to take a back shot of you, so your face isn't identifiable."

"I worry that it could turn our investigation into a circus," said Ben.

"Could we get the reporter to delay his story until the case is solved?" asked Alan.

Ben shook his head. "They keep their own counsel," he said. "They're not much for doing what we want them to do. They're more interested in selling newspapers, and if they got a juicy story in their grasp, the first one who comes out with it sells the most newspapers, leaving the others begging."

"I'll have to think about it, anyway" said Tasha, "but you know, in many ways I have a sense of relief right now. I've gotten a terrible burden off my chest. It's been haunting me for twenty years now. I think I might finally sleep tonight."

Tasha stood up and walked toward the bedroom, without saying goodnight, leaving the glass of vodka on the kitchen table.

"Very interesting," said Ben, "I think we've got a better idea now of a possible motive, but we still don't know who's doing the killing."

"After listening to Tasha, I'm wondering if there's not a bigger connection to Ivanovich than the other two who were killed," said Alan. "If revenge is a motive, he certainly would be one I'd want to drop an anvil on. He should be watching his back."

"The Medvedevs were assassins," said Vera. "They died in ways similar to how they killed the Romanovs. Where Ivanovich didn't actually kill the royal family, he betrayed them and profited from their desperation. He didn't help them find what they needed when they couldn't help themselves. Maybe his karmic punishment is financial ruin. Revenge comes to him by destroying his theaters and shows."

"But that doesn't seem nearly enough," said Ben. "I'm

with the Champ on this. If Nikolai had acted sooner as he promised the royal family, the Romanovs might've been spared their lives. I think that son-of-a-bitch should suffer the most—speaking theoretically, of course."

"Of course," said Vera.

◇◇

Ben and Vera waited in the lobby of the Camlin Hotel with
Tasha, while Alan went up to the tenth floor on his own. He
knocked on the door of 1007 and stepped to the side, as
Ben had shown him. He heard voices inside the room and
thought he recognized Sylvie's, saying she'd get the door.

Sylvie opened the door, dressed as if she were about
to go out for the day. She smiled at Alan, and her eyes
twinkled. She glanced over her shoulder and stepped into
the hallway, pulling the door closed behind her. "Where
were you last night?" she asked softly.

"We got busy with the case, and I couldn't get free. We
were at it until three this morning."

"But you thought about me?"

"I did indeed."

Sylvie reached out and stroked Alan's arm gently,
grasped his hand, and pulled him a little closer. "I missed
you, too."

Alan scratched at the back of his neck nervously. "I'm
here on business this time."

Sylvie released his hand, leaned against the door jamb,
and folded her arms.

"First of all," said Alan, "I trust you completely on what

you said about Alexander never having really channeled before, not like he has with this Anna who's stealing his show."

Sylvie nodded.

"And you know about the shooting last night at The Moore Theater with Wang Tao."

Sylvie nodded and her eyes widened. "We read that in the papers this morning. So, how about that? Not that we're happy with how it turned about, but that's pretty uncanny how Alexander called it."

"Amazingly accurate, your dynamic duo, Alexander and Anna."

"The front desk tells us that reporters want to speak with Alexander today, but he's going to put that off until later this afternoon."

"This may sound bizarre to you, but we think we know who this Anna is—or who she might have been when alive."

"What are you saying?"

"I can't tell you everything," said Alan, "but we've had three murders involving people in theater. We believe they are in some way connected to the Romanov family executions in Russia which appear to be driving the revenge. People connected to the assassination have been lured to Seattle to be murdered. Madam Zarenko it turns out is Grigori Rasputin's daughter, and she and her ex-husband could still be targets."

"I'm sorry," said Sylvie. "I've heard the name Rasputin, but I don't remember who he is or had been."

"Spiritual adviser to the Romanov family. He helped Tsarevich Alexei with his hemophilia, using mysticism or hypnosis, nobody's sure. This endeared him to the Tsarina and the Tsar, who kept him close in the castle after that for when they needed him."

"The murdered spiritualist?"

"That's the one. Tasha is his daughter and she had been close to the royal family, but her husband is the one who betrayed them. That louse might be the biggest reason they didn't escape Russia and were murdered in the basement in the place they were staying. Anna had been the children's maid or nurse, and she just might be the one Alexander is channeling. I have Tasha with me in the lobby, and she would like to meet with Alexander, if you can arrange it."

"And she hopes he will channel Anna for her?"

"Exactly."

"I don't know if he can turn Anna on and off like that, Alan. What does Tasha hope to gain from this?"

"We're hoping Anna might point us toward whoever is doing the killing. Tasha has a pretty good idea of how a séance should work. She watched her ex-husband perform a few."

"Then she knows it's almost always fakery, and they're especially expensive."

"We're hoping this will be the one that's not."

"Not a fake or not expensive?"

"Both."

Sylvie reached out and stroked Alan's arm again. "Alright, I'll ask Claude. We were about to catch a bite to eat, but maybe he'll be willing to delay it for a few minutes After all, it's not like we're little kids anymore and have to eat on time. If Claude insists on a fee, just go with what he asks and I'll forget to collect it from you. Then you can take me out to El Gaucho's later tonight and ply me with liquor for my affection."

Alan smiled broadly as Sylvie leaned forward on her tiptoes and kissed him on the cheek.

* * *

Sylvie left the door ajar for Alan, but when he returned

from the lobby with Tasha, Ben, and Vera, he knocked, to be polite, while calling out and pushing the door open slowly.

"Come on in," said Sylvie, "and have a seat. "Alexander will be with us in a moment."

After a moment the bedroom door opened and as with their last visit, the well-dressed Alexander paused in the middle of the doorframe for a second, as if waiting to make a grand entrance, and then he walked past the others to Vera, offering an extended hand, palm upward, to her. She took his hand, and he lifted hers, bowing and kissing her knuckles.

Vera made the introductions to Madam Zarenko, who had dolled up special for the occasion. Alexander kissed her hand, as he had Vera's. Alan fought the urge to punch him, figuring Alexander got far too much mileage out of playing the suave European gentleman. The reality he knew is that Alexander crafted his hustle while working bars with other con artists in Alaska during the Gold Rush. Alan didn't particularly care for the way he treated Sylvie, but then she struck him as smart enough to know what she wanted in life. She went after it with gusto and would only let people use her if it suited her purposes. He looked forward to seeing her again, after the show, when she'd have her way with him, and he'd love her for it.

Alexander gave a courtesy nod to Ben and Alan, before taking a seat, which suited Alan fine.

"This is a rather exceptional request," said Alexander. "Wealthy patrons often ask me to help them contact members of their immediate family, to beg forgiveness for past indiscretions or abuses, to find hidden heirlooms or keys to safe deposit boxes, or to learn more about the circumstances in which they died. But I've never had anyone ask me to contact someone not of their family. And most amazingly of all, you would like me to contact a nurse who worked for the Russian royal family, who's been dead for over twenty years. Most unusual."

Tasha nodded quietly.

"I'm intrigued," said Alexander. "Anna is as much a mystery to me as she is to those who watched me channel her while on stage. She completely interrupted my show. Normally, I would ask for privacy for this kind of a session, but Anna's obviously not been shy about revealing herself in front of 2,700 audience members, and I understand you've performed in front of large audiences yourself, or so I'm told."

"That's correct," said Tasha.

"So, you don't mind if the others are present in the room with us?"

"I'm fine with company, but my personal experience with séances is that they have always been in darkened rooms with candlelight. I'm willing to do what you think is best."

"You've had experience with séances?" asked Alexander.

"When Nikolai Ivanovich and I were married, a long time ago in another world, I went with him when he performed séances in his early days, he liked the darkened room. But then, he left me unimpressed with his skills."

"Oh, I see," said Alexander, "he's the darkened parlor sort. I'm afraid that he's exactly the kind that Harry Houdini would expose, finding their wires, smoke, and mirrors. Think about it for a moment. Why would a spirit need a darkened room to show themselves? The answer is: they don't."

Tasha nodded.

"Well, what you see here is your standard hotel room with no props from my stage show. I'll have Sylvie pull the drapes and light a few candles on the piano behind you. Hopefully that will be sufficient for the mood, in case Anna really likes that sort of thing, and she hasn't bothered to tell me. If not, Sylvie can also play background music for us, something dark and heavy. She's quite good on the piano, you know."

"I think having the room as quiet as possible would be best for me," said Tasha.

"I make no promises about Anna appearing, because she and I are just getting to know each other. She doesn't work for me. She's not on my payroll. I don't know what hours she keeps or where she goes when she's not interrupting my stage performances."

Tasha smiled.

"Normally, it's me, who needs to take a few deep clearing breaths to relax myself enough to get in the proper mood, but since we both might end up communicating with Anna, why don't I lead you through this. We'll take a deep breath, like this, starting by pushing out our diaphragms and blowing—"

Alexander's head snapped to the side and dropped to his chest, as if he'd been punched in the jaw during a bar fight. His mouth sagged open stupidly.

"Matryona Rasputina is that you before me?" asked Alexander in a woman's voice, Alexander's lips barely moving.

"Anna?" said Tasha, her eyes welling with tears.

"Why have you come?"

"To apologize for not being a loyal friend to the family and you."

"The time for friendship is long past."

"I'm so sad about what happened. I can't sleep at nights because of it. I don't know that Boris realized what would happen to all of you."

"Boris gambled with the lives of my babies and he will pay for it, as will the others. No one should die the way we did, punished as if we had betrayed our country, all of us, especially poor little Alexei, always so sick. He never could hurt anyone."

"Will there be more deaths, Anna?"

"Regrettably, yes."

"Regrettably?" asked Tasha. "Do you not control it?"

"Nyet! These are things beyond my control."

"Are they in the control of someone who is among the living?"

"Yes, someone close to me."

Tasha unfolded the stationery that Alan had given her earlier and read out loud. "'Filipp. We are in grave danger. Remember all in your prayers to the Holy Father. Anna.' It's dated June 21st, 1918. Did you write this?"

"Yes, of course, to my brother. You and Boris had taken the tsar's jewels but showed no signs of helping us. We were desperate for help, looking everywhere."

"Is Filipp in Seattle right now?" asked Tasha.

"Yes, but you will not find him in time to save—"

Alexander rolled his head and blinked his eyes rapidly. Then he inhaled deeply and glanced around the room. "She came again, didn't she?"

"That's correct," said Sylvie.

Alexander stood up and cleared his throat. "Be a dear, Sylive, and get me a glass of water, would you please?"

Sylvie poured a glass from a clear pitcher on the counter, next to the ice bucket. Alexander drank half of the water before pausing and glancing at Tasha. "Sylvie will fill me in on what I missed over lunch, but did our new friend tell you what you came to find out?"

"Mostly, but not all. I wanted to ask her to tell the family how much I've missed them, and I regret what happened. I wish that it all could be undone."

"But it can't be undone, Madam Zarenko, and that's

the problem with apologies," said Alexander. He set the glass down and began to rub his temples with his thumbs. "Somebody else wants a few words with you," he said, "Apologies aren't a magic cure for transgressions with the ability to erase the past and replace it with a future more to your liking. Here's a life lesson from poker: 'a card laid is a card played.' There are no do-overs with cards or with firing squads. The best you can hope for is compassion and forgiveness from those you've transgressed against. But the problem is that 'we' are under no obligation to grant forgiveness.

"I was about to say that's the 'royal we,' as in meaning everybody," said Alexander, "but I think the voice I'm hearing is indeed a royal one, but I digress. He says that you can merely ask and hope that we hear your prayers and are moved by them."

"I'm sorry, but I'm not one for prayer," said Tasha. "I haven't said prayers of any sort since my father's murder. I figured there couldn't be any point praying to a God Who had allowed the death of a holy man like my father's, such a horrible murder at that."

"Perhaps that is your problem then," said Alexander. "You blame God and haven't forgiven Him. More than anything else, this may explain your unease with your life and your inability to sleep at night."

"This isn't me speaking, by the way," said Alexander, "in case you're wondering, this is someone I'm hearing inside my head. It's a male voice, distant but not as overpowering as Anna's. A Russian accent nonetheless. I'm seeing someone very regal, like King George the Fifth—wait, that's not him at all. It's his cousin, Nicholas II, the tsar. That explains the Russian accent, but my word their resemblance is uncanny. I had no idea. He's elevated very far on the other side and his voice is but a whisper. What I'm hearing is that he 'strongly wishes—make that *strongly pleads* with you—to pray for forgiveness. You must make peace with your soul and pray for forgiveness'—then something I can't hear—'that will be your salvation.'"

Alan glanced across the room at Sylvie, catching her eye. She shrugged her shoulders, indicating this to be unchartered territory for her and Alexander.

"Whose forgiveness do I need to pray for?"

Alexander straightened his neck and rolled his lips. "The voice is gone now, but if I were in your shoes and someone from the other side made that kind of effort to contact me, I'd heed what they told me to do. I'd start at the top and work my way down. Make a list of those you've offended, if you think it will help."

Alexander paused a moment and scrunched his brow, as if listening to an inner voice. "I'm not a religious person per se," said Alexander, "and parts of this are new to me, although I've been working at my craft for years. But I have a very warm feeling right now, peaceful, like I've spoken with a saint, someone close to God. Is that possible? Does the Russian Orthodox Church believe in saints like the Roman Catholics? Do they canonize people as saints? I have a feeling that this will happen someday."

"We do have saints," said Tasha. "I'm sure my father is one."

"Then you have friends in high places, Madam Zarenko, and it appears they still might be willing to look out for your best interests. And with that, ladies and gentlemen, I must excuse myself for lunch."

The uniformed usher bowed slightly at the waist as Nikolai Ivanovich entered the Coliseum Theater lobby, while holding his arm extended, indicating the left aisle with a sweep of his hand. "Mr. Moran is waiting for you, sir, on the main floor, front row, and he's dressed very much for the part today."

"Dressed for the part? How so?" asked Ivanovich, stopping to visit with the usher.

"When he came inside he put on a Phantom's mask to go with his black cloak and hat."

"I don't think I know the Moran family. They live up on Orcas Island and don't get down here much. Did you see his face?"

"Oh, yes," said the usher. "Rather ordinary looking gentleman, I'd say. Slightly prominent nose, if you ask me."

"Jewish?" asked Ivanovich.

The usher shrugged. "I can never tell, sir."

"It's probably not important, but what's with the ice bucket and champagne on the counter?"

"Compliments of Mr. Moran. He said he'd like chilled champagne served during the movie."

"That's encouraging. Are we expecting other guests?"

"Not that I am aware."

"The popcorn smells delicious. Bring us a few boxes. Butter for me and one of each for Mr. Moran to choose from. Unless of course he has a caterer who will be showing up soon."

The usher bowed at the waist. "I'll bring the popcorn, sir, and Mr. Moran said he'd like to start the movie in five minutes, promptly."

"Really? He's already acting like he's purchased the theater. Well, let's keep Mr. Moran as happy as possible, shall we?"

"As you wish, sir."

The house lights were subdued but offered enough light to see Mr. Moran's silhouette, his caped collar flared high and outward, touching the brim of his black felt hat like a vampire. As Ivanovich drew nearer, the plastic half mask Moran wore became visible, revealing a clean shaven jaw and the firm neck of a man perhaps in his early forties. As with the version of the movie they were about to see, the mask had eye holes but otherwise covered the face to just below the nose, where a short veil of white lace dangled, obscuring the lips, showing great attention to details from the movie.

Ivanovich slowed as he neared the front aisle. "Mr. Moran, I presume."

"Indeed," said the gentleman, as he rose to his feet and extended a white gloved hand, while his other draped low at his side, clutching a walking stick, similar to the one Ivanovich carried, except instead of a lioness' head, Moran's had a tiger carved in scrimshaw.

Ivanovich offered his hand, transferring the walking stick to his left as the men shook. Ivanovich shut his eyes and winced in pain. Moran eased up on his grip and released Ivanovich's hand. "Something the matter?

"It's nothing really. I burned my hand the other evening," said Ivanovich, "and it's slow in healing."

"May I see it?"

Ivanovich shook his head, as if composing himself, while extending his hand. Moran touched Ivanovich's fingertips lightly and examined the burn—and his ring.

"That's nasty," said Moran. "It's still raw. Is that from the fire at the Paramount?"

"No, nothing heroic like that. I did it in my apartment, while using an iron to press a shirt for a walk-on part I had. My fault completely. Instead of sending the shirt out like I should have, I decided to touch it up and save everyone the bother."

Moran nodded his understanding. "Very nice ring. It looks regal, and it's so big you can't possibly slip a glove over that beauty."

"A memento from Russia I can't seem to part with."

"Your walking stick is very handsome, too, sir. Another Russian treasure?"

"Paris, actually, and yours looks quite smart," said Ivanovich. "They're great for keeping the dogs at bay when taking the evening stroll, don't you think?"

"Up on Orcas Island we mostly have deer, but they're really no bother when walking about. It's the cougars that worry me. They're not always well behaved."

The men took their seats, allowing the space of an empty seat between them. In the pit at the foot of the stage, orchestra members began warming up, tuning their instruments, arranging music sheets, and adjusting their chairs, speaking between themselves in Russian.

"So what finally got you off your island?" asked Ivanovich. "Why did you leave?"

"My father loves the life up there just fine, but I keep an apartment here in town, which I like to slip away to often as

I can. It turns out I'm more of a city boy than a woodsman, a conservationist, or a hermit. None of those titles seem to work for me. I appreciate nature, sure enough, but personally I like the hustle and bustle of Pike Place Market, which is the very sort of thing my father said wore him out, the hustle and bustle. Most don't remember that he'd been the mayor of Seattle, back during the Great Fire of '89. The stress of that debacle and rebuilding the city afterward took its toll, and so he had to get away for his health, retire early, which meant he took all of us with him up to the island.

"So now I'm looking for somewhere to invest my money that will keep me active in city life down here. I like what I see with motion pictures. I think they're the future of entertainment and vaudeville won't be able to compete much longer. Just take a gander to a year back and change to '39. We had *Gone With The Wind, Stagecoach, Wuthering Heights, Beau Geste, Ninotchka, Mr. Smith Goes to Washington,* and *Goodbye Mr. Chips,* every movie a box office winner and a major force in cinema. There's nothing that can top that for entertainment, except maybe Alexander's live act, the magician you have at The Orpheum. That man can pack a palace."

"Agreed, and since his accompanying retinue is so small, compared to other shows, he's very easy to accommodate. He's self-contained and can easily fill every one of the 2,000 seats we have here – that is when he's not contracted with me, of course."

"My bias is towards motion pictures," said Moran. "We have our own theater on the second floor of the estate and a world class pipe organ for accompaniment, when we have a silent film. We've learned to rely on movies shipped up to us by ferry. But watching movies alone has spoiled me. I learned to run the projector so I could watch them again and again, after the others had gone to bed. Consequently,

I've developed an overpowering sense of destiny about films, and I want to share the movie experience with as many others as possible."

"Moving pictures have been good for me," said Ivanovich, "and I agree that the cost and logistics of a stage show can eat up cash reserves."

"I'm very interested in your theater here. That is, if the numbers work out for me. I also might be interested in restoring your Paramount Theater too, if the price is right. Such a shame about the fire. Quite ghastly. Did you and the police ever get to the bottom of it? The newspapers haven't had much to say about its origins."

"I'm afraid the police and private detectives are still working on it," said Ivanovich, "but I don't think they've gotten very far. In the meantime, I'm losing revenue every day that the door is padlocked because it's officially called a crime scene—or in their lingo, 'the theater of the crime'."

Moran checked his pocket watch, stood up, and waved towards the projectionist's window. "Young man, start now, please. Then he faced towards the orchestra pit, "Maestro, are you ready please?"

A head with a military styled cap suddenly appeared higher than the curtained rail lining the pit. The maestro raised his baton, and the house lights dimmed, as the head usher brought the three boxes of popcorn that Ivanovich had ordered.

"Most excellent," said Moran to the usher, before nodding his thanks to Ivanovich. "I love the smell of melting butter, and this is the proper way to watch a movie. But I'm going to have to step out of character for a few moments, take my gloves off for the popcorn when the movie starts. I wouldn't want to get greasy butter all over them."

Moran canted his head toward the usher. "Would you be so kind as to bring the champagne down, pour each of us a glass, please?"

"Certainly, sir," said the usher with a deep head nod.

The orchestra started with a rousing number, heavy on the oboe, giving the music a festive but formal sound, gradually slowing and shifting to something foreboding and somber as the screen credits rolled high above them. More strings were added to sweeten the sound.

"I confess I have a bad habit of talking all through movies," said Moran. "It comes from watching so many with family or by myself. Like the director who made the movie, I'm busy giving stage directions, like I know what I'm doing. The family shushes me all the time. I'll try not to be too big of a pest for you."

Ivanovich smiled indulgently.

"Your orchestra is quite good," said Moran, leaning slightly towards his host.

"All Russian émigrés, except the organist," said Ivanovich. "He's from Berlin and is a bit temperamental. You'd think the Russians and he were still fighting either the Great War or the new one in Eastern Europe. I don't know for sure, but I think he's a Jew with communist leanings, but a brilliant organ player, nonetheless."

"How interesting," said Moran, fidgeting slightly with his left glove.

"Impressive resumes for all of them. The Russians were once members of the St. Petersburg's Mariinsky Orchestra. They played for the tsar and his family. They command top dollar, and we gladly pay it."

"Well, bully for them, but given your name, Nikolai Ivanovich, do you speak Russian at all?"

"Not so much," said Ivanovich. "We spoke mostly English growing up, but I can follow a conversation."

"That must come in handy. Does it give you a feeling you're visiting your homeland or never left it?"

Ivanovich smiled again, with a touch of weariness. "It's been a long time, but there's a certain comfort in hearing the familiar."

Before long, the head usher returned with the bucket of champagne and two glasses on a tray. He stepped to the side, unwound the wires holding the cork in place, and gently allowed the cork to pop, smothering it in his hand as he deftly poured the bubbling nectar into two fluted glasses.

"To success and your homeland," saluted Moran.

"Success and Mother Russia," said Ivanovich, matching the toast with his scarred hand.

Both men took sips from their glasses and sat back in their seats. Moran finally took off his right glove and began eating the buttered popcorn.

"This is great, this is living," said Moran. "If I owned a theater, I'd have a private collection of films and watch a movie every night. Eat my weight in popcorn, and wash it down with champagne. I hope you don't mind my bringing it along tonight."

"This is not the first time champagne has been served inside this theater," said Ivanovich. "If your tastes run toward the adventurous, private film collectors will approach you with fists full of money. They host parties after hours where they screen their private cult movies with their friends. You certainly can say 'No' to them, but they pay handsomely and tidy up afterward. You'd never know they were here."

"Would those be fantasy movies?"

Ivanovich nodded. "Indeed. They cover the gamut: foreign art films, horror, and erotica of every taste. 'Birds of a feather' as the saying goes. These people seem to find each other and embrace shared tastes of things others might consider peculiar."

"Intriguing. More champagne?" asked Moran holding

up the bottle.

"Please," said Ivanovich, holding out his glass.

Moran turned sideways in his seat and reached across his body to pour, but he couldn't stretch far enough. He stood up and stooped into a crouch, while steadying Ivanovich's glass with his gloved hand, pouring champagne with his other.

Ivanovich's hand trembled, shaking the glass and spilling out some of the bubbly.

"I'm sorry did I spill on you?" asked Moran.

"It's quite alright," said Ivanovich. "But I must be absorbing the alcohol through the broken skin. Stings a bit but should go away."

"Clumsy of me," said Moran. "So how about Russian cinema, Nikolai? I love finding old documentaries of the Romanov family back during their reign. I can't get enough of Russian history, but you certainly can't find much of it in this area. Thankfully, there is some, you know. As I've traveled around Europe I discovered that I would find more the further away from Russia I roamed, with the United States being the exception, of course. America doesn't have much use for anything Russian yet, except for caviar, art, literature, and its music. I hope that changes. You can't find anything on the Romanov's in Seattle, and I certainly found nothing at all in Russia during my travels. It's as if the Bolsheviks and Yankees are trying to pretend the family never existed."

The tremors in Ivanovich's hand continued to worsen as the skin reddened quickly. The champagne glass spilled and fell from his hand into the folded seat between them.

"Should I get someone to clean this up, or can it wait until we take a break?" asked Moran.

"It can wait," said Ivanovich, his words slurred as if his tongue were thickening, and then his eyes widened as he stared at Moran.

Moran peeled off the white glove on his left hand carefully, starting at the heel of his palm and rolling the fabric forward, revealing a rubberized surgeon's glove underneath. Moran shook the white glove to the floor and kicked it away from him with the toe of his shoe.

"You should take off the ring you're wearing before your fingers swell up around it," said Moran.

"Is this poison?"

"No, not poison, Boris, it's venom. Snake venom. Rattlesnake, if you want to be exact. It has a generous mixture of southwestern rattler venom in it – Mojave Rattler to be precise. This venom will paralyze you, and if untreated or delivered in large doses, it will certainly kill you, which of course is my intention. I understand it's a very painful way to die, which is only fitting for you. Now, I'll have that ring."

"How do you know my name?" asked Ivanovich, his voice slurring more now. "This can't be robbery. What's this about?"

"It's all about your past and the ugly imprint you've left on history, Boris, but more importantly," said the Phantom, "it's about my sister Anna. It's also about the entire Romanov family that you helped destroy through your selfishness, with your pernicious greed."

Ivanovich threw his weight forward over his knees and stood up unsteadily. He grabbed his walking stick and unsheathed his sword.

The Phantom sprang from his seat, drew his own sword, stepped backward, and tossed his cape out of his way and over his shoulder, taking up the en garde position.

"You poison me, you cur, and you expect a fair fight?" asked Ivanovich.

"It's venom, not poison!" said the Phantom. "There is a

difference. I am Anna's brother, and I didn't come here to fight fairly. Do not mistake this for a dual of honor, because you have no honor. That's been proven time and time again. I've searched for you my whole life, and I have come here to see that you suffer and die ignobly. The only honor at stake is that of the Demidova family, which demands revenge for your transgressions. For the last time, Boris Soloviev, I'll have the tsar's ring."

<hr />

The three detectives gathered with Tasha outside of the
Camlin Hotel, next to the Packard.

"Frankly, I'm amazed," said Vera. "I've seen entertainers
who've claimed to be psychic go through their routines with
moans, groans, and chants, making deliberate transitions
from one character to another, like actors getting into their
parts before going on stage. But I've never seen it where the
host body gets knocked out like a prize fighter, and then
later has no recollection of what he said while channeling—
like he'd suffered a concussion. And if that weren't enough,
Alexander can also channel when he's awake and aware of
what's going on, but differently, this time seeing an image
of the tsar in his mind's eye, who he mistakes for the tsar's
first cousin, the late king. Quite remarkable. I've never seen
anything like that."

Tasha nodded her concurrence. "I haven't used my birth
name since before my father took me to St. Petersburg. The
few who learned of my name were the Romanov sisters and
Anna, because of Maria Romanov, of course, the second
oldest. The family thought it necessary to call me by a name
different than Maria since we visited there so often, so it
wouldn't be confusing to anyone, but that didn't happen.

So I reverted back to Maria and have been that ever since. No one else addressed me by anything other than Maria, so there's no way Alexander could have possibly known."

"I gravitate towards craftiness," said Ben, "but Alexander puts on a convincing show. He's given me a lot to think about, which I can't explain. I have a feeling he's just as surprised by this as we were, but truthfully, at the moment I'm more worried about Ivanovich's safety. I think his days are numbered, if not his hours and minutes."

"I'm with Ben on both counts," said Alan. "There's part of me that says Alexander's a showman who always covers every angle, but there were tangents here I'm sure he didn't see coming. He couldn't have. My problem with believing what I saw is I don't want to be taken for a fool, flimflammed by a clever conman, but like Ben said, I saw a lot I can't explain."

"I agree about Ivanovich being in danger," said Vera, "we need to do something about him, despite what a worm he's been."

"Can I come along with you?" asked Tasha.

"I don't know if that would be a good plan," said Ben. "We have absolutely no idea what we might encounter when we find him, and having you with us means we have to factor your welfare when making decisions."

"Ben, I throw knives at people for a living, moving targets at that, and I do it while I'm almost naked. Not much is going to scare me. I'm not a helpless little girl."

"Did you bring your throwing knives?" asked Ben.

"No, detective, they're still inside the Paramount," said Tasha. "Can we go get them, please?"

"Later," said Ben. "Something in Alexander's tone said we have no time to waste."

*   *   *

Ten minutes later, the foursome entered the lobby of

The Moore Hotel. With it still being a police investigation, Ben took the lead and approached the front desk, holding his badge discreetly. "We'd like to call on Nikolai Ivanovich, if he's in, please."

"He left an hour ago to meet a gentleman," said the male clerk. "Is there a problem?"

Ben rolled his lips as he paused for a moment. "We have reason to believe he might be in imminent danger. Do you know where he might've gone?"

The clerk gazed at Ben's badge a moment and then quickly glanced around the lobby. "Everybody's concerned about people getting killed on stage. Has this something to do with that?"

Ben nodded slowly, not pushing his point.

"I suppose it's okay then," said the clerk, as if satisfying an inner argument. "He's meeting a potential buyer for a theater, a man by the name of Moran. The gentleman sent his driver over an hour ago to pick up Mr. Ivanovich. They're meeting at the Coliseum Theater."

"At Fifth and Pike," said Ben.

"That's right."

"It's a little early for a vaudeville act, isn't it? Are they running a movie?"

"Private showing," said the clerk, "before today's matinee."

"Is that something theaters normally do?"

The clerk shook his head. "Very rare, at least during the daytime, and in fact the request surprised Mr. Ivanovich. The client insisted he wanted to see Rupert Julian's *Phantom of the Opera*. Said it's his favorite."

"That's a silent," said Ben.

"Correct you are, detective—with Lon Chaney. He's superb in the movie and helped direct it, but if you ask me, Mary Philbin and Norman Kerry were rather wooden.

Mr. Ivanovich had me call in the house orchestra, the organist, and concession staff. The gentleman insisted on refreshments with his movie, and he wants to see the ushers in attendance. He wants everyone in their uniforms."

"He's bringing in the orchestra?" asked Alan. "All that for the two of them?"

"That's my understanding."

Ben nodded his thanks and put his badge away.

Vera's eyes flared wide. She started toward the front door, walking quickly, followed quickly by the other three. "I say we take a taxi over so we don't have to worry about parking."

* * *

The taxi stopped at Fifth and Pike in the middle of the street, in front of The Coliseum Theater. "If you can hold on a minute," said the driver, "I'll make a left turn into the alley, back out and pull up to the door."

"This is fine right here," said Ben, digging into his wallet, pulling out a five spot and handing it to the driver. "Keep it."

Vera and Alan were already opening the rear doors. Traffic stopped behind them, mid-block. A guy in a delivery truck had the irritated look that indicated he might say something nasty, but then he paused to gape at Vera and Tasha as they finished crossing the street and stepped up on the curb. The car behind him honked.

Ben led the way to the ticket seller's window and flashed his badge.

"I'm sorry, we're not open yet," said the ticket seller, her voice amplified electronically, coming out through an outside speaker. "We're having a private showing. It's two hours until the matinee."

"We're not hitting you up for a free movie," said Ben, "we're here on official business."

248

The cashier pointed towards the door closest to her. "We've never had trouble with the police. Go ahead, it's unlocked."

Standing next to the door, Alan pulled it wide for the others as they hurried past, in front of him. Across the lobby, two usherettes stood shoulder to shoulder in the aisle way entrance, watching something in front of them, by the stage. Startled by the detectives' approach, they jumped out of the way.

"Arghhh!" came a scream from down in the theater.

Halfway down the aisle the head usher stood frozen in his uniform, watching two men, one with a sword, fighting it out in front of the first row, the one wearing half a mask as light on his feet as a matador, the other, a larger gentleman, staggered like a dying bull in the caged arena, pawing at the ground, gathering courage to mount a final charge to gore its tormentor in a lost cause to even the score.

As the detectives drew near to the usher it became clear that the larger man resembled Ivanovich in stature, except with face bloodied and head distorted. He had several cuts about his cheeks and blood ran freely from where his ears had once been. It also appeared from a distance that he might be missing two fingers from his right hand.

"There's some kind of poison on the blade of his sword," said the usher to Ben and the others. "I heard them talking about snakes."

"Halt! I'm a police detective!" shouted Ben, while holding up his badge with one hand and drawing his revolver with the other.

Vera stepped into a row of seats and nodded for Alan to follow her to the other aisle way. He drew his Colt and kept it discreetly low, at his side.

Next to the orchestra pit curtain, Ivanovich dropped heavily to his knees and fell forward, ending up on all fours, bracing himself with stiff arms. Below the combatants, the orchestra continued playing an accompaniment to the movie on the screen, which showed would-be rescuers running down steps below the Paris Opera House.

Inside The Coliseum, the real life Phantom raised his sword as if preparing to stab the helpless bull one final time, but he stopped and turned towards Ben's voice. "You are too late, detective. He has suffered the stings of many snake bites and there is no way he'll recover. At this point it would be a mercy to end it all for him, but truthfully, I actually don't mind watching his suffering. It's well deserved."

"If you don't believe me, ask him yourself," the Phantom continued, "but I assure you that at this point he favors death."

Ivanovich groggily nodded his head and moaned in a creaking voice, "Please ... finish what you started."

Vera and Alan continued sliding through the row of seats and emerged at the other aisle, which also led down to the front row.

"Please don't interrupt my performance," the Phantom called to them, "or it will end horribly for you as well. I have enough venom left to kill a hundred men or more, but I have no quarrel with you. My family's honor and redemption are at stake here, and sweet revenge has finally been ours. My fate has been inextricably linked to Boris Soloviev's betrayal and greed. I don't wish for it to involve others."

"Kill me," pleaded Ivanovich in a weakened voice.

"There, you heard him yourself," said the Phantom, as Ivanovich slumped to his side. "The paralysis has consumed him. Soon he will no longer be able to talk. His throat will swell, and he will suffocate."

Ben moved closer toward the front row, while across the row of seats, Vera and Alan did the same. The Phantom raised his sword higher with one hand and while holding its sheath outward with the other, as if preparing to stab Ivanovich. "No closer," he said, glancing back and forth between the detectives.

Ben raised his pistol and aimed towards the Phantom. "I've sworn to protect and serve everyone," he said. "Despicable as Nikolai may be, I can't let you finish him off in front of me."

"You would rather he continues his suffering before he dies?" asked the Phantom.

"That's the way it's got to be," said Ben. "If you stab or cut him again, I will shoot you."

"If you miss," said the Phantom, "you'll hit one of the innocent musicians behind me."

"Please do as he says," said Tasha.

"Well hello, Maria Rasputin. You shouldn't be here at all. I left you for dead on the stage at the Paramount, where you should have burned to a crisp, but it appears I got too greedy, tried to tidy too many loose ends all at once, with one fell strike. It didn't go as planned."

"You must have finagled a pardon from those who died because of your selfishness," the Phantom continued. "So, why did you come here now? To witness more Russian justice? Or did you want to give me another chance to take your life? Is that it? Do you have a death wish? You obviously don't appreciate how family vengeance works, or you would've pursued Rasputin's murderers and avenged your family's honor. But then perhaps there's a decent bone in your body, which I am unaware of, and you came to gloat at the destruction of your vile husband?"

"Ex-husband, Filipp," said Tasha.

"Oh, clever girl," said the Phantom. "But then not so clever, Maria. My sources tell me your divorce to this scoundrel is not official, and you can't just quit on a marriage."

Tasha's shoulders shrugged heavily as she sighed. "I

spoke to Anna today, Filipp."

"But how is it that even possible?" sneered the Phantom.

"Alexander, the psychic who claims he's '*the man who knows*' channeled her for us. That's how we knew where to find you."

"And what did Anna have to say?"

"That we would be too late to save Boris," said Tasha.

"She's right about that."

"And then she stepped aside to let the tsar, himself, speak through Alexander. You should know that he and his entire family, as well as your sister, are in a holy place, Filipp. Alexander thinks they're saints now. If they are indeed, your murdering people in their name would be an atrocity against all that's holy and a stain on their good names. The tsar's message urged forgiveness."

"The tsar and Anna spoke to you?"

"We were there," said Alan. "We saw it, and I'm not a regular believer in that kind of thing."

"What is my birth name?" asked Tasha. "Did Anna ever mention it to you?"

The Phantom slowly lowered his hand with the sword, while Ivanovich hacked out choking sounds on the floor in front of him. "Maria Rasputin. If not that, I have no idea."

"No one here in this country does, and few in Russia remember ever hearing it," said Tasha. "Only the royal family and those very close to them knew me as Matryona Rasputina. My father changed my name to Maria when we moved to St. Petersburg to live closer to the royal family. This morning, we caught Alexander unprepared to perform, but he went ahead as a favor. And despite his lack of preparation, Anna called me by my given name, and it sounded like her voice, the one I remember, not the psychic's voice. It could only have been Anna speaking through him, because afterward he had no recollection of what happened during the session."

"Are you begging for your life?" asked the Phantom, "because it's too late now to save Boris Soloviev."

"I'm not begging for my life," said Tasha, "but I will ask you for your forgiveness. That's what Tsar Nicholas wanted me to do."

"Let's hear it with meaning, then," said the Phantom.

"I, Matryona Rasputina ask you, Filipp Demidova, along with all those I've wronged by my actions and inactions, to forgive me, please. I just want to end all this and be able to sleep at night."

"Nicely done," said the Phantom, sheathing his sword, which had a thick gel of some kind on the blade. "Please celebrate with a glass of champagne. The bottle is quite safe, but don't touch the glove on the floor, unless you plan to join Boris on his journey to hell."

The Phantom drew his cape from behind and pulled it around his shoulders. Almost instantaneously, he thrust his hand towards the floor as if throwing something.

POP! POP! Two blinding flashes of light showed brightly, one between Ben and the Phantom, the other in the direction of Vera and Alan. All three detectives leaned backward reflexively, and then recovered and cautiously moved forward towards the lingering smoke. The orchestra had stopped playing with the sound of the first flash, and when the smoke began to clear, it became apparent the Phantom had disappeared.

Alan ran ahead, but Vera stayed with him stride for stride, while Ben approached from the other direction, spreading his arms out like a football lineman, blocking his aisle. Behind him, Tasha cautiously followed.

Alan slowed as he neared Ivanovich's lifeless body, being careful not to step on his severed ears and fingers, which were on the floor, a few feet apart. He stepped up to the brass railing and glanced over the curtain into the pit. Below, the members of the orchestra sat on their stools and gazed up at him with expressionless faces. All wore Russian military dress uniforms with side caps, except for the organist, who dressed more like a doorman at the Rainier Club.

"Did he come this way?" Alan asked.

The conductor shrugged his shoulders, as if Alan were speaking a foreign language.

"The Phantom!" Alan shouted, while raising his shoulders and hands, implying in the universal body language that he expected an answer.

Still no response.

Vera stopped next to Alan. "We know they speak English, because the clerk called them on the phone to ask them to come in today," she said.

"Apparently the code of the street applies here, too," said Alan. "No sense helping the police catch a fleeing murderer."

*   *   *

In the pit below, the Phantom took the sealed vial of snake venom he had hidden in his sleeve and slid it into his dress boot. He crawled out from under the scaffolding noiselessly, while carefully draping his black cloak around him as he scurried past the orchestra members. As he reached the organ, the organist stuck out his foot and caught the Phantom by his ankle, tripping him, sending him crashing to the floor.

"Arbeit macht frie!" spat the organist.

"Bolshevik!" said the Phantom, as he scurried to his feet and felt the sting in his ankle. He ran towards the rear of the theater, looking for a door that would take him outside to freedom.

*   *   *

Alan and Vera glanced over the railing, searching for the source of noise. The organist yelled something and then sat back down at his stool. To his side, a darkened shape scurried away.

"That's German," said Vera. "Work will free you. It's a slogan the Germans use to taunt their Russian prisoners with."

Alan pulled the short curtain to the side, squatted down, and slid underneath the rail. He turned to help Vera, but found her following right behind, not as worried as he about how much of her shapely legs showed to anyone looking her way.

Alan raised his Colt to belt level and led the way through the pit, ducking underneath the stage, with Vera hot on his heels. "Look for the first door that goes outside," said Vera. "He'll want to put distance between us. I don't think he'll hide."

"But be careful of that blade," said Alan. "If it's been dipped in venom, there's likely plenty more in the sheath."

◇◇◇

Alan pushed open the backstage door to the alley and let it swing wide into the recessed loading dock, a few concrete steps down from the alley. The Phantom's mask lay on the bricks at the top of the steps near a manhole cover. Alan ran up the steps and glanced to the north and decided against it. Too long a stretch to reach Pine, where Pike lay much closer to the south. Something his father had told him years ago reminded him to take the short route, where a man on the run could make quick turns. He ran towards Pike, and Vera followed, a good sign that she trusted his instincts. At Pike he slowed at the last moment, in case the Phantom had decided to wait in ambush. To the east he spotted the Phantom's hat and cape discarded next to a building. They won't last long here he figured, given the scavengers in the area.

"This way," he said, glancing back to Vera.

Alan turned his semi-automatic over, palmed the butt of the handle, and slid the barrel up his coat sleeve, opting for a lower profile on the crowded sidewalk in the heart of the City's business district. They hurried toward Sixth Avenue, choosing a pace that allowed them to scan the crowds for someone else running.

"I don't know what he really looks like when not in costume," said Alan. "I've seen the Magician, the Roughrider, and the Phantom, but all of them have been disguises."

"He wouldn't wait for the traffic to clear," said Vera. "Let's head north. I figure he'll double back to Pine, where he can duck into a department store."

Alan and Vera jogged lightly down the street, as if they were trying to catch a bus. Near Pine, a gentleman darted into traffic and crossed the street, dragging his right leg behind him. He grabbed at the leg, as if trying to guide the stubborn limb into moving faster than it could, while his other hand, carrying a walking stick, pumped furiously.

"There he is," said Vera and Alan at the same time.

The two detectives cut across the street, midblock, dodging between delivery trucks and Yellow Taxis. Ahead of them, Filipp Demidova stopped at the entrance to I. Magnin, a high-end retailer who catered to Seattle's moneyed tier. Demidova paused for a moment, holding the door for a woman wearing a fur coat to enter ahead of him, and then he ducked in through the door, behind her.

"I'd say he's been injured," said Alan. "Like John Wilkes Booth, making his escape. Maybe he broke his ankle."

"But why would he hide inside I. Magnin's, after holding the door for a lady?" asked Vera. "I think he has a purpose in going there."

When they reached the store, Alan stared through the glass doors inside before he pulled one of them open for Vera. "She's by the cosmetics, but I don't see him," Alan said.

The detectives hurried past the display counters and then heard a crash, followed by a woman's shriek, in the back of the store. "The jewelry shop," said Vera.

The detectives raced towards the sound, passing startled shoppers and clerks. When they reached Leykin's, an independent franchise inside the store, they found Demidova down on one knee surrounded by broken glass, the display case in front of him smashed. Alan pulled out his detective badge and let his pistol slide into his hand, where he gripped it firmly and pointed it at the back of the Phantom's head, while at the same time Vera drew her pistol and set her purse on a nearby counter.

"Don't move, Filipp, we have you covered!" yelled Alan, making his intention clear to everyone in the area.

Demidova still holding his walking stick pitched forward and rolled onto his side and glanced up at Vera and Alan. "Who are you?" he asked.

"Detectives Stewart and Deward," said Alan. "We're working with the big detective in the theater."

"Oh, yes, I remember you now," he said, easing onto his back, clasping his sword across his chest. "It appears that as the French say, I've been 'hoisted on my own petard.' So be careful where you touch me. I have rattlesnake venom on me that's been unaccounted for. I slipped the vial in my boot, but apparently, it has broken and is now the source of my bane. You will also find the sword's blade is covered in petroleum jelly mixed with more venom, so be careful with that and what you touch."

"Thank you for telling us this," said Vera. "Is there anything else you'd like to say?"

"The jewels in the case above..." Demidova stopped, apparently having difficulty speaking.

"The display card reads, 'From the estate of Nikolai Ivanovich,'" said Vera.

Demidova nodded. "Not his but the Russian royal family's."

"I see," said Vera.

Demidova extended his gloved hand towards Vera. "Excuse the blood on the ring," he said, "but this belonged to the tsar himself. Please take it."

"What would you have me do with it?" Vera asked.

"As his wife, Matryona Rasputina will inherit what's in the case here, now that her vile husband is dead. I won't be here to dispute that, and it's probably a lost cause anyway. But this ring once belonged to the tsar and probably his father before him, and on it goes." Demidova paused to work his tongue, having great trouble swallowing. "The tsar gave it to Boris Soloviev to use to arrange safe passage for the royal family, but Boris reneged on the deal. And since the deal hadn't been completed, Boris and Matryona have no right to keep it. No claim to it. Since it can't be returned to the Romanovs, and the Bolsheviks lied about what they did to the family, I say it's mine by possession. But I will have no use for it where I'm going, so I bequeath it to you."

"I can't accept this," said Vera.

"If you don't, who will?" asked Demidova.

Vera shook her head. "I don't know."

"My whole life has been dedicated to revenging these treacherous deaths. Plotting, scheming, manipulating, and killing those who needed it, when I could find them, but in the end I have nothing left to show for my work. There's no joy in this for me. I will be forgotten. It's as if my life ended when my sister and the Romanovs were murdered. Mine is yet another life wasted. You take the ring and decide what you want to do with it. Buy yourself a movie theater, like the Coliseum or the Paramount. There should be a number of them on the market right about now, unless his wife decides to keep them for herself."

Vera squatted down, extended her free hand, and Demidova rolled the large ring into her hand. "You have a regal bearing about you, pretty lady. You remind me of the tsarina with her proud carriage. You could wear a tiara."

"Thank you, Filipp."

"Now, step back, please. I need room to breathe. It's becoming very difficult."

Vera stood up and moved next to Alan. Behind them more customers and staff came up and crowded around.

"Thank you all for coming tonight," said Demidova. "I hope you enjoyed the show, although it's the worst bit of magic I've ever performed. Now, if you will excuse me, I have family waiting for me. I hope the greeting from them is warm but not fiery. It's time to end this."

Demidova pulled the sword partially out of its sheath and raked it across the palm of his hand. Blood ran freely onto his suit and white shirt. His hand began twitching immediately, and he wheezed horribly, like he couldn't take in any air. Vera leaned into Alan, put her head on his shoulder, and whispered. "I hate watching him suffer like this."

"At least this death is not one of our making," said Alan.

Suddenly, Demidova's twitching and wheezing stopped. Instantaneously his face relaxed, and he finally looked at peace with himself.

"We should call this in and have the dispatcher let Ben know where we're at."

Alan caught the eye of a sturdy but well-dressed woman working the jewelry counter. "Do you have a blanket or screen we can put up for his privacy?" he asked.

"I'll call maintenance. I'm sure they'll have something."

"Great," said Alan, "and would you also call the police for us, please? Or if I can use your phone, I'll make the call."

"Certainly, sir."

Alan put his hand on Vera's hip reassuringly. "What are you going to do with the ring?"

"I have absolutely no idea, but I have to tell you that buying a theater is out of the picture. I've been down that road before and have no inclination to going back. And it doesn't seem right that I should keep something with all that historical value. But I'm not so soft in the head to think that it should be returned to the Bolsheviks. After all, they cold-bloodedly murdered that family and stole all the jewels that were left—shamelessly, at that. I'd rather save this for Jennifer than give it to them. But then maybe I'll donate it to Whitman College, where they can create a wing to study Russian History. We'll see. There's no rush."

* * *

Following breakfast with Ben at the Five Point Cafe, Alan and Vera adjourned to their offices at the Washington Federated Union headquarters. Alan followed Vera through the back way into the office they shared. They would check for telephone messages with the receptionist later. Waiting on Vera's desk, a large bouquet of flowers and bottle of champagne tied with a red ribbon. An envelope leaned against the bottle.

"Another admirer of yours?" teased Alan.

Vera smirked and shook her head, while opening the note. "I doubt it." She hitched a leg on the corner of her desk and scanned the note quickly. "How nice. It's for both of us."

Alan leaned against Vera's back, inhaled her perfume, and read over her shoulder:

Congratulations, Detectives Vera and Alan!

I am pleased to hear that you located the man who had been terrorizing Seattle theaters and killing the performers. I hope my counsel assisted you in your timely capture of this man, ending his murderous spree. I must say that I sincerely enjoyed working with you on your case. The newspapers and radio reports have been most kind to me, and I thank you for that. The new management at the Orpheum Theater is pleading with me to extend my show in Seattle because of high ticket demand, but unfortunately Sylvie and I are committed to touring Europe for most of the next year. Despite the winds of war, people need entertainment, which engenders hope, and I'm all for bringing that to where it's needed. We have already booked future dates in Seattle, which will be the first stop on our return to the states. We look forward to seeing you again—and perhaps helping you in the future.

I am sincerely yours,

Claude Alexander Conlin, The Man Who Knows

"How nice," said Vera. "Very nice penmanship. Written in a woman's hand, I'd say."

"He probably dictated it to Sylvie," said Alan.

"Of course," said Vera, "and that would explain the X and O on the lower corner of the page."

"Where? I didn't see that!"

THE END

"Neil Low is a senior captain with the Seattle Police Department and serves as the agency's Night Commander, responsible for rapid response and coordination of emergency services during large events, civil unrest, tragedies, and serious crimes, such as homicide, kidnapping or arson. Fugitive, and Gangs; Advanced Training and the Range; Internal Affairs; and Domestic Violence and Sexual Assault.

Neil was the agency's first commander of the Ethics and Professional Responsibility Section and has commanded sections in almost every other area of police operations, including: Metropolitan Section, which has K-9, Mounted, Harbor, and SWAT; Homicide and Violent Crimes, which also has Robbery, He is a Vietnam War veteran and a cum laude graduate of the University of Washington's Bothell campus, where he also wrote for the school's weekly newspaper, The UW Bothell Commons. A Seattle native, he now lives in Snohomish with his wife and three daughters.

His novels include:
THICK AS THIEVES
SIGN OF THE DRAGON
UNREASONABLE PERSUASION
UNHOLY ALLIANCE
DEADLY ATTRACTION

His short story collection, LOW STORIES, is only available on Kindle..

Acknowledgements:

Writing is very much a solo pursuit, but I don't know of any author who does it completely alone, without the help of peers, family, and friends. There are many we owe thanks to for their behind the scenes encouragement and support. In my case I am eternally grateful and wish to acknowledge those who have helped to make this, my sixth novel, possible. I continue to be blessed by the support from my lovely wife, Lesley, as well as our three daughters, Amanda, Michelle, and Meghan, who realize the importance of writing for me. It is my oxygen. And as with my five other novels and short stories, portions of this were conceived or written at the University of Washington's Bothell campus library, where I find solitude and freedom from interruptions while nestled inside my favorite nook on the second floor. As it was when I was a student there, the library continues to be managed by Sarah Ledley, whose alter ego, Miss Ledley, enjoys recurring guest spots in my novels, although carefully disguised in the persona of a far more mature librarian. Special thanks go to Jim Ritter and Judy at the Seattle Police Museum, who have been very helpful with my police research, some of which includes historical correspondence they allowed me access to so that I could capture the feel of the corrupt "bygone era" of the 1940s. Thanks, again, go to the amazing Steve Montiglio for his original cover art and interior graphics. I also wish to acknowledge first draft reader Marie Trujilo for her keen eyes and attention to detail, as well as acknowledging again, Dr. Jeffrey Abrams, my recently retired chiropractor, for his gritty stories about old fashioned police work (comparing Philadelphia to Seattle), which proved very helpful for character development of my recurring cast. And of course there is Peter Atkins, whose subtle hand at editing helped smooth out the rough edges of my manuscript. Of course none of the above would have been possible without the expert help and guidance from my very wonderful publisher, Kristen Morris, of Tigress Publishing. The inspiration and concept for this story came while discussing writing with her here in Seattle. An attentive listener, she has been the perfect sounding board for my character and plot development. Special thanks on technical issues involving murders go to Homicide Detective Cloyd Steiger and Cold Case Detective Michael Ciesnyski, who graciously share the knowledge, insight, and time. Again, to all of you, thank you.